DEAR MOTHER

OTHER TITLES BY REA FREY

When She's Gone

In Every Life

Don't Forget Me

The Other Year

Secrets of Our House

Until I Find You

Because You're Mine

Not Her Daughter

PRAISE FOR REA FREY

"Rea Frey is at the top of her game in this twisting, binge-worthy thriller about trust, betrayal, and the thorny tangle of memory and trauma. Compelling, deep, and character rich, *When She's Gone* will have you tearing through the pages until the haunting conclusion. Put this on your must-read list."

—Lisa Unger, *New York Times* bestselling author of *The New Couple in 5B*

"With the backdrop of cutthroat competitive sports, *When She's Gone* is a page-turning story about a mother who will do whatever it takes to protect her daughter. Tense and twisty, Rea Frey's newest psychological thriller will have you turning pages late into the night. Read this one with the lights on!"

—Lauren Nossett, award-winning author of *The Resemblance*

"Rea Frey sticks the landing in *When She's Gone*, a taut, gripping thriller that takes mean girls to a whole new level. You'll be desperate to turn the page!"

—Hannah Morrissey, author of *When I'm Dead*

"In *Don't Forget Me*, Frey writes with authority, weaving together themes of family secrets, domestic violence, and childhood trauma. The characters are complex and believable and the plot expertly crafted. A highly compelling page-turner!"

—Wendy Walker, bestselling author of *What Remains*

"You had me at neighborhood murder club! *Don't Forget Me* is a fast-paced, exciting read where every neighbor is a murder suspect. Rea Frey has once again woven together an enticing tale of suspense. One bit of advice: Don't trust anyone."

—Georgina Cross, author of *One Night*, *Nanny Needed*, and Amazon bestseller *The Stepdaughter*

"Chilling from the first page to the final line, *Don't Forget Me* is a fast-paced, riveting read with layers of family secrets, each one darker than the last. I tore through this book, desperate to see whether my theories were correct—only to be blown away by an ending I never could have guessed."

—Megan Collins, author of *The Family Plot* and *Thicker Than Water*

"In *Don't Forget Me,* a deviously clever story, Frey brings a top-notch thriller alive with insane tension and a shocker story. You won't soon forget this stellar read."

—J. T. Ellison, *New York Times* bestselling author of *It's One of Us*

"Poignant, emotional, and yet marvelously malevolent, *Don't Forget Me* is written with Frey's traditional gorgeous prose while simultaneously being suffused with dread. The final outcome is deeply shocking and terrifying. Certain to keep readers turning the pages!"

—Christina McDonald, *USA Today* bestselling author

"Rea Frey's *Don't Forget Me* is a suspenseful and unnerving thriller that peels back the layers on a quiet suburban neighborhood and shows the reader—and the characters—what's really going on behind closed doors. The secrets that get revealed are both shocking and surprising—and they may make the reader think twice about everyone on their street. Rea Frey has outdone herself again, and this is her best book yet!"

—David Bell, *New York Times* bestselling author of *Try Not to Breathe* and *She's Gone*

DEAR MOTHER

A THRILLER

REA FREY

This is a work of fiction. Names, characters, organizations, places, events, and incidents are either products of the author's imagination or are used fictitiously. Otherwise, any resemblance to actual persons, living or dead, is purely coincidental.

Published by Thomas & Mercer, Seattle

www.apub.com

EU product safety contact:
Amazon Media EU S. à r.l.
38, avenue John F. Kennedy, L-1855 Luxembourg
amazonpublishing-gpsr@amazon.com

ISBN-13: 9781662532283 (paperback)
ISBN-13: 9781662532276 (digital)

Cover design by Damon Freeman
Cover images: © David Manson / ArcAngel Images;
© Kriengsuk Prasroestsung / Shutterstock

Printed in the United States of America

For my mother, who taught me generosity, patience, and how to trust my instincts. (I'm still waiting on the patience part.)

For Janina, a mother who does her best every day, who shows up fiercely for her human, who says yes to it all: yes to the pleasure; yes to the pain; yes to the uncertainty; yes to this unruly, extraordinary life.

For Jessica, the best dog mom—a reminder that motherhood wears many faces (and sometimes, fur).

And for every mother—
our work here is never done.

We dream in our waking moments, and walk in our sleep.

—Nathaniel Hawthorne

Part I: The Wake

BELOVED FOSTER MOTHER OR SECRET MONSTER? GAIL ARCHER DIES UNDER MYSTERIOUS CIRCUMSTANCES—25 YEARS AFTER DEADLY FIRE

By Eliza Harrell | May 11, 2026 | The Cedarloch Sentinel

Cedarloch, WA—Twenty-five years after the fire that killed three children and shattered a community, Gail Archer—the woman at the heart of it all—has died, cause unknown.

Though she was once hailed as a generous foster mother who opened her home to children in need, Archer's reputation took a dark turn when one of her foster children, Marcus (15), went missing in the Cedarloch woods, never to be recovered. Only a few years later, a 2001 fire claimed the lives of Celia (12), Ben (15), and Jude (17)—siblings through foster care.

The fire, later ruled accidental, broke out in an underground bunker on Archer's 20-acre property, trapping the children inside. Two surviving children, Archer's biological daughter, Isabelle (13), and Harper West (13), another foster child of the same age, were found safe at home.

Archer was never charged with a crime, but questions lingered. Why were the children in that bunker? How did the fire start? Where was Gail, and why did she do nothing to save them?

For years, Cedarloch has been divided—some defending Archer as a misunderstood woman trying to do good in a broken system, others convinced she got away with something unthinkable.

Now, with her sudden death, the town is left to wonder:

Did Gail Archer take her secrets to the grave? Or is the truth finally about to surface?

"It was always just a matter of time," says retired sheriff Theo Mullins, who led the original investigation and now consults privately. "There were pieces that never fit. Maybe now, we'll find out why."

Isabelle Archer, now in her late thirties, returned to Cedarloch this week to settle her mother's affairs. When asked for comment, she declined—but sources confirm there are more questions than answers here.

In a town still haunted by these losses, one thing is certain: The past isn't finished with Cedarloch. Not yet.

1

Isabelle stood over the graves.

Her daughter scratched her nose and sighed. "Where are they?"

Despite being back in this place, to say goodbye to a mother she hadn't spoken directly to in years, Isabelle smiled. "Don't you mean *who* are they?"

"No." Maisy scrunched her nose. A few freckles dusted the skin pinked by the harsh beginning of summer. "I mean where."

Maisy was eight, a smart child but sensitive, like her father, Jack. How could Isabelle possibly explain the trappings of religious beliefs or drum up a more spiritual explanation? Isabelle shifted, considering. "Well, where do you think we go when we die?"

"I think we come back as something new."

Isabelle patted her on the head. She loved that Maisy could reduce one of life's biggest questions to something so simple: *We come back as something new.* After the atrocities Isabelle had experienced growing up, she'd lost that sense of purity. She would move heaven and earth to sustain it in Maisy, for as long as she possibly could. They stood like that for a moment, as Isabelle paid her respects to her three siblings, buried deep in the woods behind the Archer house. And now to her mother, a fresh, much larger grave beside them.

Isabelle shuddered. You shouldn't outlive your family. It wasn't natural. But then again, nothing was "natural" in Cedarloch.

Carved from the forest more than a century ago, Cedarloch was a place where men chased timber and opportunity. At its peak, the town thrived on endless pines and the sawmill that chewed through them day and night. But the forest gave out before the people did. The mill eventually closed, the loggers left, and the woods began to reclaim what had been taken. Back then, the only way in or out was by boat, floatplane, or hiking in. Now that it had a population of just fifty, if you lived here, you chose to be here.

Isabelle was happy to see that they'd carved some roads into the dirt, and she could now get her truck up to the cabin, at least. When she was younger, she had to trek two miles to get into town. She used to dream about swimming across the Lady of the Lake or boarding the town ferry and spilling into other territory. Finally, when she was old enough, she had.

By then, grief was one of her closest companions. Even though she'd never grown up with a father, once she lost her two foster brothers and foster sister, the pain had marched in, swallowing her up completely. After, she'd been afraid of everything, shrinking into herself until she felt like a shell.

It seemed almost everyone she loved disappeared.

After a moment of paying their respects, they trudged back toward the cabin, cracking over dried brambles and thicker sticks. The trees were just as she remembered them, expansive and all-consuming. The ground beneath them was a bed of dead needles, spongy beneath their soles. She cast a palm out, let her fingers trail along the various barks, which peeled back like skin. Isabelle pointed out the names of trees and plants that she remembered. *Wyeth's biscuit-root. Yarrow. Devil's club. Pacific willow. Western red cedar. Subalpine fir. Ponderosa pine.* Maisy loved wildlife, had an affinity for flowers. Maybe they'd start a garden this year. Yes, that was what they'd do. A garden. Something to grow. Something to nurture.

Isabelle tried to tell herself they wouldn't be here long. They'd clean the cabin, get it ready to sell, and disappear. On the drive up, Maisy had been shocked to hear she'd had a grandmother all this time who lived mere hours away. Isabelle had seen the hurt in her eyes, and she understood why. She'd kept this secret from Maisy, kept someone away who could have loved her and spent time with her. But how could Isabelle possibly explain that she could never trust her mother with Maisy? Everything her mother touched turned bad. She couldn't let that happen to her own daughter.

Her other foster sister, Harper, would disagree with Isabelle, of course. They were former best friends turned sisters. Gail had taken in Harper once Harper's mother died unexpectedly. Then, after the fire, it had been only Harper, Isabelle, and Gail again.

Back then, Harper and Isabelle would often stay up late into the night whispering about Gail, afraid of what might happen to them too. Gail was a complicated woman. She loved order and control. She ran a tight ship, had high expectations, and often withheld love and kindness as punishment. Isabelle often felt her mother had been slightly softer with her, because Isabelle was Gail's only biological child, and yet she had never felt deeply connected to her mother. Even now, while Isabelle searched for grief, what she really felt was relief.

Isabelle left Cedarloch the first moment she could, but Harper stayed behind. And Harper had been good about staying in touch over the years. Letters. Texts. FaceTime. A handful of visits here and there. But it was always on Isabelle's terms, always Harper coming to her, even though Harper had her own farm to tend to and a child to raise. Isabelle was stubborn like her mother and had refused to visit Cedarloch. Jack made a joke that her mother died just to get her to come home. Maybe in some supernatural way, Gail had.

And maybe one day she could explain to Maisy how complicated her childhood had been. But not now.

"Your mom sure had a lot of stuff." Maisy stopped, huffed, threaded her fingers into her doll's matted hair. She gestured to the oversize trash bags lined up outside the back door, like dead bodies wrapped in tarps. Harper had gotten a head start before she arrived, which Isabelle was grateful for. There were so many bags, she'd had to call to see if she could get a dumpster out here. She knew it was a fat chance, and she was right. There was one a mile outside of town. Thank God for her ex's pickup truck. Something she'd convinced Jack to keep after a bit of a fight.

"Yeah, she did." Isabelle gnawed on the inside of her cheek until it was raw, wondering if it was the right thing, bringing Maisy here. But because Jack would be traveling on assignment, they traded summers. This one was hers, so she didn't really have much of a choice. "Hopefully we can get out of here in a day or two, Bug."

Maisy nodded, her large gray eyes raking over the woods. "Must have been lonely growing up here."

"Actually, it wasn't. My brothers and sisters and I would play like we lived in these woods. We weren't afraid of anything." Isabelle was shocked to realize, as she said it, that it was mostly true. They'd felt they owned this land, exploring it, conquering it, claiming it. With her siblings, she always had someone to play with, someone to talk to.

After the fire, Isabelle spent years trying to shed the survivor's guilt she could never seem to shake. Harper had survived, too, of course, but the void her siblings left couldn't be filled by only one person. It couldn't be filled by anyone.

Though Isabelle didn't like to discuss her past outside of therapy, one question plagued her for years: Why had she and Harper been spared? And then there were the darker questions, the ones she couldn't ask, the fears she couldn't touch.

"Mama? What's this?"

Maisy's voice broke the silence as she kicked at something in the dirt.

"Let me see." Isabelle's mind was all over the place. So many things to clean, collect, toss, and sell. It shocked her, all the random objects collected in one's life. And after? They became someone else's problem to deal with. As if the grief wasn't hard enough, you had to sift through all those reminders too.

Isabelle crouched and brushed away the dirt. She recoiled, a small gasp startling Maisy. They looked like bones. A rabbit, maybe? She dusted away a bit more of the dirt, tracing the outline of what appeared to be a finger. Smaller than hers.

No.

She swallowed, her gut aching. "Come on, sweetie. Let's go inside."

Maisy protested, but Isabelle ushered her in through the back door, into the must of the house that was still so cluttered despite hours of Harper's initial head start. Her heart pounded wickedly as flashes of memory hit her consciousness. *Bones. Dirt. Shovels.*

She needed to forget.

2

Inside, Maisy tugged on Isabelle's arm, urging her to finish what they'd started.

Luckily, Maisy loved to organize and clean and had been a big help so far. They moved toward the hall that led to a tiny cluster of rooms at the rear of the house, where she and her siblings had shared two bedrooms between the five of them.

"Do you miss your mom?"

Maisy's voice startled her as Isabelle hauled a bag of trash toward the back door. Maisy followed, dragging a smaller, lighter one.

How did she answer this? "You know, Bug, it's sad to say, but I don't really." Isabelle settled for the truth, figured it was better to teach Maisy not to sugarcoat things, not to tell people she felt one way when she clearly felt another.

"You don't?" Her eyes went wide. "Why not?"

She groaned as she opened the back door and tossed out the bag. It landed with a thud next to the others. "My mother was complicated." Maybe best to leave it at that. She hadn't spoken about her mother—to anyone—in years, and she didn't want to start now. After her siblings died, awful, terrible accusations were flung her mother's way, so much so that Isabelle had started to believe them too.

The media had had a field day after her first foster brother, Marcus, had gone missing. He'd simply vanished one day after wandering in the woods, and the world had thought the worst of Gail. Then, as with most things, they'd forgotten, until three more children under the same roof died only a few short years later. Now, with Gail's own death, the reporters had reared their heads again, cracking everything open to get to the bottom of a mystery Isabelle herself had never been able to solve. Jack often wondered if this was why she became a journalist: to suss out the truth.

But it was natural for Maisy to want to know about her grandmother. Isabelle searched for a funny story or warm memory to share, something to humanize Gail, but mostly what she remembered was her mother being tired: tired from raising five children on her own, tired from cleaning the house, tired from homeschooling them, tired from constantly cooking food and working and living off the land. Because of where they lived, they'd all become wildly independent. They could do most chores around the house and knew basic survival skills, like chopping wood, starting a fire, foraging, getting clean water, and providing simple wound care. You had to, living in a place like this.

"What about your brothers and sisters?"

Isabelle's stomach churned. "Yes, I miss them very much." That was the honest answer. She missed them so much sometimes, it made her feel paralyzed.

"What happened to them?"

Isabelle paused as she considered how to explain. She wanted to be the type of mother who could answer a simple question. A woman who could smile, say the right thing, and pretend life had turned out the way she wanted it to. But Isabelle wasn't that woman, and she wasn't sure she wanted to be that type of mother either. Yes, she wanted to protect Maisy, but she wanted to honor the truth too. In the space that question left, they walked back and forth from room to room, dragging out bags and small pieces of furniture they could donate or sell.

"Well," Isabelle grunted as she carried a particularly heavy end table from the living room, "there was an accident. A fire." The truth, then. Isabelle would continue to share the truth.

Maisy stopped and looked at her, confused. "A fire?"

Before she could explain further, there was a knock on the front door. "Yoo-hoo? Anyone home?"

Isabelle was thankful for the distraction but surprised. From what she knew, her mother had become somewhat of a recluse these last few years, living completely off the land, canned food, and whatever else she owned . . . which, judging by all the cleaning and sorting, was a lot. Besides her visits from Harper, Isabelle wasn't sure who else her mother had in her life.

She set down the end table and walked to the front. Rita, the funeral home director, waved her hand in apology. "Hi, Isabelle. I'm sorry to just barge in like this, but, well, I had some papers I needed you to sign and thought I'd come to you. Thought I'd save you a trip."

"Quite a trek." Isabelle wiped her hands on her shorts. "I could have come into town."

"Eh, it's nothing." Rita waved a hand dismissively and smiled down at Maisy.

But it wasn't. Their property sat on twenty acres. Protected. No one in Cedarloch had neighbors in the traditional sense. If you wanted to visit someone, you laced up your hiking boots, brought a weapon, and packed a canteen of water.

Shockingly, Gail had left the house only to her, not Harper. Isabelle was stunned, since she was the one who'd distanced herself from this place—and Gail.

It wasn't until Isabelle was back here, on this land, that she wondered if maybe she shouldn't sell the property. Yes, tragedy had struck here, but it was still part of her legacy. She glanced around now. Could it ever feel like an escape and not a tragic homecoming? Maybe she could sage the crap out of it, pass it down to Maisy someday. But did she want that for her daughter? Knowing what happened here and how desperate Isabelle had been to leave . . . no. She didn't want to pass that along to Maisy. Someone else could deal with it.

Rita squatted down to Maisy's eye level. "And what do you think of all this, young lady? Seeing where your mom grew up?"

"It's neat," Maisy said.

"Cedarloch is a neat place," Rita said, winking at her. "Stick around long enough, and you'll see why."

Isabelle signed the papers—something about the death certificate and her mother's insistence on being buried on the property without a coffin, like Isabelle's siblings—and handed them back. "We won't be sticking around."

Rita cocked her head. She'd barely changed over the years. Frizzy brown hair now bore thick hunks of gray. Her skin was thinner, like paper, pocked with sun freckles. However, it seemed a diet of sun, water, and fresh seafood had also kept her sharp and physically able. "No?"

"No." Isabelle frowned. She'd never understood the people here. So married to this place but so tight lipped about the bad things that happened here. Extremely tight-knit yet ready to throw you under the bus if they suspected you of anything. As if they all had amnesia. As if they'd all forgotten that after her siblings died, everyone had treated them at first with sympathy, then with contempt, then landed somewhere in the middle: indifference. By the time she was eighteen, Isabelle felt like a ghost. She had a few allies, sure, but most people steered clear. It made for some tense teenage years. Once she left, she'd settled into a loud, bustling city full of curious people and had become an investigative journalist instead.

"That's too bad," Rita said, tucking the papers into her backpack. "Maybe you'll change your mind. I know Harper would love to see you stay awhile."

"I won't." She held the front door open, and Rita, taking her cue, lifted her hand in another wave.

"Don't be a stranger, Izzy. Bye, Maisy."

Isabelle shut the door. Wasn't that what she was now? A stranger? Maisy shifted from foot to foot.

"You hungry, kiddo?"

She nodded. Isabelle smiled, looking Maisy over. Dark, unruly hair, with massive kinks of curls she got from Jack. Large gray eyes rimmed in jet-black lashes. Gangly limbs. Maisy was all thin, sharp edges, but

Isabelle knew puberty was coming, knew that her little girl would soon morph into a young woman, and then a grown one. If she did her job right, Maisy wouldn't need her. She'd be fine on her own. But Isabelle had such a short time to instill all the good stuff, to protect her, teach her, and hold space for her. She studied Maisy's clothes—her shoes, especially.

They hadn't prepared well. Isabelle had gotten the call from Harper in the middle of the night, like most bad news, and they'd come as soon as it was light out. Maisy had on Skechers when what she really needed was hiking boots. Maybe there was a store in town? Or maybe they wouldn't be here long enough for it to matter.

"We'll work a bit more and then head into town. Pizza, maybe?"

"Sure." Maisy eyed the cabin again, her eyes roaming everywhere. In Portland, they lived in a small, tidy condo. There was no green space, but they were across the street from a park. Before she and Jack split, he'd had his condo and she'd had hers. With the nature of their work and so much travel, having two places worked for them. Maisy had simply grown up with it, so when they separated, it hadn't come as a shock.

Isabelle loved their home in the Pearl District, mainly because it was the opposite of what she'd had growing up. It was full of restaurants and shops, and was walkable to almost everything. Jack lived in Dunthorpe, the crown jewel of Portland luxury living. Despite her mostly urban upbringing, Maisy seemed curious about the sprawling land here, the seduction of it.

Though Isabelle considered herself more of a city girl now, when she was a child, this entire twenty acres had been her playground. She'd been free to explore and roam for hours at a time. Often, she and her siblings would stay out the entire day, coming home, muscles aching, only to get up in the morning and do it all over again. She'd forgotten this part of her existed, the part who knew how to be in the wild, who *was* wild. Instead, she'd let herself become domesticated these last twenty years. Isabelle had craved it, in fact. But standing here, she remembered a different version of herself.

Tonight would be their first night staying in this cabin. Harper insisted they come stay with her, but Isabelle wanted to remain close to the cabin, so she could get an early start tomorrow. She'd already made up her, Celia, and Harper's old room for Maisy. She would sleep in the boys' room.

She waited for Maisy to ask her again about her siblings, but when she didn't, they went back to work. After the last bag was tossed outside, Isabelle tented her hands around her hips and exhaled, glancing at the sky. Hopefully rain would hold off so they could haul everything to the dumpster tomorrow.

"All right, let's head into town."

Before Maisy started walking to the truck, she stared into the woods and then stopped, pointing at something behind the trees. "Who's that?"

Isabelle had already opened the driver's side door and was hoisting herself into the cab. "Who's what, Bug?"

"That person."

Person? Dread filled Isabelle's belly as she hopped back out of the truck and stood where Maisy was, following her outstretched finger toward the tree line.

Isabelle searched for a buck or a fox, so common in these woods. She'd already warned Maisy about the bigger dangers, like black bears, and the more elusive wolverines. "I don't see anything. I'm sure it was nothing." Isabelle looped an arm around Maisy's slight shoulders and ushered them toward the truck. She glanced back to the trees again.

There was nothing to worry about, she told herself.

Nothing at all.

Then

Isabelle

Isabelle and Harper raced through the woods, Celia close behind.

Since they'd built the tree house a month ago, it seemed the five of them were always there. Tonight, Isabelle had packed a small bag because they were doing a sleepover. Her mother had given her a hard time for bringing some of her favorite treasures, but she loved to pretend she lived in the middle of the woods and the five of them had to fend for themselves. Just like the Swiss Family Robinson.

Jude and Ben said they were too old to role-play anymore, and Isabelle was disappointed; just because you were a teenager didn't mean you had to lose your imagination, did it? Her mother said she was the most creative of the bunch, which was a rare compliment coming from her.

Celia lagged farther behind. Lately, clumps of Celia's hair had been falling out. Her eyebrows were disappearing, and since she was a fair-haired, freckled girl, it made her self-conscious. "Wait." Celia wheezed a bit, stopped, braced her hands on her knees.

"You okay?" Harper asked.

Celia had also been getting more and more winded. Come to think of it, so had the boys. They were listless, not as active as they usually were. Isabelle thought maybe they were passing a virus around, but she felt totally fine. Harper had complained of a few stomachaches but didn't seem as bad as the others. Whatever it was, she hated to see them suffering.

Celia stood, panting through her mouth. "I've been feeling so lightheaded." Celia was a bit of a hypochondriac. She'd once bought a medical dictionary at one of the neighbor's yard sales, and ever since, was convinced she had a whole host of diseases. But when she started to lose her hair, Isabelle and Harper had pored over the book, trying to put Celia at ease. The symptoms had started only with Celia, but when Ben, Jude, and Harper started issuing complaints, too, Isabelle, ever the problem solver, had been determined to get to the bottom of it.

"Don't worry. We'll look it up." Even as Harper said it, Isabelle panicked a little. What if they *couldn't* get to the bottom of it? What if they all had some contagious disease, and it was a matter of time before she got it too?

Every time Isabelle expressed concern to her mother, Gail would dismiss Isabelle and call her dramatic. The neglect was cruel, and Isabelle was starting to feel out of her depth with knowing what to do.

Her mother firmly believed in the body's ability to heal itself. In the last few years, they'd all suffered through colds and flus, shivering or coughing late into the night. They took turns trying to make natural tinctures to help. Word got around, but neighbors had long ago stopped dropping medical supplies on their doorstep.

Maybe Isabelle could run into town tomorrow, see if she could get some meds from the pharmacy. Even though she wasn't the oldest, sometimes it felt like her job to take care of them. Because they all knew Gail wouldn't.

Isabelle waited until Celia was ready to walk again and linked arms to help steady her sister. "Where's the first place you want to go when you're eighteen?"

It was a game they often played. In their room the three girls had a globe they would take turns spinning, dragging their fingers against the bumpy terrain. Wherever it stopped, they'd research that city or country and decide if they wanted to go there someday. So far, Celia only had a short list: Auckland, Austin, Paris, Tokyo, and Cairo. While Harper played, she loved Cedarloch and had no plans to leave. Isabelle knew Harper wanted to take over her real family's farm when she was old enough. She couldn't leave her legacy behind.

But Isabelle's list of cities was up to twenty-five. Every time her finger paused on a place and she read more about it, she became obsessed. She imagined her life, what her home might look like, and what it would feel like to host her siblings for family dinners.

This was what tonight would be like. A family dinner. Just the five of them. She'd brought a freshly baked loaf of sourdough. For the last six months, Isabelle had been trying to perfect the recipe. Gail couldn't tolerate bread, so Isabelle had grown up not eating it. Still, she wanted to make something nice for everyone. Celia had burgers already cooked, wrapped in aluminum foil. Harper had made a pie. The boys were bringing a salad and some baked beans. It felt so adult of them, marching out into the wilderness to spend the night alone.

As the woods cleared, she glimpsed the tree house. The boys had painted it red and blue. It was two stories. The downstairs, or "the Parlour," as the girls had named it, was open and designated as a hangout, while the upstairs was for sleeping and holding important meetings. It was a proper tree house with a roof and everything. Luckily, it wasn't too hot tonight, so they could hopefully sleep in peace.

"Ahoy! Who goes there?" Ben stuck his head out of one of the tiny windows upstairs and smiled. Now that he was fifteen, his voice had dropped, he'd shot up a foot in the last few months, and he'd lost at least ten pounds. He had white-blond hair that had been recently buzzed, because his hair had also started falling out. Isabelle was petrified it would happen to her too. Lately, she'd become obsessive about raking her fingers through her own hair and then having Harper count the strands that landed in her palm. How many were too many?

"We come bearing gifts!" Isabelle shouted, lifting the loaf of bread.

"I'll be the judge of that." Jude appeared around the corner, a scary mask he'd carved from teak positioned over his face. "Bread, please."

Isabelle rolled her eyes but handed over the loaf. He pinched off a tiny end, lifted the edge of his mask, and chewed. "Isabelle, wow." He ripped off the mask. "This is delicious."

Her heart warmed. Isabelle thought she'd nailed this recipe, but because she didn't ever eat the bread, she wasn't sure. Now she was. Jude never lied.

"Thanks."

At seventeen, Jude was the oldest, and they naturally defaulted to his leadership. Though they'd all built the tree house together, he was the one who kept them in line. But she was worried about him too. Dark circles bruised the hollows beneath his eyes. His right hand trembled, like he was afraid of something.

"You okay?" It was the second time she'd asked one of her siblings that question in under five minutes. She shifted her heavy backpack and glanced from him to Ben to Celia to Harper. What was wrong with them? She hated feeling this helpless, like there was nothing she could do.

"I'm great," he said, raking a hand through his dark, messy hair. "Counting down the days until I conquer the world." He offered his lopsided grin, and Harper rolled her eyes.

"Everything you need is right here."

"Oh, yeah?" He tipped back the aluminum foil on Harper's pie and stuck a finger in it.

"Hey!" she shouted. "Gross."

"We're all family." It was something they always said, but it wasn't really true. They were all brimming with hormones and acne, and none of them were related by blood. Sometimes Isabelle thought it was the worst idea, having all of them crammed into such a tiny space. And other times, she couldn't imagine growing up with anyone else.

When it had been Harper, Isabelle, and Marcus, she and Harper had banded together, staying as far away from their foster brother as possible. After he disappeared, Isabelle felt like they could breathe again. But when her mother brought in Jude, Celia, and Ben, the five of them had instantly clicked. In three years' time, they'd become a real family. It was all she'd ever wanted.

But lately, Jude was eager to remind them that next year, he would get to venture off to college. Isabelle couldn't imagine life without him. The thought of it made her want to cry.

They got set up, laying out blankets and pulling out paper plates and plastic forks. They ate and talked, and Isabelle couldn't remember the last time she felt so happy. Sometimes, when they ate dinner together in the cabin with her mother, the conversation felt censored. But here, among the trees, with only the five of them, they could speak freely.

"Can we just live out here?" Celia asked the group. She tore off another hunk of bread and smeared butter on it.

Isabelle smiled at the thought and raised her hand. "I would."

Ben raised his hand. "Me too."

Harper followed suit. "You know I would."

They waited on Jude to respond. He was staring over the railing at something in the woods. "I'd be up for that," he said at last.

Isabelle let out a breath. The moment she got away from the cabin, she was reminded of what awaited her in the future. What awaited all of them. Freedom. Exploration. New places, new people, and a whole world outside of Cedarloch. Jude was right to be excited. Because no matter what they did or where they went, they would always have each other.

"Let's play truth or dare," Ben suddenly said, sitting up.

Harper clapped her hands. She loved this game.

Jude rolled his eyes but lay on his side, propping his head in his hand while Celia groaned.

Isabelle pulled her legs into a cross-legged position. She hated dares, and everybody knew it. But not wanting to be the odd one out, she shrugged.

"Jude, truth or dare," Ben said.

"Duh, dude. Dare."

Ben rubbed a hand over his buzzed hair as he contemplated. "I dare you to run back to the house and steal a bottle of wine." He hiked one eyebrow in a challenge.

Harper laughed, and Isabelle and Celia gasped. Their mother had become somewhat of a wine drinker and now kept the alcohol locked out of sight. How would he even get a bottle? How would Gail not know?

"Too easy." Jude hopped up and was already making his way down the ladder. "Be back in a sec."

Isabelle fidgeted. Would she be expected to drink? She'd never had alcohol before. What would it taste like? What would she feel like? "Are you going to drink some?" she asked Celia and Harper.

Harper shrugged. "I mean, why not, right? You only live once."

"Yeah, you only live once," Celia parroted.

Isabelle wasn't sure if she believed that. She believed in ghosts and reincarnation and was pretty sure she'd been around the planet a few times. It brought her peace sometimes, thinking that if she couldn't figure it all out in this life, then there was always the next one. Gnawing on a hangnail, she debated what to do if Jude offered her wine. Her heart began to beat wickedly at the mere thought of having to decide.

Before she could contemplate how she could get out of it, Jude was climbing back up the ladder, winded, one bottle of red wine clutched in his fist and another wedged beneath his arm. "Ta-da!"

"How'd you do that so fast?" Ben asked, clearly impressed.

"I knocked her over the head with it," Jude said.

Celia cackled while Harper frowned. Though Gail wasn't Harper's biological mother, she might as well be. Harper had known Gail much longer than the others. Lately, Celia had whispered to Isabelle in the dark that she thought Gail hated all of them because they weren't her real children. That Isabelle was the chosen one because she was her only biological child. Isabelle spent a lot of time explaining how that couldn't be true, but it made her sad that Celia felt that way. Did the boys? Did Harper? Did *she*?

She'd heard Jude and Ben talking about how since Isabelle was the only one who wasn't sick, maybe Gail was making them sick on purpose and sparing Isabelle. The idea was awful. Her mother was a lot of things, but she wasn't a monster . . . was she?

The wine had a screw top, so Jude had it off in seconds. Celia and Harper held out their mugs. Isabelle did the same while Jude poured. Maybe she could pretend to drink it? She sniffed. It smelled like grape juice but a bit more pungent.

Jude held up his mug. "To family," he said. "And to the best friends I've ever had."

Isabelle felt the back of her throat nearly close up, because it was true. She loved her siblings so much, would do anything for them. Even though it had only been three years, it felt like a lifetime. It was hard to remember life before them. They all took a sip. Isabelle tilted her mug back and took a small taste. It was sour, but it wasn't awful. She swallowed, almost proud of herself.

"Jude, you're next," Ben said.

"Oh, right." He took another swallow, swished it around his mouth, gurgled it. "Isabelle, truth or dare."

Everyone would expect her to say truth. It was what she always chose. She took another sip for courage. "Dare."

All three of them looked at each other and then began clapping and cheering. "A dare for Isabelle!" Harper said. "Someone, please, remember this moment."

Isabelle rolled her eyes. Already, the wine was making her chest warm. She felt looser, more relaxed. She downed the rest, then reached out her mug to have some more.

"I like this version of you, Izz," Jude said, topping her off. "Archers, huddle." Jude, Celia, Harper, and Ben grouped together, whispering, while Isabelle drank more wine.

Finally, they all cleared their throats and sat back. Jude's eyes were shining. "We dare you to walk to River's house and flash him through the window."

Isabelle nearly choked. Flash River? River Foust? Everyone knew she had a crush on River. And that River liked her back. But *flash* him? She'd never done anything remotely like that in her life, but the wine made her feel bolder, so unlike herself.

"Fine." She stood, her legs wobbly.

Jude nodded to Harper. "Go with her so we know she actually does it."

"On it," Harper said.

The two of them took turns down the ladder and then stalked off into the woods toward River's house, which was only five minutes from the tree house.

"Are you really going to do it?" Harper asked. "They'll never know if you don't."

"Who knows?" Isabelle said. "Maybe."

They walked in silence. With every step, Isabelle felt more relaxed and also sleepy. When she nearly took a wrong turn, Harper gently grabbed her wrist and steered her in the right direction. She let herself be led. Before she'd even decided what she would do, they were at River's cabin. What if his parents were home? What if they saw her? She and Harper stood there until Isabelle felt a sharp sting.

"Ow. Why do you always do that?" Isabelle cradled her arm. Harper had pressed her fingernails into her flesh, leaving angry half moons on her skin.

"I didn't mean to." Harper stalked ahead and knocked on River's window. He had a room at the back of the house. She knew Harper had a crush on him too. Who didn't, really?

Harper ran back giggling. "He's inside! He's inside! Do it!"

Isabelle took a breath. She was only thirteen, but she'd gotten her boobs early. They were good boobs, she thought. Well, decent, at least. She walked up to his window and saw him peering out. Before she could change her mind, she lifted her shirt and smashed her chest against the glass. She counted to five, dropped her shirt, and then began to run back toward the tree house. Harper squealed as she hooked her arm through Isabelle's to help her get away.

"I cannot believe you just did that!" Harper's voice echoed through the trees. "Who are you, Isabelle Archer? I didn't think you had it in you."

Neither did she. But she'd done it. She'd actually *done* it. And nothing bad had happened. Maybe tonight could be the start of something different. A change. More bravery. Being able to actually take a few risks.

They giggled all the way back to the tree house. When it came into view, Harper shrieked that Isabelle had actually gone through with it, and the boys clapped for her.

When Isabelle made it to the top of the ladder and took her seat, she felt different, like she'd done something important, more grown up.

For the first time, she wondered what else she might be capable of.

3

The drive into town was bumpy but quick.

They parked at the edge of the main strip so they could walk. There was one direct road that curved around the entire lake, sealing it in like soup in a bowl. Jagged green mountains jutted up around them, dotted with stray homes overlooking the crystal-blue water. Everyone else's homes were tucked inside the trees, spread out, spacious, hidden.

The land opened up to her as it always did, with its expansive peaks and valleys and stunning water peppered with houses, boats, and aged wooden docks.

It only took twenty minutes to walk the entire perimeter of downtown Cedarloch, so that was what they did. Isabelle found herself almost nervous as she pointed out old, familiar haunts and marveled at new ones. It was then and now all wrapped into one.

"Feet okay?" she asked as Maisy lagged behind.

"I'm hungry."

"Right." Isabelle's appetite had disappeared since the news of her mother's death, her last biological tether gone. She'd never known her father, never wanted to after the few stories her mother had shared. All she'd ever known was Gail. All Isabelle had carried was the shadow of who Gail might be, the unspeakable things she might have done.

They'd passed a pizza parlor, Dough, a block back. It was late, but she hoped they were still open. They circled back and grabbed a table outside. Isabelle felt her shoulders relax as she stared out at the water. This, she had missed.

"Know what you want?"

Isabelle was pleasantly surprised to see they had gluten-free crust. After they ordered, Maisy started up again with the questions. What happened after her siblings died? Why didn't they see Harper more? What really happened to her mother? What was she going to do with the cabin? What was her favorite part about being back?

Isabelle tried to answer as best she could, starting with the first question. Again, she glanced out at the water, at the majesty of the mountains that seemed to puncture the sky. "Well, after the fire, it was only me, my mom, and Harper again," Isabelle explained.

"Was that hard?" Maisy asked as she sipped from her straw and kicked her feet against the legs of her chair.

"Very, but it was also kind of normal." Isabelle explained that she and Harper had been best friends first, and that their mothers had also been best friends. After Sandy died, Gail had taken Harper in without question, and right after, her mother had also taken in Marcus. But Harper was her oldest friend, her closest companion.

"Then why don't we see her more?" Maisy asked again. "If she's your best friend?"

Isabelle almost told Maisy that when you got old enough, best friends didn't matter so much. But she wasn't sure she believed that; somewhere along the way, Isabelle had stopped prioritizing friendships like she once had.

"Because we live in different cities."

"But she comes to visit sometimes."

"She does." Isabelle paused. "Harper knows I don't like coming here."

After she left Cedarloch, Isabelle was convinced her mother had something to do with that fire, had maybe done something horrible to Marcus too. She worried for Harper, alone with Gail, even though Harper moved back to her family home when she was old enough and had built her own life, separate from Gail. But Harper had always been too trusting, especially when it came to Gail.

"But she's your best friend!" Maisy was indignant.

"We're not really best friends anymore, Bug," she explained. "Sometimes, when you're friends with someone your whole life and then you move away, you make new friends."

"I don't have a best friend."

Isabelle's heart ached at that statement because it was true. Back home, Maisy had playdates but hadn't found a true best friend yet. "You will, Bug. You will."

After their bellies were full, they drove back to the house, the headlights chopping the trees, making shadows and ghosts of plain objects. She kept glancing over at Maisy to see if she was scared. She'd purposely avoided taking Maisy anywhere near the woods most of her young life . . . for more reasons than one.

Back inside, the cabin felt stripped and sad. Despite her best efforts, they hadn't made a huge dent in cleaning the house. Harper had told her not to worry about it at all, that she was happy to handle it, but it was Isabelle's responsibility. Gail left the house to her, not Harper, so she would take care of it.

Tomorrow, she would call a real estate agent and see if she could simply sell it as is. Hire a company to clean out the rest. She didn't want to spend any more time with her mother's belongings. They brushed their teeth in the tiny bathroom and changed into pajamas, and then Isabelle tucked Maisy in.

Maisy's large eyes inspected her surroundings. "I can't believe this was your room."

And Harper and Celia's too. Her mother hadn't touched it since she and Harper were teenagers. After the others passed, all the rooms were left untouched, half of this room resembling a shrine to her dead sister. All of Celia's favorite belongings—books, markers, marbles, a record player, her rock farm—were waiting for her as if she were still coming back. Once Celia was gone, they'd gotten rid of the bunk beds and pulled in a twin bed from the boys' room. It was morbid to think about Harper having slept in Jude's old bed, but they didn't have a lot of money back then and had to make do.

"Do you think you'll be able to sleep, Bug?"

Maisy clutched her doll and nodded.

"Do you miss home?"

She nodded again.

"I know, sweetie. Me too. We'll be home soon. Love you. Sleep well." She kissed her forehead, flicked off the light, and shut the door.

Next door, her hand froze on the knob to Ben and Jude's bedroom. Would it still be filled with all of their most treasured items? Isabelle gently closed her eyes, recalling a normal summer night. What would Ben and Jude be doing? Jude loved to whittle. Ben loved to draw. Often, she'd barge into their room to find Jude with a knife and Ben on his belly, sketching. She'd beg them to come play. They would tell her to scram. Usually, she could convince them. She smiled at that. Isabelle had always been very good at persuasion.

She sighed and opened her eyes. They were cemented on the door. How long had it been since she'd thought about her brothers and Celia? How much had she blocked out? That grief had been too vast, losing them. It had cut her deeper than anything else. Looking back, she wasn't sure how she'd survived it.

Isabelle hadn't touched these rooms yet, hadn't dared pack them up. It felt sacrilegious almost, since her mother was so hell bent on keeping them the same, and she found herself furious that this mess had been left for her to clean.

After a deep breath, she twisted the knob, stepped inside, and flicked on the light. Dust danced through the air. The room was thick with it. She crossed over to the windows, tried to lift them. It seemed they were painted shut. She grabbed her utility knife, dragged a short blade along the seam of one window until she could pry it open. It released with a crack.

Her eyes assessed everything. One twin bed with plaid covers was neatly made, everything in its exact place. LEGOs, magazines, whittling tools, drawing supplies, and textbooks lined neatly on a shelf. Her mother used to joke that she, Harper, and Celia were the messy ones and her boys were the neat freaks.

The bookcases were still stocked, science projects on display, as well as Jude's whittling. He used to love to carve masks. She'd forgotten how good he'd become. She picked one up now, dragged her fingers over it. It was almost chilling. When Halloween came around, Jude would come up with scary creations and chase them all through the woods, like they were part of their own horror movie.

She set the mask down and went to grab a Swiffer, knocked away thick cobwebs, and cleaned surfaces covered with inch-thick dust. She could not imagine peeling back the covers of Ben's bed and sleeping here tonight. No way. She couldn't do it.

Creeping back out of the room, she paused at the door and listened for Maisy. Satisfied she was asleep, Isabelle walked outside and searched for a signal.

She had a text from Harper.

> Hey, Izz. Just wanted to check in. Sorry I couldn't be there today. Ivy had a bunch of camps and the farm kept me busy. Maybe you and Maisy can come by tomorrow? Would love to see you both.

It shocked Isabelle sometimes to know that Harper had taken over her family's farm, that she'd chosen a life here, even with all the loss and pain. Though Harper kept checking in to see how Isabelle was taking the loss of Gail, it should really be the other way around. Gail had been sick for the past few months, and Harper had to step in. They were still waiting for the autopsy report, but it seemed like she'd simply died from natural causes, though the media liked to insinuate otherwise. Harper suspected Gail died from a broken heart.

Isabelle felt guilty she hadn't come home when Harper told her Gail had taken a turn. Harper thought it would be a chance for Isabelle to make amends or to maybe make peace with the past. But Isabelle didn't want anything to do with Gail. She'd stolen three people that she loved. She didn't have anything to say to her. Even when she'd stood over her grave, waiting for a wave of emotion to hit, all she'd felt was rage.

Isabelle offered a quick reply, saying she'd touch base with Harper tomorrow, before pocketing her phone.

The old, battered picnic table was still here, littered with starched pine needles. She brushed them aside, climbed on top, and lay back, gasping when the infinite flood of stars consumed her vision. It had been so many years since she'd seen this many stars without the constant light pollution of the city. She'd forgotten. Before the tree house was built, she, Celia, Harper, Ben, and Jude used to gather out here for sleepovers, staring at the star-dusted sky until they fell asleep.

She was drifting off when something jarred her awake.

Her eyes flew open, heart immediately pounding, and slowly, she sat up. You had to be careful out here with predators, never react too fast. Her hand went to her pocket, feeling the indentation of her utility knife. She panned the trees, but the sound had come from behind her. Like a slap. She sat all the way up, her eyes adjusting to the inky darkness.

A brush of something moved past her in the distance. A deer?

Then her brain computed. That wasn't a deer. It was fabric. Pajamas.

"Maisy?"

She scrambled off the table and walked toward where she thought her daughter had gone. Straight into the woods. What in the world was Maisy doing out here? Somehow, Isabelle had already lost sight of her. Or maybe it wasn't Maisy? She pushed her fists into her eyes, willing herself to wake all the way up.

She called her daughter's name again, strained to listen. The woods were dense, the trees so deep you got swallowed up the moment you entered them. Before she went on a wild-goose chase for nothing, she jogged back to the screen door and tiptoed down the hall. Isabelle paused. The bedroom door was wide open. She smacked on the light and stared at the empty bed.

Darting back outside, she panned left and then right. "Maisy?"

Why would she be out here? Where would she even go?

Before she could think too hard about the answer to that question, she approached the perimeter of the woods and stepped through.

"Maisy? Where are you, Bug?"

She strained to listen, but she only heard the sounds of actual bugs. Her heart ratcheted in her chest. Right then, a flash of yellow, out of the corner of her eye. Up ahead and to the left. Isabelle took off running, not paying enough attention. A branch scraped the flesh of her bare arm; another arched back and slapped her on the neck. She ignored the searing sting and moved forward, her feet stumbling for purchase on the uneven terrain.

Maisy was a city kid. She was used to parks, not woods. What if Maisy saw a deer? Or a bear?

"Maisy!" Her voice echoed in the eerie stillness, and her heart thudded dangerously in her ears.

Finally, up ahead, through a thicket of trees, she spotted her. "Maisy! Are you okay?"

As she neared, Maisy was standing still, something clutched in her fist. Her fingers were covered in dirt, her eyes glazed, unmoving. Isabelle shook her hard, and when Maisy didn't respond, Isabelle dropped her hands and jumped back as if she'd been shot.

Maisy was sleepwalking.

Carefully, without saying another word, Isabelle steered the girl back the way she'd come, as gingerly as she could. Inside, she wiped her daughter's hands clean, removed the object, and tucked her back into bed. She locked the windows and rigged a chair beneath the doorknob from the outside so Maisy couldn't escape again.

Sleepwalking. Maisy had never done it before. And Isabelle had never shared her own sordid history with it. Isabelle used to sit up nights when Maisy was younger, terrified she would turn out like her, but when Maisy had no episodes, Isabelle assumed they were in the clear. Now, the devastation of it was swift, as if her daughter had received a horrible, irreversible diagnosis.

Because Isabelle knew what this meant.

She knew how dangerous sleepwalking could become. That worry, rotting you from the inside.

Isabelle sat cross-legged in front of Maisy's door, prepared to sit there all night if she had to. Prepared to do whatever it took to keep her daughter safe.

4

"Mama! Mama!"

Thud. Thud. Thud. The wild, staccato rhythm of fists against wood jarred Isabelle awake. Orienting herself, Isabelle unpeeled her body from the hardwood floor. The door she'd rigged shut jiggled, threatening to dislodge. Maisy hated small spaces, hated feeling trapped. What had she been thinking, blocking her in?

"Hold on, Bug. I'm coming, I'm coming." Isabelle's body ached, but she ignored her stiff joints and removed the chair so Maisy could come out. Her cheeks were tearstained. She glanced at the chair.

"Did you lock me inside?" Her little chest heaved, and Isabelle felt instantly guilty.

"You sleepwalked." This probably wasn't the best way to tell her, but her own mother had sugarcoated it for years. If she'd only *known*, Isabelle could have handled it. Just like she would handle it for Maisy.

Her face scrunched. "I what?"

"Last night, you sleepwalked. Do you know what that is?"

"Yeah. Mr. Richards has a kid who does it." Maisy glanced down at her hands and nightgown, which were smeared with dirt.

Isabelle could see the mix of confusion and fear on her face. It was always terrifying, the thought of rising from your bed, going places, and not remembering. Not once in all the years that she did it could Isabelle recall a single episode. She'd tried so many times, but there was always just a void.

"Well, it's nothing to worry about," Isabelle reassured her. "I used to do it. I outgrew it, and you will too." She motioned toward the dining room chair. "I was worried you'd try to leave your room again, so I wanted to be safe."

Maisy yawned and moved past her to pee. That was the other thing she remembered. On the nights she sleepwalked, the next day, she had a fatigue she could never shake. She didn't want that for Maisy. She didn't want any of this for Maisy. They would get to the bottom of it. She was sure there were advances they'd made since she was a kid. She'd start researching, stay on top of it.

When Maisy was done, she immediately launched right back into questions about what happened last night.

"You were holding something," Isabelle said, just remembering.

Maisy looked at her hands again. More dirt lined the beds of her nails and beneath them. She stared at them in disbelief, as if her tiny fingers were doused in blood. Isabelle understood that disbelief, had lived with it her entire childhood.

Where had she put it? Ah, right next to the television. She picked it up now. It looked like a little talisman, something Jude would bury during scavenger hunts. This one was carved from a deer antler, and it was in the shape of an owl.

"That's pretty."

"My brother Jude made it." Isabelle ran her fingers over all the intricate edges. "He used to make these for us as presents and then hide them in the woods to find as prizes. Guess we missed this one." Surprisingly, her eyes filled with tears, and she cleared her throat, handing it over to Maisy, who inspected every inch of it.

"Mama needs coffee." She moved to the kitchen, praying her mother had a spare bag of coffee somewhere. She panned the space. Dishes filled the sink, crusted over with food. Her mother used to be obsessive about the tidiness of her kitchen. Never a meal eaten without immediate dish washing and drying. It was so ingrained in her now, some people assumed Isabelle had OCD. Everything was always in its place. What had happened to Gail to make her let it all go? Even after her siblings died, they stuck to their routine.

She scoured the sage green cabinets until she found a bag of local French roast and a few filters for the coffee maker. Thank God.

She was surprised Harper hadn't been in here to clean in the last few weeks. Or maybe she had, but her mother kept messing it all up. Guilt tapped her on the shoulder once again, reminding her that she'd left Harper here to care for Gail, when it should have been Isabelle's responsibility.

Once she had that first delicious sip of caffeine, some of the fog lifted. She was already making a list of to-dos in her head. They'd crammed in a lot yesterday but not enough. At least they'd paid their respects to her mother, whose body had already been stuffed into the earth, thanks to Harper. Her mother had always insisted on green burials, but when Isabelle had glimpsed the shovel beside the grave, so she could scoop dirt on top, she'd frozen.

Bones. Dirt. Shovels.

She had said a few words, Maisy looking on uncomfortably. Then they'd started cleaning and hauling out trash, but there was still so much left to be done. Before she could calculate how much, her phone buzzed. She assumed it would be Jack. He'd asked if she needed him to come help, but she'd politely declined. Though it had been her idea to separate, they were still great friends, and she didn't want to drag him into this. She didn't want to drag anyone into this.

To her surprise, it was Harper again.

Meet at my place at 9? I have good coffee and will make you breakfast. Ivy is dying to see Maisy!

Ivy and Maisy had also only met a few times, when they were little. They were nearly the same age, just as she and Harper had been when they became best friends. She wondered what Ivy was like now. When Harper was young, she was a bit of a pushover, always doing whatever Isabelle wanted to do. In fact, Isabelle had sometimes walked all over her, ignoring her feelings, being bossy, something she still felt bad about.

She glanced around the kitchen again. They didn't have anything for breakfast, and she didn't have the energy to start cleaning and bagging yet.

Okay was all she typed back. She sighed and turned back to Maisy, but she wasn't anywhere in sight. "Hey, Bug?" She searched the rooms and then looked outside, where Maisy was out back, playing with the owl and her doll at the picnic table.

Isabelle sipped her coffee and smiled as she stepped outside the screen door and leaned back against the cabin wall. In another life, this might have been an ideal situation, coming up to her family home for a getaway with her kid. If she rented out this place instead of selling it, she could probably make a fortune, especially from folks who were obsessed with true crime. She rolled her eyes at her own insanity and stared out at the woods again, remembering last night.

For the first time, she could put herself in her mother's shoes. How terrified Gail must have always felt, not knowing when Isabelle might venture off into these woods, and what might happen to her if she did. Gail had often locked her, Celia, and Harper inside their room and put that burden on her sisters to make sure Isabelle didn't do anything stupid. In many ways, Isabelle felt as though she were being punished for sleepwalking, and Celia and Harper were simply caught in the crossfire.

Isabelle checked the time. It was already after eight. They needed to shower, put on a fresh change of clothes, and make the trek through the woods to Harper's family farm.

"Want to go take a shower and then see Harper and Ivy?"

Maisy turned to her and nodded without question, scooped up her belongings, and walked back toward her. Before going back inside, Maisy stopped at the screen door, then turned, her eyes trained on the woods again. Her little breath hitched, and Isabelle's eyes followed her sight line.

"What is it, Bug?"

Maisy opened her mouth, then snapped it shut. "Nothing." She walked back inside, but Isabelle felt the hairs on her arms prick up. She took a few steps toward the trees, panning them again. What did Maisy think she saw?

And why was she so drawn to the woods last night?

Once she heard the shower running, Isabelle took the opportunity to follow the path she'd taken last night through the trees. She wasn't 100 percent sure she was retracing her steps correctly, but her memory was sharp, always had been. It had to be when you grew up in the forest.

It was only when she came to a stop mere feet from where they'd been last night that she saw it. A tiny mound in the dirt where Maisy had been digging, and what lay beyond. Her body clenched, as if prepared for an attack. The four headstones stared back at her.

Maisy had unknowingly sleepwalked right to her family's graves.

5

Harper lived west, about a mile through the woods.

When Isabelle was younger, she could make this hike by memory any time of day or night. Now, with Maisy traipsing clumsily behind her, Isabelle deliberately slowed her pace, trying not to obsess over the fact that her child had inexplicably started sleepwalking and had made a beeline for her family's headstones.

It would be pointless to ask Maisy why; anything one did while sleepwalking was a question for the subconscious mind, not the conscious one. Instead, Isabelle shared stories from her treks to Harper's house when she was younger, and Maisy shared random facts she was learning from one of her favorite podcasts, *Earth Rangers*. Maisy was an auditory learner, like Isabelle. If only Isabelle had podcasts growing up. Instead, she'd been subjected to ghost stories and tall tales around campfires. Her mother reading from fat novels when she was younger, or listening to children's stories on the old record player. She could still hear the crackle of those records, feel the anticipation of getting lost in someone else's words.

Nearly half an hour later, they emerged onto a beautiful sprawling property of five acres. A horse fence housed three mares. There were chickens, goats, and an old mutt that barked the moment they approached. To the right, the familiar red wood of the farmhouse greeted them. Isabelle placed a protective hand in front of Maisy, though she assumed the dog was trained.

Harper banged out the back screen door, mug of coffee in hand. "Preacher, come." The dog did as he was told, disappearing around the fence. She waved when she saw them, and Isabelle broke into a grin. As they approached, Maisy made comments about the animals. She loved animals. The zoo was one of their frequent outings back home. They passed other little treasures—raised beds of fresh herbs and vegetables, a box of bees, and a few cows off grazing in the pasture. Isabelle's whole body relaxed as she took it all in.

"Long time, no see, stranger," Harper said, pulling Isabelle into a swift, firm hug.

She melted into her oldest friend, her honorary sister. It had been too long. Seeing her again reminded Isabelle of how close they'd once been. They were *survivors*. The only ones. That was a bond you didn't share with just anyone.

"You look good, Izz." Harper smiled, her blue eyes crinkling. And so did she. Harper's skin was tanned, muscles long and lithe, like those of a yogi. But her hands were rough, calloused, a worker's hands. Harper glanced down at Maisy. "Hi, Maisy. Do you remember me? It's been a while."

Maisy tucked into Isabelle's side but nodded shyly.

"Want to meet the goats and chickens and then pick some veggies for an omelet? Do you like omelets?"

Maisy launched into her likes and dislikes as a smaller version of Harper exploded out the door. Ivy stopped next to her mother, all bony knees and elbows, freckled face, and a wide gap-toothed smile. Harper placed a protective hand over her head. "You two have met, but it was a while ago. Maisy, how old are you now? Sixteen?"

Maisy giggled. "No, I'm eight."

"Well, Ivy here just turned nine. She can show you the ropes. You girls be good, yeah? We'll be right inside."

Maisy cast Isabelle a look, and she nodded to tell her it was okay. A stab of guilt, as sharp as anything, hit her right in the heart. In another life, in another world, maybe Maisy could have grown up on the land, like Ivy. Maybe they could have already become best friends.

Though the outside of the house was the same, inside was nothing like she remembered. The farmhouse had been gutted. What was once homey had been replaced with an expensive, modern touch. It was breathtaking.

"Harper, wow. This place belongs in a magazine."

"Ha. It's already been in one. Coffee?"

"Sure."

She paused in front of a Sub-Zero fridge. "Cream? Sugar?"

"Cream, thanks." Isabelle accepted a fresh mug and took a sip. It was delicious. "Good coffee too?" She sighed. "You could rule the world, Harper West."

"I do, mostly." Harper laughed and showed her to a comfy sofa. Isabelle removed her shoes and curled up in her socked feet as Harper took the oversize chair next to her. Outside the floor-to-ceiling windows, she could see and hear Maisy squeal in delight as she fed a horse a carrot.

"Harper, this is really something." Though Isabelle didn't know everything about her life, it certainly looked good from here. "I'm so glad you kept the house and farm. Sandy would be over the moon."

"You think?" Harper swirled her fingers absently on top of her mug. She glanced around. "I think this might be a bit too updated for my mother's taste. But I always knew I wanted to take it over, to honor her memory."

"You've definitely done that."

"Thanks for saying that." She cocked her head. "So how's it been? To be back?"

"About how you'd expect." Isabelle hunted for what to say. There weren't enough words in the world to properly thank Harper for checking in on Gail, for being here for her when Isabelle chose not to. "About the house."

Harper waved a hand nonchalantly through the air. "It's fine."

"But it's not fine. She should have left it to you, not me. You could actually *do* something with it."

"Like what?"

"I don't know. Airbnb it? Sell it? Flip it?"

She shrugged. "Wasn't meant to be."

Isabelle searched for any resentment in her words but couldn't find it. She exhaled. "We can split the proceeds."

"Please, don't worry about that right now. We'll figure it all out, okay?"

"Okay." Isabelle glanced outside again, then back at Harper. "Can you tell me how she was before she died?"

Harper sighed but nodded. "Gail had been acting strangely these last couple of months. I'm ashamed to say I didn't make it out there as much as I used to. She'd . . . well, she'd really let the place go. I tried to help, but she'd get so angry at me. You know how she used to get."

Isabelle remembered. Gail was tough, both verbally and emotionally. A product of her own upbringing by her parents, but it didn't make their lives any easier.

"So, I'd go sit with her when I could, or have a cup of tea, but she seemed off." She shrugged. "I suggested she go get a checkup, but I'm sure you know how well that went over." Harper rolled her eyes, and Isabelle nodded. Her mother had loathed doctors. "And then, when I was taking her some groceries, I found her. She was already gone." Harper's voice got thick, and she cleared her throat, finally dragging her gaze back to Isabelle's. "I know you have your suspicions about her, Izz, I do. And I get it. But what I've come to realize is that she was a lonely old lady who'd truly lost everyone she ever loved. It made me sad for her."

"Lost? Or killed?" Isabelle snapped. "I saw the article."

Harper sighed again. "Don't read that trash. This town is so desperate for something to grab onto, they'd say any old thing." She waved a hand in the air again. "It's nonsense."

It was what Isabelle thought, too, but something about it still nagged her. "What about the timing? You think it has anything to do with the kids' anniversary?"

It was coming up in a matter of days. Twenty-five years. She didn't like to think about it.

"Maybe. But that would mean . . ." Harper trailed off.

That would mean suicide, and Gail was too proud of a woman to do such a thing. "Do you believe she killed them?" They hadn't had this conversation in decades, but it still mattered to Isabelle. She wanted Harper on her side. She wanted Harper to see what she saw.

"What does it matter what I believe?" Harper said. "I loved Gail. She took me in after my mom died. She treated me fairly. I'll always be indebted to her for that."

Isabelle clenched her jaw. Harper had always been soft for Gail when the rest of them weren't. If Harper wanted to have love in her heart for a monster, then that was on her. Isabelle just couldn't feel the same way.

"So how's Jack? Still journalist of the century?"

Isabelle was grateful for the subject change. She smirked. "Yeah, something like that."

"And you two? You're still not together?"

"Not at the moment." Isabelle and Jack were a great fit. Good chemistry, a stable foundation, wonderful coparents. But he wanted more—the house, the marriage, the whole traditional life—and Isabelle couldn't give it to him.

"Well, no one would blame you for not being able to commit after everything you've been through. Lord knows that's why *I* never got married."

Those words smacked Isabelle right in the heart. Because, out of everyone, Harper knew exactly how hard it was to want to get close to anyone after you lost everyone. Years ago, Harper had gotten knocked up and decided to keep the baby but not the relationship. She'd always been hush-hush about who the father was.

Harper swept her long hair over one shoulder. "How's work?"

"It's good, but I'm not working this summer. Jack's heading to the Middle East, so Maisy's on my watch." She and Jack had a deal. Since they were both investigative journalists, they didn't work at the same time. That way, the one on the job could become totally immersed in their work, and the other could focus on Maisy.

"I still can't believe you procreated with Pulitzer Prize winner Jack Pearce. Wild."

It was wild. Though Isabelle was nowhere near as successful as Jack, she never felt threatened by his prestige. Instead, she felt inspired by it. She'd been so very green when they first met. He'd showed her the ropes. They'd fallen in love, and then she'd gotten pregnant, which had inevitably changed things for both of them.

"Do you think there's a chance you guys will get back together?"

Isabelle shrugged. She'd been the one to break it off, much to Jack's disappointment. She stroked a soft leather pillow, fingering the buttery fabric. "I guess time will tell. What about you?"

"What about me? I'm boring. No love prospects on the horizon, that's for sure." She gestured around her. "I take care of the farm, take care of Ivy. We have a simple life but a good one."

"I think that's lovely, Harp." And she did. Isabelle was always jealous of people who wanted exactly what they had—nothing less, nothing more. Those were the people who really had it all figured out. No constant chasing or uncertainty, only pure, sweet acceptance.

"You hungry?"

Isabelle nodded. They rounded up the girls, who brought in fat baskets of produce: tomatoes, basil, bunches of purple onions, and sprigs of oregano. A half dozen eggs. Harper guided Maisy and Ivy through cracking the eggs and chopping the herbs, and they settled on making a frittata. By the time Maisy was done, Isabelle was rethinking her entire parenting strategy. At home, Maisy never asked to cook, so Isabelle didn't offer. Mostly, she put together quick dinners or they ate out.

"Mama, can Ivy show me her room?"

She looked to Harper to make sure it was okay. "Of course, Bug."

They vanished up the stairs, and both she and Harper seemed to be thinking the same thing, like this was a glimpse into another life, if only Isabelle was willing to forget.

"You set on selling the cabin?"

"Yeah, I am." Isabelle sipped the last lukewarm dregs of coffee as the fresh scents of parmesan and basil filled the room.

"No homesteading in your future?" Harper joked.

"No, I don't think so." The land felt cursed, all good memories she'd had before her siblings' deaths erased the summer Isabelle turned thirteen.

"Understandable." Harper busied herself with pulling down plates and cutlery, and Isabelle checked her phone. She responded to a few random texts, then opened her email and stopped. The preliminary findings for the autopsy report were already back. It would take weeks to get the full report, but this would put her at ease, at least.

"The preliminary autopsy report just came in," she said.

"Oh?" Harper stopped what she was doing and turned, eyes concerned. "And?"

Isabelle scanned the document, assuming she'd find the general run-of-the-mill "death by natural causes" terminology. But she didn't. "Oh, my God," she breathed, pinching and zooming in. She read the sentence three times and then looked up. "They found thallium in her blood."

Harper's face scrunched. "Thallium? Is that a drug?"

"It's poison." Isabelle's heart thudded violently against her ribs. In her late twenties, she'd done an entire exposé about thallium, which was a metal from the earth's crust. It had been the most personal piece she'd ever written. It had gotten Jack's attention. In fact, it was the entire reason they'd met.

She could never prove it, but Isabelle thought her mother had been slowly poisoning her siblings using thallium. With research, she was almost positive. Once the piece went live, her mother had reached out to her, enraged. Isabelle had blocked the calls. Part of her felt guilty for dragging her mother through more proverbial mud, but the piece wasn't all about her childhood. It also delved into murderers who used thallium because it was harder to detect than other poisons, but if someone knew to look for it, traces could show up in blood, in hair, or under the nails, even decades after the fact. Similar to rat poison, it was mostly banned in the nineties. She wasn't sure how anyone would even get it now.

"So what does that mean?" Harper asked.

"It means she didn't die of natural causes," Isabelle said, even checking herself as she said it. Was it possible her mother could have ingested thallium somehow and not known? No, she was almost positive.

"So someone *poisoned* Gail?"

Isabelle blinked, hearing the absurdity of that statement. Gail Archer, once beloved mother and saint, who took foster children in to give them a good home. Then, it was Gail Archer, suspected child killer, the kind of title and accusations one could never really shake. If someone had poisoned her, did Isabelle even have to guess why? She frowned. But why now? Why like this?

She swallowed, her racing thoughts all clashing for space. Her mother didn't die naturally; she'd been poisoned. Which meant her mother might have been murdered.

And someone in this town was responsible for her death.

6

The first thing she did was call Jack.

She bit her nails, pacing Harper's gorgeous backyard. "Pick up, pick up. Please, pick up." Jack's schedule this summer was insane. He would be in the Middle East for most of July and August. June was a heavy prep month.

"Hey, you. I was just thinking about you. How are you and Maisy doing?"

His voice was deep and warm, and she instantly felt her body relax. Though she had dated a lot in her life, Jack was the only man she'd ever felt truly safe with. Truly seen. She skipped the niceties. "I'm sending you something."

She waited until he confirmed receipt of the email. There was a loaded silence as he reviewed it. "Izz, is this for real?"

"Apparently. I mean, *thallium*? What are the odds, right?" That piece had landed her in all the major trades. Whoever did this must have known that. Was someone sending Isabelle a message?

"Izz, this changes things. You and Maisy. I'm not sure . . ." His voice faded. It was an unspoken fact between them. Their jobs were dangerous. Jack would be gone until September. They couldn't both be on assignment, both be at risk. One of them needed to offer stability and comfort for Maisy. This time, it was her.

"We're fine. I can handle it." But could she? If someone had purposely murdered her mother, then didn't that mean she could possibly be in danger too? "I'm going to see Theo." Theo was the only sheriff in town. She'd told Jack about him when they'd first met and Isabelle had wanted to dive back into the case, poke a little deeper to see what happened the night her siblings died. Theo had worked the case back then. He'd known her mother for a very long time. Seemed like a good place to start. "I'll get to the bottom of it."

"You sure I can't come up? Try to help?"

"And dazzle the town of Cedarloch with your presence? I wouldn't subject you to all your adoring fans, Jack Pearce."

He laughed. It was still one of her favorite sounds. It filled her entire chest with heat. "I miss you, Izz. So much. You know that, right?"

She sighed. Though she'd ended things a few months ago, he'd tried to rephrase it as going on a break. She'd loved their life, loved the autonomy it brought, but something in her couldn't let him all the way in. "I miss you too." It was true. She adored Jack. Besides Maisy, he was her absolute favorite person, and that was why she had to keep her distance.

"Keep me posted, okay? Kiss the Bug for me."

She smiled, despite the situation. "I will. She currently just fed farm animals, picked vegetables and herbs, and assisted in making a frittata."

"Bring her home immediately."

Isabelle barked out a laugh and hung up. Feeling a little lighter, she went back inside, hoping to get some intel on Theo.

The girls were at the table, eating their frittata and chatting. "Girls, finish your food. We'll be right back." Harper wiped her mouth with a cloth napkin and motioned for Isabelle to walk with her down the hall so they could chat in private.

Harper closed the door to a massive office. Books, arranged by color, studded the entire back wall in built-in bookshelves. A Lucite desk and a funky, patterned chair were perched in the middle of the room on a cream rug. "Everything okay?"

"Who's the sheriff now? Still Theo?"

Harper shook her head. "Yes and no. Technically he retired, but no one else has stepped up. There's not really any crime here, but if there's a problem, he's the one you'd talk to."

She nodded. He'd been an ally for her mother before her siblings died, but then when the tides had turned, he'd come after Gail with a ferocity that still shocked her. If it wasn't for him, the entire town wouldn't have turned on her like they had. Theo had put Isabelle and Harper in a hard position, both fearing Gail and also feeling strangely protective of her.

"You gonna go see him?"

"Yep."

Harper crossed her arms. "Look, if you want to leave Maisy here for a few hours, she can help with farm chores. She'll be so tired tonight, I can nearly guarantee she'll be out the moment her head hits the pillow."

Instantly, Isabelle saw Maisy in her bright pajamas last night, stalking assuredly but unknowingly through the woods. She debated. On one hand, she didn't really know Harper anymore, did she? But on the other, she didn't want Maisy to have to deal with any of this. Not until she knew more. Plus, it was only a few hours. "Are you sure?"

Harper waved a hand. "Consider it done. Trust me, Ivy will be thrilled."

Isabelle squeezed her arm. "Thank you, Harper. For reaching out. For today. For everything."

"What are friends for, right?"

Were they still friends? She hoped maybe they could be again. Back in the kitchen, she explained to Maisy that she needed to run some errands. Harper had them rinse their dishes and prepare for chores. Maisy was so excited, she barely said goodbye as Isabelle headed back through the thicket of woods.

So many questions raced through her head, and Isabelle mourned the fact that no matter how much she dug, she might never learn the truth. Isabelle hadn't spoken to her mother in years, despite being the last familial tether she had. They'd had a massive falling-out before she left Cedarloch, and Isabelle's stubbornness ran deep. Her mother knew that. Everyone here did.

Now, she regretted it. She regretted not knowing what was going on in her mother's life.

Not knowing who would want Gail dead.

Then

Ben

Ben had never seen Isabelle drunk before.

It disturbed him for some reason; he hated that they were all getting older, that pretty soon, Jude would move out, then him, then Isabelle, then Harper, and Celia would be left all alone. He'd never thought of the timeline in this exact way before, how their unit would disband one at a time. What if they grew apart? What if they moved to opposite ends of the world?

"Dude, hello! Are you drunk?" Jude lay down beside him, elbows behind his head, staring at the star-dappled sky through the gaps in the trees.

Was he drunk? Maybe. Ben felt thick in his bones. He didn't usually drink, and with the way he'd been feeling lately, now he was fuzzy, as if he could fall asleep any moment. Every time he sat up, he got dizzy, so he decided to stay lying down. His mind was still sharp, surprisingly. Below him, in the Parlour, he could hear the girls talking and giggling in hushed voices, just like they did in their bedroom most nights. When he was younger, he would desperately eavesdrop, wondering if any of the girls' friends liked him. But no one had a crush on him. With his white-blond hair and pale skin, he often got called an albino. He wasn't, but the words still stung.

After being tossed from foster home to foster home before Gail adopted him three years ago, he was used to it all. Terrible foster parents. Abuse. Being poor. Being bullied. He knew there were stereotypes about people in foster care, but from his experience, it was mostly true.

"Whatcha thinking about?" Jude asked.

Ben shrugged. "Life, mostly. How strange it will be when you move out."

"Aw, buddy, we still have one more year."

One more year. Ben rolled over, propped his head on his elbow. "I know, but I can't imagine it." He swallowed hard. Jude was the best older brother he could ask for. He was kind and patient and was the only male figure he'd ever really trusted. Maybe he could graduate home school early, go with Jude wherever he went? He perked up a bit at the thought of it.

"You're looking a little pale, man," Jude said. "You feeling all right?"

It was the common question ping-ponged among him, Jude, Harper, and Celia. *You feeling all right? You feeling all right?* It didn't make sense that Isabelle felt fine. It made him wonder, in the black of night, if she was behind this. But Isabelle wasn't a bad seed, not like some of the girls he'd lived with before. He could sniff out a freak a mile away, and she wasn't one. He hoped not, at least.

"I'm all right." He wasn't all right, not by a long shot. When his hair had started falling out, he'd nearly cried when he asked Jude to shave it. He loved his hair, and with it buzzed, he felt naked. Exposed. There was nothing to hide behind. And he was so tired all the time. No matter how much sleep he got, there was a fatigue deep in his bones he couldn't ever seem to shake.

"Boo!" Isabelle's head appeared at the top of the ladder, nearly startling him to death. He slapped a hand against his chest and then pushed his way up to sitting. Even that was an effort.

"Give me a heart attack, why don't you."

"Let's go do something crazy." Isabelle's eyes twinkled.

"Define crazy," Jude said.

"I don't know. Let's go roll somebody. Or egg somebody!"

"Yes, rolling!" Harper called from down below as Celia complained that she didn't want to go.

"Like they won't know it's us?" Ben countered.

"Come on. We never do anything fun anymore." She pouted. "Let's get into some trouble!"

This wasn't like Isabelle. The wine was really having an effect.

"Whose house?" Ben asked. He didn't know why he was playing along. He wasn't going to toilet paper anyone's house.

"Hmm." She worked her bottom lip between her teeth. "Maybe River? Or Ms. Rita? That way, if we get caught, they won't hate us."

"No." Jude smirked. "Let's roll *Theo's* house."

"Sheriff Mullins?" Ben swallowed even harder. "We could get in serious trouble, man."

"It's our bravery test for the evening." Jude steepled his fingers together and wiggled them as though hatching an evil plan.

"Harper and I will run home and get the toilet paper and eggs." Isabelle dropped back down before Ben could protest.

"You really think this is a good idea?" Ben asked. His stomach cramped after eating so fast. He was hoping they could chill and maybe build a fire, talk for a while.

"Sure. Why not?" Jude started to descend the ladder and jumped the last few rungs.

"What if we get in trouble?"

Jude grinned up at him. "What if we don't?"

Ben nodded, but he had a pit in his stomach. While he waited for the girls to return, he tried to tell himself nothing bad would happen.

It was only some harmless fun.

7

It had been two decades since Isabelle had seen Theo.

Back then, she'd had the occasional run-in, but after Celia, Jude, and Ben died, his presence was an unwelcome constant. Theo's house was sprawling, perched on the other side of the lake with a long, freshly painted dock and a few shutters in need of repair.

The forest dumped her out facing the back of his house. There Theo sat, sipping coffee in an Adirondack, his gaze fixed on something off in the distance. Harper had shared that his wife had died a while back.

Isabelle carefully stepped through the trees. Though he wasn't a sheriff anymore, his hand braced against his side. She was almost positive Theo had never used a gun, had never gotten to play a cop like he saw on TV.

"Isabelle Archer?"

His voice was thick and scratchy, raked with pain. If he was surprised to see her, his face didn't show it.

"Sheriff Mullins."

He waved her off, sighing. "It's just Theo now."

That was right. The retirement. What was it like to go from sheriff to *just Theo*? He'd changed, weathered, shrunk.

"You look well, Isabelle."

Did she? Isabelle didn't spend much time thinking about appearances. She never had. The last time she'd been here, she was only eighteen. Still gangly and awkward, in her own right. She caught a glimpse of her reflection in his shiny patio door and took a moment to study herself. Tall and strong, with long brown hair, usually swept up into a messy bun. A prominent nose, like her mother's, high cheekbones, a wide mouth with a freckle above her lip.

"Take a seat." He gestured to the second Adirondack chair she imagined was once reserved for his wife.

"I was sorry to hear about Barbara," she said, sinking into the cool wood.

He faltered, his eyes growing soft and wet. He cleared his throat, mumbled a *thanks*. How cruel time could be, Isabelle thought. You retire and think you have your whole life ahead of you. And then someone dies.

"So what can I do for you?"

"When's the last time you saw Gail?"

Theo scratched his jaw. "A long time. She kept mostly to herself."

"Know anyone who'd spent any time with her lately?"

"I didn't keep up with your mother's social life, if that's what you mean. I told that reporter the same thing."

"What reporter?"

He waved a hand. "Eliza what's her name. Works for *The Cedarloch Sentinel*. Been sniffing around here for a few days now."

Media had reached out to her as well, though she'd declined to comment. "Well, I received the preliminary findings for Mom's autopsy report," she explained. She sometimes wondered, all these years later, if he felt any guilt about how he'd treated Gail after the fire. How, when there were no logical answers and the town demanded them, he'd pointed a finger at her mother instead. It had become a sensational case, made all the more sensational because of how they'd handled the burials. Though her mother had gone through the proper channels to bury the kids on property, people assumed she was trying to hide something. But still, there was no concrete evidence ever linking Gail to those fires, so she'd gone free. Though Isabelle often thought her mother was guilty, there was still something about others coming for her that made her want to defend Gail too. Made no sense really, but it was how she felt back then.

He scratched his jaw again. "And?"

"Here." She passed her phone to him, and his eyes sifted over the findings. "Thallium?"

"It's a metal," she explained. "I did a piece on this a decade ago. Seems like too much of a coincidence, if you ask me."

He sat up straighter, his curiosity clearly piqued. "And there's no way to ingest it naturally?"

"No."

"Huh." He handed her phone back. "And you're here because . . . ?"

She huffed, just like she used to as a kid. "I'm here because I believe my mother was murdered, and I want to know who did it."

He let out a low whistle. "That's a mighty strong accusation. What proof do you have?"

She stabbed her phone. "The autopsy report, for starters." She thought for a second. "Who saw her body?"

"Frank." Frank Robbins was the only coroner in town. "Why?"

"Because thallium poisoning causes a host of issues." Isabelle stabbed a few notes into her phone. "I'd like you to get involved, Theo. Help me get to the bottom of this. Unless there's somebody else I can talk to?" Even as she made her ask, she wasn't sure he would go for it. But then, on the other hand, maybe this could be a chance to unwind some of the past, do a good deed.

He cleared his throat. "No one's taken over yet. It's just me." After a beat, he nodded. "I'll look into it." He stood, signaling the chat was over.

"Where are you going to start?"

He sighed, his eyes drifting past her again, to the forest. "I'll see who was up by the cabin in the last week or so. Establish your mother's routine. Your mom have any cameras out there?"

She blinked at him. The thought hadn't even occurred to her. "I don't think so, but that's a great point. I'll check." Isabelle hesitated before asking the next question. "Do you think this has something to do with what happened back then?"

"You mean with the fire? The kids?" He shook his head. "I don't think so, Isabelle. Why would it?"

She swallowed, looked at him. "Because the anniversary is coming up," she said quietly. "Twenty-five years."

"Sounds like it could have been suicide, then. Maybe she poisoned herself?"

Harper had the same thought, but again, Isabelle couldn't see Gail choosing to go that way and said as much. "No one would purposely kill themselves this way. It's literal torture."

"Noted." He stuffed his hands into his pockets and stared at the tree line. "Like I said, I'll ask around. See what I can find."

Satisfied, she nodded once and thanked him.

"Hey, Isabelle."

She turned at the lip of his deck.

"Bring that little girl of yours by. I'd like to meet her."

She nodded once, then disappeared through the trees.

8

Cedarloch Funeral Home was Isabelle's next stop.

She typed out a text to Harper to make sure the girls were okay. Within minutes, Harper sent back a video of Maisy feeding the cows and chickens. She smiled at her sweet girl, cheeks pink, thrilled that she wasn't merely tagging along on this trip but had already found some unexpected joy and a new friend.

Isabelle snaked through the trees, which dumped her back onto the main road. The funeral home sat on the other side of the lake. As she walked, she mulled over her chat with Theo. Though she was thankful he was willing to look into things, she didn't exactly sense any urgency from him either. She knew his past with her mother was complicated, but still. If someone was possibly murdered in this town, then he should want to get to the bottom of it. Even if the woman in question was Gail "the Child Killer" Archer.

Isabelle had already worked up a light sweat by the time she reached the funeral home. It was a drab building, painted gray. Inside, bright-blue carpet and plaid furniture clashed for attention. Embalming fluid and the sickly-sweet fragrance of fresh flowers hit her immediately, an unfriendly combination that nearly made her eyes water. As kids, they'd often run in here on dares, but she'd been lucky enough to not have to ever sit through a funeral. Mainly because her mother insisted on backyard burials with no visitors when Celia, Ben, and Jude died.

She shivered as icy air blasted from rusted vents. "Hello?"

After a few minutes, Rita appeared from the back, a piece of paper in hand, her eyeglasses on a chain around her neck. "Look at that. You're still here."

"I am. Is Frank here?"

"Frank! Visitor!" Rita eyed her outfit, nodded to her shoes. "Better get you some boots if you're going to stay awhile."

Isabelle felt the fight revving up in her, just as it used to. "As I said before, I'm not staying."

"Mm-hmm." She posted a hand on her hip. "Where's your girl?"

"Harper's."

Rita nodded as Frank walked out in gloves and an apron. Clearly, he'd been working.

"Hey, Frank." Isabelle had a soft spot for Frank. He'd been so kind to her after her siblings died. He wasn't the coroner back then, but when Ronald, the coroner who'd performed her siblings' autopsies, moved away, Frank took over. Though it wasn't typical for a coroner to do their work in a funeral home, in Cedarloch, it made sense. He worked downstairs; Rita ran the business upstairs. The two had been thick as thieves for years.

"Isabelle Archer. I don't believe it." He snapped off his gloves, tossed them in the trash, and reached out for a hug.

The chemicals invaded her senses again as she offered him a quick embrace and stepped back. "Is there somewhere we can talk privately?"

Rita and Frank looked at each other. "Use the office."

Frank led her back to the shared space. The desk was covered with two empty Coke cans and an array of papers. Once they sat, she launched right into it. "Did you perform my mother's autopsy?"

He nodded. "I see you got my report?" Frank folded his thick arms across his chest and rocked back and forth in the office chair.

"I did. What do you make of it?"

He winced and sat forward, interlacing his fingers on the desk. "I make of it that someone poisoned your mother. And almost got away with it too."

She tilted her head. "Why almost?"

"I might not have even tested the hair had it not been for her . . . physical condition."

"Which was?"

"Would you like to see?"

Isabelle hesitated for only a moment. She'd seen many coroner reports and photographs of dead bodies over the years. People who did unspeakable things to other human beings. But this was different. This was her mother. She nodded anyway, and he moved to unlock the filing cabinet behind him. "I was going to reach out directly, but I knew once you saw the report, you'd come."

"Had you talked to Gail much these last few months?"

He slammed the cabinet door shut and slapped the file down between them. "Yes and no. She'd come into town to get supplies once a week, but other than that, not much. Really kept to herself these past few years."

Once again, Isabelle felt the vise of guilt grip her heart. If she'd only known how Gail was doing and what was going on in her life, maybe this wouldn't feel like such a wild-goose chase. If she'd reached out to her once in a while, would she still be alive? Frank flipped open the file and rotated it so she could sort through it on her own. "It's not pretty, Isabelle."

"It never is." Silently, she flipped through the photos, asking permission to snap photos of her own so she could send them to one of Jack's guys. Tears filled her eyes almost immediately, but she cleared her throat and tried to stay professional. The images almost looked like a sick caricature of the woman she remembered. In her mind, Gail was still middle aged. But this woman was older, more fragile, slight. And as Isabelle suspected, she had the telltale signs of thallium poisoning.

Frank pointed to a strand of hair that had been photo enlarged. "She had a disorganized cuticle and atrophy of the hair bulb. Common with thallium." He sniffed. "She also had toxic encephalopathy with high concentrations of electron-dense granules."

Isabelle squinted at the photo. "Caused by thallium deposition?"

He grinned, as if they weren't dissecting what killed her mother. "That's correct. I'm impressed."

"Don't be. I studied this. Wrote about it, in fact."

"Well, that's certainly a coincidence."

"Or not." She pointed to the photos again. "Continue."

He snapped back to the task at hand. "She also had erosive gastritis. Can't completely rule out other causes, but that can be a symptom too." He flipped to the next photo, her mother hacked and prodded and sewn back together with what looked like numerous black zippers pocking her waxy, ashen skin. He pointed and ticked things off one by one. "She had renal autolysis."

"Which is?"

"Self-digestion of cells after death. She also had some mild glomerular sclerosis and alopecia, which suggests that this might not have happened all at once."

Isabelle's head snapped up. "What?"

Frank adjusted his black-rimmed glasses. "With the amount she had in her system, coupled with the other side effects, it looks like these symptoms went beyond a lethal dose. Theoretically, she could have been drip fed thallium until it killed her. It's tasteless, undetectable, really, as you probably already know, so the body excretes some but not all. She could have had all sorts of symptoms and not known what was going on."

"And she didn't go to a doctor, Harper said."

Frank laughed. "Your mother never met a doctor she didn't hate."

Wasn't that the truth. Gail had nearly been ostracized from the community early on when she fed them all homemade remedies whenever any of the kids got sick. Isabelle suddenly remembered parcels showing up on their doorsteps: antibiotics and ointments from the townspeople. Ben used to stash them so their mother didn't see.

"But if someone put it in her food or drink, then that means she had visitors at the cabin?"

"Most likely, yes."

That narrowed it down, at least.

Frank pointed back to the photos. "You see these?" He gestured to the white lines on her fingernails. "Mees' lines. Another symptom." He flipped to the final finding. "She had some myocardial damage as well. Again, hard to pinpoint to the thallium specifically, but in this case, most likely."

"I went to see Theo about it."

He looked up. "Oh, yeah? How is old Mr. Mullins? Still grumpy as an ox?"

"Affirmative. And not in a rush to help," she said.

Frank massaged one of his hands. "Yeah, he wouldn't be. He and Gail had history."

"Don't you mean beef?"

He paused, then shook his head. "No, I mean history. Romantic history."

"What?" Isabelle sat straight up, one word blinking like a neon sign. *Motive, motive, motive.* She almost laughed, it was so preposterous. "But they hated each other."

"Oh, this was before all that. And before all the bad stuff, they were in love."

Theo Mullins and Gail Archer in love? No one would have been able to keep that a secret. Theo was tall and good looking, the only Black man in town. Plus, he'd been married. Her mother had always been single. Or so she'd thought.

"Did they have an affair?"

"You'll have to ask him about that."

No, she'd have to ask someone else. "I appreciate this, Frank." She handed the file back to him. "If you were me, what would you do?"

"I'd get out of here, kid. Go back to your life. Go back to that sweet daughter of yours. Forget about this place and everything that happened here."

From anyone else, it might have sounded insensitive to suggest she simply leave her mother's mystery death unsolved, but he'd always wanted more for her. He was one of the few people in this town who'd wanted her to leave and make something of herself.

"You know I can't do that."

He sighed, rose, and replaced the file in the cabinet. "That's what I thought you'd say."

"I'll probably have more questions," she said as she stood.

"And I'll probably be right here, ready to answer them."

She reached forward to kiss him on the cheek and said goodbye to Rita, and the moment she was outside, she texted all the photos to Jack.

I'll send them to Omar, with the report, he texted back. We'll get to the bottom of it.

But would they? That was what everyone said after Celia, Ben, and Jude had died, when no one could figure out who—or what, exactly—caused the fire. Because they'd been trapped in an underground bunker, the fire had burned so hot and so long, it was a full day before they were found, and no one could ever determine who started it. What made her think this was going to be any different?

She pulled up the Notes app on her phone and wrote a few more things down. She hadn't put two and two together about the date of her mother's death until they'd gotten here. Either whoever poisoned her timed her death to be near the anniversary, or it was a coincidence.

And in terms of suspects? Well, Theo just got a hell of a lot more interesting, for starters. But someone else must have come to her mother's house, as it sounded like Gail and Theo hadn't spoken in a long time. She knew Harper had been there. And Rita. From what Frank said, it seemed like someone was putting the thallium in her food or drink. If she could find out who'd been visiting the Archer house, she could find out who'd been potentially poisoning her mother.

Lost in thought, she pocketed her phone and stared out at the gently bobbing water. The lake glittered like a million diamonds, each tiny crest of wave dazzling beneath the reflection of the sun. Expensive lake homes jutted around the perimeter. Jet Skis, boats, and kayaks bobbed in the water, tied to various docks. To the naked eye, this place appeared like some sort of small-town utopia.

As she began to walk, she shuddered. Deep down, she knew it was anything but.

9

By the time she arrived back at Harper's, Isabelle was out of breath.

It was lunchtime, and she felt guilty she'd taken so long. When she knocked on the door, Harper waved her in. "The girls are giving Preacher a bath."

"You really put them to work, huh?"

Harper shrugged. "I run a tight ship."

"I believe it." Isabelle shoved her hands into her jeans pockets and offered a tight smile. "Thanks for watching Maisy. We'll get out of your hair."

"You sure? You're welcome to stay for lunch."

Though she appreciated the offer, Isabelle needed to do some digging and figure out this thallium connection, if there was one. She hadn't thought about her article in so long. She'd never been sure anyone in this town had even read it besides her mother. "Thanks, but we should get back."

Harper nodded. "I'll go grab her."

"Quick question first."

Harper turned on the stairs.

"Did Mom have any cameras at the cabin that you know of?"

She scrunched her nose. "Cameras? I don't think so. Gail wasn't super into tech."

Isabelle loitered in the living room while she waited, her eyes raking over all the beauty that Harper had curated in her absence. It was like time had stood still but also expanded, changed, offering Harper something real here.

"Mama, I don't want to go." Maisy appeared at the top of the stairs, her shirt damp with soap bubbles. Her little cheeks were flaming red, the tops of her shoulders pink from a morning spent in the sun.

"I know, sweetie, but we've got a lot to do back at the cabin."

Harper put a hand on Maisy's shoulder. "Izz, if she wants to stay for the rest of the day, she's welcome to. The girls can hang. I can feed them, and they can watch a movie on the projector later? We can do popcorn too."

Maisy hopped up and down. "Yes! Please, Mama? Please?" She tented her little fingers under her chin. Isabelle didn't know whether to thank Harper or be annoyed, but she settled on the former.

She addressed Harper. "Are you sure? I don't want to put you out."

"Are you kidding? We're making up for lost time! Plus, Ivy loves having someone around. Makes my job easier." She glanced down at Maisy, then back at Isabelle. "So is that a yes?"

Isabelle knew if she said no, Maisy would throw a sizable tantrum. And this way, at least, she could make phone calls and do some sleuthing in peace. "Only if you're sure."

"Yay!" Maisy left to help Ivy with the dog, and Harper marched back down the stairs.

"We're happy to have her. Really. Go do your thing." She squeezed Isabelle's arm and gave her a reaffirming nod.

"Okay, well, I owe you. I'll text you in a bit?"

"Sure thing. I'll keep you updated." Upstairs, the girls squealed, and Harper chuckled. "They're clearly having an awful time."

"Just the worst." Isabelle smiled, gave Harper a quick hug, and let herself back out. Her legs were tired, her feet aching, but she had no choice but to trek back through the woods and toward her mother's house . . . to search for what, she wasn't sure.

By the time she approached the cabin, she almost felt like she'd had too much time to think. Isabelle remembered the night the children died so vividly; everything had started out normal. They were doing a sleepover in the tree house. But the kids had been sick, exhibiting symptoms none of them could trace. It was what had spurred her deeper investigation into mothers who poisoned their children. Even though Isabelle had never trusted her mother again, she'd always been too afraid to ask her outright if she'd done it.

Isabelle knew Gail was a complicated woman. Jack seemed to think she might have gotten in over her head as a foster mom and wanted a way out. Isabelle could never quite get there in her mind. If you were overwhelmed by foster children, you didn't slowly poison them. You found another way to get help.

As Isabelle came out of the forest, she stopped. All the trash bags had been cleared off the property, deep tire tracks raked through the mud. But she didn't see a vehicle. She spun around. Who would have come up here and done this? She appreciated it, but she didn't love the idea of someone else on this property. On her mother's land. That conditioning Gail had instilled in all of them—that you protected your land at all costs, that you owned it, that it was your responsibility, no matter what—ran deep.

The back door was ajar. Had she left it unlocked? She couldn't remember. She toed it open, called out. "Hello?" Inside, she heard a grunt, and the hairs on her arms bristled. Isabelle searched for a weapon within reach and palmed her utility knife, ready to flick open the blade if she had to.

Footsteps shuffled around the corner. Isabelle stiffened, took a few clumsy steps back on the deck as a rugged man spilled out the back door, his eyes dark and brooding. He softened when he saw her, and that was when she recognized him. River Foust.

Her mouth went dry as she took him in. The boy she knew had been replaced by someone with more edges, someone who'd maybe lived a rougher life. She catalogued him: fitted jeans, a sleeveless T-shirt, a shaved head, dark skin, tattoos, muscles for days.

"Isabelle Archer."

"What are you doing in my house, River?" She'd also forgotten how confident River could be. If he wanted something, he took it. No questions asked. No apologies.

"Harper called me." He swiped his head with a rag and stuffed it in his pocket.

"Okay, *and*?" Isabelle gestured for him to explain himself.

"She said you needed help. So I'm here to help."

"By breaking into my home?"

He laughed, revealing two rows of perfectly white teeth. Veneers. He'd gotten them when he was younger because he'd knocked so many loose playing hockey. He'd been good, if she remembered correctly. Thought he'd go pro. "You call it breaking in. I call it helping out an old friend."

"Friend?" She hiked an eyebrow, dropped it, then berated herself for flirting.

"Yes, Isabelle. A friend." He took a step toward her, and she automatically stepped back. This man-child had broken her heart, and she hadn't seen him since.

Isabelle glanced behind her. "Thanks for hauling those out."

"Welcome."

She pointed toward the house. "Mind telling me what you're doing in there, though?"

"Come see for yourself." He opened the screen door, as if it were his house. She moved past him, inhaling that familiar scent of cedar and smoke mixed with something slightly sweet, like vanilla.

Her anger vanished as she looked around. All the remaining trash bags and clutter had been cleared. The cabin had been cleaned and staged with the remaining furniture, and it even smelled good. She walked to the kitchen, which, despite how old it was, now gleamed.

"How did you do this?"

"I work construction. Have a crew. Hookups to a local cleaning service too." He reached his arms up to the low beam separating the kitchen from the dining room, biceps flexing. Her eyes snagged on a snake tattoo that wrapped its way around most of his upper left arm. "Impressed?"

She hated to give him the satisfaction but nodded. "Very." Moving from room to room, she was amazed he'd been able to do all this in half a day.

"Needs a paint job, but Harper called in a favor from Buddy Wright, a hotshot Realtor the next town over. He thinks we can get away with selling as is."

"*We*?" God, this man was cocky. Did he expect a share of the profits when she sold too? That old chip on her shoulder, that if she wasn't careful, people would take from her, just as life had taken from her, reared its ugly head. At the children's bedroom doors, she hesitated.

"I didn't touch them," he said now, more tenderly.

"Thank you." She swallowed the emotion and turned, feeling a flood of gratitude for what he'd done today. Technically, she no longer had a reason to stay in Cedarloch, other than meeting the Realtor, signing some paperwork, and then waiting for a call to tell her the house was sold. She and Maisy could get on the road tonight. Or at first light tomorrow. But she couldn't do that, could she? She had to dig more into her mother's death, had to know what happened to her in her final days. "You've saved me weeks, River."

"Buy me dinner as a thank-you."

As nice a thought as that was, she had Maisy. "Can't. Need to pick up Maisy."

"She's at Harper's, right?"

How close were these two? "Yeah."

He laughed. "Then trust me, Maisy can stay a little longer. Ivy loves having friends over. Come on. What do you say?"

She should say no. She had to find out more about the way Gail died. As Isabelle considered, she realized it wasn't such a bad idea to start with River. Pick his brain. Ask questions. Maybe they could eat somewhere a bit more populated in town, where a few locals might be.

"I'll text Harper and see what she says."

"I'll pick you up at five."

"Five? That's practically lunch."

"Remember where you are, Belle."

The nickname surprised her. She hadn't heard it in twenty years. "Fine."

"It's a date."

"It's not a date."

He paused on his way out the door, where his truck must be parked out of sight. He turned to look at her, breaking into a grin. "Whatever you say." He tapped the doorframe twice before exiting. "See you tonight."

Then

Celia

As they marched through the woods, Celia noticed how loose and talkative Isabelle was, more energized than she'd been in months.

Though Isabelle didn't seem to be affected by whatever she, Jude, Harper, and Ben had, Celia knew how exhausted Isabelle stayed because of her sleepwalking. At first, it terrified Celia. When she'd wake up and find Isabelle's bed empty, only to later learn she'd let herself out of the house and into the woods . . . it was like a horror movie. Who would do that? And why? Celia was a heavy sleeper, but if she woke up before Harper did, she tried to guide Isabelle back to bed before she did something stupid.

Sometimes Gail locked the three of them inside their room, but she didn't seem overly concerned by the sleepwalking, too busy with trying to make ends meet. Gail didn't talk about finances, but Celia knew money was tight. Every day, Celia compiled a fresh list of worries and kept them hidden in a journal by her bed. Lately, money was on it. One more thing to add to the list.

Harper and Isabelle carried backpacks of toilet paper and a dozen eggs. They knew Celia was feeling weak, so she was thankful she didn't have to carry supplies too. Gail would be furious once she found out they'd stolen from the house. She calculated the cost of both in her head and wondered if she could sell one of her crocheted dolls at the next farmers market to cover the cost of what they'd taken. Celia hated how guilt clung to her, followed her around sometimes like a ghost. Isabelle thought she was too sensitive. Celia liked to think she cared.

They all traipsed through the woods, shushing each other, which only made them all get louder and laugh even harder. Up ahead, Harper's arm was looped through Isabelle's. No matter how hard she tried, Celia could never get as close to them as they were to each other. Celia often felt left out. The boys had each other, and Harper and Isabelle had each other, but who did she have?

Even after three years, Gail had not taken to Celia. There was still a formality between them. Celia longed for the type of relationship between a mother and daughter that she read about in books. Once she had a daughter, Celia would give her everything. She would tell her how she felt about her constantly, and never, *ever* diminish her feelings.

Worry number seventy-six: What if she couldn't have kids?

Sheriff Mullins's house sat on the opposite side of the lake. It would be a miracle if they didn't get caught. She was sure that he, as sheriff, had some sort of automatic lighting system. Or even cameras. Had any of them thought this through?

Celia's foot snagged on a root and her ankle twisted. She cried out, and Isabelle turned back to check on her. "You okay?"

Celia's ankle throbbed, but she continued. She would not be an even weaker link on this journey. She was already physically the weakest, even when she was feeling her best. Now that she had no energy and strange symptoms, she felt useless. The boys tried to ignore whatever was going on with them, especially Jude. They seemed mostly unaffected by their symptoms, carrying out their chores and their schoolwork as they always did. Harper complained, like Celia, but her hair wasn't coming out as fast as the others'.

Celia's stomach cramped, and she curved her hand over it. She'd eaten too fast.

Worry number seventy-seven: Could eating too fast puncture an intestine?

Celia wanted to scream. Maybe she should. But then that would give them away, and everyone would be mad at her. She got so frustrated with herself sometimes, she wanted to rip her brain straight from her skull. Often she feared she might be going mad. How did anyone ever escape their own thoughts? If she could figure out a way to do it, she'd be a millionaire.

"Shh, shhh!" Jude stopped up ahead, turned, and pressed a finger to his lips. "Okay, troops. We're going to get in and get out. Eggs are for windows only, no cars. We ready?" From his own backpack, he extracted a can of shaving cream. Celia's stomach twisted. She hated doing things like this because she knew what a pain it was to clean up. But they'd make fun of her if she sat this one out. As the youngest, she was often still thought of as a baby. Maybe tonight she could prove them all wrong.

Ben tossed her a roll of toilet paper, and Harper pressed two eggs into her palms. They were heavy and cold, and she shivered.

Worry number seventy-eight: Could she get salmonella from holding an egg?

Her siblings snickered as they moved quietly through the forest surrounding Sheriff Mullins's house, tossing up toilet paper rolls and watching them rain down again if they missed a branch. Jude got his hooked over a branch on the first try and mimicked a crowd going wild. Ben emulated Jude's exact movements. Celia rolled her eyes. She loved Ben, but he needed to find his own way. His own voice.

Celia tried to scout out a proper tree and found a shorter one. She aimed the toilet paper roll up and threw it, her shoulder jerking painfully from the effort. The roll sailed over a branch and cascaded back down. She yipped in excitement. She kept tossing it until the leaves were covered. Now for the eggs. She didn't know where to throw them. If she tossed them at a window, wouldn't Sheriff Mullins and his wife wake up? What if he came out here with a gun?

Worry number seventy-nine: Being shot to death before she turned thirteen.

Suddenly, she heard the staccato thunk of eggs bursting against hard surfaces, and her siblings' stifled giggles. Wanting to get it over with, she stepped up to a rear window, took a breath, and threw. The first egg exploded violently against the clear sliding glass door and oozed in thick, yellow streaks toward the ground. Before she could throw another one, a figure appeared behind the window. She could see the whites of their eyes, and she shrieked and jumped back, alerting everyone that someone was watching them.

They all yelped and began to fly back through the woods. Once again, Celia's foot caught on a root, and she pitched forward, landing hard in the dirt. Her chin smacked against the earth, her teeth clacking painfully together.

Worry number eighty: Knocking out her two front teeth but not having the money to get them fixed.

Crawling forward, she cranked her head back to the window, but there was no one there. Panic seized her chest. Ben, Isabelle, Harper, and Jude were fading away. She didn't know her way back by heart. What if she got lost?

"Guys!" she called out. Fear mangled her voice, made it shake. "Wait for me!"

She climbed back to her feet and stumbled clumsily toward the break in the trees.

Before she got there, a large hand clamped on her shoulder, yanking her back.

10

Cedarloch Fish House was the most popular restaurant in town.

The moment she stepped inside, Isabelle marveled at how little had changed. It smelled like the lake and crispy fried fish. River asked for a table outside, overlooking the water. A cool breeze ruffled her hair. The restaurant was packed. She forgot how early the locals ate here. Dinner at five sometimes turned into a three-hour affair. Live music, endless drinks, and catching up on town gossip.

That wouldn't be them tonight. She had to pick up Maisy. Guilt worked its way through her system again. She couldn't believe she'd left her with Harper all day. She reasoned that Maisy had probably had one of the best days in a long time, though. A silver lining, at least.

She and River chatted about their lives over drinks and appetizers. He almost made it as a hockey pro, got injured, took another job, then moved home several years back. He liked construction, liked that it was real, honest work. He was still single. While she found that hard to believe, she understood it deeply. Isabelle used to feel like that, making conscious choices to stay untethered. Now, however, when she tried to picture her world without Maisy, she couldn't. There was no one she loved more on this earth. No happier accident.

Once they breezed through the small talk, Isabelle got down to business. She filled River in on enough details to explain the seriousness of the situation.

"You think someone *murdered* Gail?" His dark eyebrows knitted together. "Who?"

"That's where I need your help." She gestured around to the other patrons. "Is there anyone else you think might have talked to my mom, been up to the cabin recently, maybe cooked for her?"

He barked out a laugh and sat back in his chair. He fiddled with the label on his beer bottle as he studied her. "Gail rarely had anyone up to the cabin. Kind of a well-known fact."

"So no one?"

He cocked a muscled shoulder, dropped it, slid his eyes over to the other patrons. "Not that I've seen. I've worked on almost everyone's property that lives here, Belle. Lake houses, cabins . . . Of course I hear things. Town gossip. Things I don't *want* to know." He grinned. "Things you would be shocked by."

"Try to stay on track."

"Right." He snapped his fingers and leaned in, closing the gap across the table. She could feel the heat between them. Isabelle cleared her throat, moved back in her chair, just as he had moments before. "What I'm saying is, no one went to that cabin. No one I know about, anyway."

"What about Theo?"

"Theo?" Something passed across his face, then was gone. "Didn't he and your mom despise each other?"

"I heard they used to be more," she admitted now. "Lovers. A long time ago."

"No shit." He drained the last of his beer, signaled their server for another. "You want one?"

Isabelle shook her head and stared at the water. Did Gail truly have no friends in the end? Never have anyone over for a cup of coffee or a game of cards? Though Isabelle was a bit of a loner herself, she still loved the company of her closest friends. She understood the loneliness out here, though, how it could eat you from the inside. But if what the preliminary autopsy report said was true, then someone *had* been to the cabin. Someone *had* poisoned Gail. Like Isabelle had told Theo, it wasn't like she would administer thallium to herself.

She paused, nearly gasping.

"What?" River could see her turning something over in her head.

"Hear me out," she said. "Earlier, I ruled out death by suicide. It didn't seem like something Gail would do."

"Right."

"But the anniversary of the kids' deaths is coming up. And if what I always suspected to be true *is* true—that she poisoned them with thallium—then what if the guilt was so great that she poisoned herself too?" The moment the words were out of her mouth, something felt true about them. Possible.

He exhaled, sliding his elbows forward on the table. "But didn't you say the side effects are awful? Like torture?"

She nodded. But what if her mother had changed over the years? What if, after all this time, she regretted her choices? What if she *had* set that fire to end the kids' suffering because she felt so awful about poisoning them? And what if, as she neared their anniversary, she decided to join them? Isabelle shook her head, cleared away the morbid thoughts.

"Sorry." She attempted a smile. "I know this is heavy conversation."

"It is, but it's what's happening, so here we are."

What would Jack think about her having dinner with her first love? Isabelle wasn't sure she'd ever mentioned River. Why would she? It was odd, though, sitting here with another man she had once known so intimately, even if it was another version of her. Another version of him.

They dug into their fish and chips, and Isabelle practically swooned. The batter was perfectly crisp, the white fish flaky and moist. "God, this is good," she said, dipping a fry into ketchup and then tartar sauce.

"The best," River said. Conversation swerved to other topics, and then a live band appeared out back. Isabelle knew they should leave, but as the band started playing a few Americana tunes, she was shuttled back to the very best parts of her childhood, where live music and fried fish had once felt like enough.

"Care to dance?" River extended his hand while other couples took to the wooden deck, twirling, clapping, and stomping their feet to the beat of the drums. Before she could refuse, River had her up and on her feet. One hand pressed into her back as he effortlessly led her around the mock dance floor. Despite herself, she threw her head back and laughed. When was the last time she'd danced?

One song turned into many. When they stepped back to their table, Isabelle was warm and happy, her limbs sore from all the movement. Then River was paying the check and walking her to the edge of the woods, where she would cut through to get to Harper's house. The sun was near setting, and that mom guilt wormed its way in again, making her realize how she'd pushed Maisy from her mind today. She didn't like that at all.

He paused at the entrance to the trees, a small path cut through the dirt. "Can I walk you?"

She shrugged. "Sure."

Under the cover of trees, it was even chillier, and she shivered in her black T-shirt.

"It's been really great to see you, Belle."

"No one calls me that, you know," she said.

"Oh, I'm sorry," he said, misunderstanding her.

"No." She placed a hand on his arm, felt a spark crackle between them. "I mean no one but you has ever called me that."

He smiled, the purple bruise of the sun framing his features as he glanced at her. "Well, good."

She was suddenly nervous as they inched toward Harper's farm. Isabelle searched for what to talk about, what would keep them on safe territory.

"I'm sorry, you know." He stopped, leaned against a tree, staring at her.

"For what?" She knew for what. She looked down at her shoes, her heart racing.

"For being a dick back then. For hurting you." He pushed off the tree and closed the gap between them, but she took a step back.

"It's fine," she said, walking again. "Water under the bridge." Something about being alone in the woods with River didn't feel right. She searched her memory for why but came up empty. They carried on and reached Harper's house in minutes.

"Thanks for dinner," she said. "And for all that you did today at the cabin."

"My pleasure. Can I see your phone?"

She narrowed her eyes but fished it from her bag. He opened it to her contacts and added himself in. "In case you need me for anything." He handed her phone back, smiled, and waited until she was near Harper's side door before waving and disappearing back through the trees. She watched him go, something gnawing at her conscience.

What was it?

Before she could contemplate more, a scream tore through the house. Isabelle rushed through the glass side door to let herself in.

11

Isabelle prepared herself for the worst.

She was surprisingly calm in a crisis, had become that way because of her job, but not when it came to Maisy. With Maisy, she was as protective as one could get. "Maisy?"

"In here!" Harper trilled.

Her voice sounded fine, so Isabelle relaxed a little, but she needed to see for herself that Maisy was okay. Then, another scream. Isabelle practically sprinted through the kitchen and living room, where she and Harper had been earlier, and spilled into the family room, which was cozy and dim. Spread out on a giant sectional were the girls, covered in blankets and pillows, a bowl of popcorn between them.

On a projector, *Coraline* was playing. Maisy had never seen it before, and her hands were plastered over her eyes. Though she loved dolls, she found some of them creepy.

This time, Ivy screamed, and the girls burst into a fit of giggles. Isabelle took in the sweet scene before her and sighed in relief.

"Hey, mama," Harper said. "Have a productive day? Wait, let's talk in the other room so we don't bother these girls."

Before stepping back into the living room, Isabelle reached down and kissed Maisy on the head. "Hi, Bug. Fun day?"

"The *best* day!" She was energized, her eyes sparkling.

"Hi, Ivy."

"Hi." The girls were glued to the screen as they talked and munched on popcorn. Isabelle longed for this very situation back home. Having Maisy's friends over for a movie or a sleepover. Seeing it here, that it was possible, that Maisy just had to meet the right friends, made her feel hopeful for the first time in a while.

In the next room, Harper was already pouring a glass of wine. "Want one?"

"I'm good, thanks."

"Here, sit."

Isabelle was tired, but her mind raced. She needed to figure out what to do next. She wasn't really in the mood for chitchat, but Harper had come to her rescue today in more ways than one. "I can't believe you called River Foust," she started.

"Why not?" Harper shrugged. "He's a friend. You needed help. And it was my home too, Izz. I didn't want you to have to do that all alone."

"Well, I appreciate it more than you know. The cabin looks almost brand new."

"He's good at his job, I'll give you that. Anything else to report?" She wiggled her eyebrows up and down.

Despite the heaviness of the day and the realization that her mother might have been poisoned or might have taken her own life, River's face flashed through her head. "No. I don't think of him like that anymore."

"Aw, boo. No fun."

"How were the girls?"

Harper smiled. "An absolute dream. Ivy has asked me at least five times if you two can please move here, so the girls can be best friends." She could tell Harper wanted to say more but didn't. "You must be beat. Do you all want to stay the night? I have two guest rooms. You'd be doing me a favor, really. No one ever comes to stay."

A sleepover. How long had it been since she and Harper had spent the night together? Staying in this fancy house versus the cabin with all its demons was a no-brainer. "We don't have our clothes or toothbrushes or anything."

Harper waved her off. "I got you, girl. But can I be the one to tell the girls they get to have a sleepover?"

Maisy had never had one. She would be over the moon.

"Go for it." When Harper was gone, Isabelle took a moment to close her eyes. She tried to settle back into her body. This day had been big. She didn't know what she had expected in coming here, but it hadn't been digging into a possible crime.

More screams, this time ecstatic, nearly burst her eardrums from the other room. To be safe tonight, Isabelle would lock Maisy's door from the inside, in case she had another sleepwalking episode. She didn't think she'd sleepwalk again so soon, two nights in a row. It had never worked like that for her, anyway, and though sleepwalking could have a genetic component, she hoped maybe this was a one-off thing for Maisy, that she wouldn't turn into a worried, sleep-deprived version of herself like Isabelle had.

Harper burst back into the room, a grin on her face. "Okay, that's settled. Let me show you to your room, my lady. I told the girls they could finish the movie. They've only got about thirty minutes left."

They walked upstairs and then padded down a long hall. Harper pointed to the right. "Down there are our rooms." She pointed to the left. "And at this end are your rooms. Do you like baths?"

"I do." At the end of a long day, Isabelle loved to take an Epsom salt bath. Wash the day off her skin.

"Then you're going to love this tub. This way." Harper slid a reclaimed barn door open to reveal one of the most exquisite bathrooms Isabelle had ever been in. A giant soaking tub took up the center, next to a steam shower, a long, modern sink, and a separate water closet.

"Harper, are you rich?" Isabelle realized she didn't know her financial situation. Shame on Isabelle for even assuming it was only farm money. It could be Harper's too.

"I wish." She tented her hands around her slim waist and looked around. "I have a lot of hookups for design since that's what I got my degree in."

"That's right." Isabelle smiled at that. She remembered how much Harper loved designing and organizing when they were young. How she'd bring blankets or fresh flowers to different spaces when it was just the two of them so they could pretend they lived on their own. When they first built the tree house, she'd helped decorate.

"My ex was super handy too. We did the remodel almost entirely ourselves."

"And by 'ex,' you mean . . ."

She snorted. "Another time, another conversation."

Isabelle smirked at Harper's intense privacy. She was much the same way. "Have you ever thought of starting your own business?"

"I have." Harper chewed on her bottom lip as she studied the room. "It would be a lot of work, but I do love design." Her eyes glazed over for a moment, and then she snapped back to the present. "Right. So towels are in the closet. Floors are heated. Glass jars of Epsom salt behind you. There are two rooms that are identical, so choose yours, and Maisy can have the other. I'll go grab Maisy a nightgown and grab you some pajamas too. Oh! And toothbrushes. They're in the top drawer there."

"Harper." Isabelle stopped her at the door and grabbed her hand. "You have been so incredible today. Truly. I really can't thank you enough."

"Don't thank me." Harper squeezed her hand. "You're family. I'm happy to help. Now enjoy that soak. You've had a long day."

She shut the door behind her. When was the last time Isabelle had let someone in like this? Someone other than Jack? Sure, she had girlfriends she saw in the city, but it was always so fleeting, wasn't it? A drink, a dinner, a visit to a museum or show. Conversation was sometimes deep but mostly surface level. Work. Relationships. Kids. Health. It was nice to be with someone who used to know her, someone who was once her very best friend. A sister.

Isabelle let herself enjoy a scalding bath, allowing her mind to simply let go of everything it learned today. Tomorrow, she would figure out what to do next. If she should leave, if she should hire someone to help her, or if Jack's guy, Omar, had learned anything new.

But for now, she would sleep like the dead.

12

The next morning, Isabelle woke late.

Her head felt groggy, almost like she'd been drugged. She couldn't remember sleeping so hard in a very long time. She stretched, used the restroom, and peeked in on Maisy, but found she wasn't in her bed. She checked the door, which was unlocked, padded quickly down the hall, and took the stairs two at a time.

"Morning, sleepyhead." Harper was already dressed in yoga pants and a tank top.

"Morning." Isabelle glanced around. "Where's Maisy?"

"The girls are doing chores," Harper said. She glanced at her watch. "Started about an hour ago."

"Really?" Isabelle hadn't heard her wake up. "I can't believe I slept so late."

"You must have needed it."

"I guess so." Though she'd slept, she was no closer to knowing what she should do. Go or stay. Leave everything behind or dig deeper. The journalist in her wanted to stay, of course. Wanted to get to the bottom of the real story, to see if what happened to Gail had anything to do with what happened the night of the fire. But was it fair to drag Maisy through all this? Probably not. "I'm going to take a quick shower, and we'll get out of your hair. For real this time."

"No rush on our end."

She walked back upstairs and checked her phone. She had three missed calls from Jack, but no texts or voicemails. She tried to call him back, but it went straight to voicemail. Of course, that was just like him to call her but not leave a message. Classic Jack. Once she was showered and changed, she gathered up Maisy's few belongings and brought them downstairs.

Harper slid her a steaming mug of coffee without her having to ask.

"You would have made one hell of a wife," Isabelle said now.

"Thanks." Harper offered a sad, distant smile. "You sure you have to go?"

"I am."

"Okay. I'll grab the girls."

Isabelle tried Jack again. Nothing. A few minutes later, Maisy stomped inside, clearly unhappy with today's plans.

"Mama, I don't want to go. I like it here. I want to stay with Ivy. We're not finished yet."

"I know, Bug. But we have to finish up at the cabin and then head back to Portland."

"But *why*? We aren't even doing anything this summer."

Isabelle didn't like Maisy's tone, but she couldn't disagree. "I understand that, sweetheart, but we don't want to overstay our welcome."

Harper butted in. "Not to complicate things, but it's really no problem at all. If you need to take care of things with the cabin today, Maisy can stay with us for a bit while you, you know, figure stuff out."

Isabelle appreciated that Harper didn't say what that "stuff" was to Maisy, but she could not just pawn off her kid again. And at the same time, if she did decide to stay in Cedarloch a little longer, she couldn't drag Maisy around from place to place while she tried to understand more about what happened to her mother. It seemed Isabelle was at an impasse.

"Look, how about this? I'll take the girls into town for a bit. Ivy has a horseback riding class. Maisy, have you ever ridden a horse?"

Maisy shook her head and looked at Isabelle. "Can I? Please?"

"Harper, I really can't ask you to do that."

"How many times do I have to tell you? You're not asking. I'm offering. Plus, you're family, which makes Maisy family. And Ivy loves having a friend around. Right, sweetie?"

"Yes!" Ivy confirmed.

Isabelle nodded. "Okay. Thank you so much. I'll let you know what's happening by no later than this afternoon."

"No worries."

Isabelle kissed Maisy on the head and headed back through the woods toward the cabin. She felt like a terrible mom leaving Maisy with Harper again, but it was a true blessing in disguise. Whenever she worked on stories at home, Maisy was usually with Jack. In fact, Maisy rarely saw Isabelle in work mode, except when she was editing. She wanted her to know her work was important, of course, but this was different. This was personal. And dark. And laced with complications, spanning decades.

She crunched through the leaves and sticks and thought again about River, about how odd it had been to see him last night. It made her realize how much she missed Jack.

At the cabin, she studied it objectively for a moment, before walking around to the front. Maybe she'd missed a clue somewhere. Maybe there was something in this house that would give her new insight into her mother's final days.

Before she could let herself inside, someone stepped off the front porch. Isabelle reached for her utility knife and had the blade flicked open in seconds before she recognized the facial scruff, the messy hair, the tan skin.

"Jack?" She lowered the knife.

"Easy, slugger," he said, eyeing the blade.

"What are you doing here?"

"Well, if Mohammed won't come to the mountain," he said, extending his arms. He glanced behind her. "Where's Maisy?"

"She's at Harper's." The mere sight of him kicked her heart into overdrive. She'd always thought he was so successful partly because he was supremely intelligent and great at his job and partly because he was so damn attractive. Because of his sex appeal *and* brains, the media loved him.

"Is that any way to say hello?" He crossed toward her and pulled her in for a hug.

She drank in his smell, the warmth of his chest, and remembered how the two of them had always fit so perfectly. "Hello," she muffled. Isabelle hated herself a little for it, but she knew with Jack here, she could get much further than she would on her own. Finally, she pulled back. "I thought you were prepping."

"I am. But this is much more important, Izz. *You're* more important." His hands were still around her waist, large and warm.

She extracted herself and smiled. "Maisy will be ecstatic."

"Will she? Seems like she's enjoying life as a farmhand," he said in a country accent.

"Oh, she is." Isabelle shifted from foot to foot. Jack was *here*. In Cedarloch. She wasn't exactly sure where to begin. They'd never actually worked a story together, and though this wasn't exactly a story because it was also her life, it meant something to have him here.

"It's beautiful here, Izz. Wow."

And it was. Isabelle knew that it was, but so much had happened to taint it, hadn't it? His eyes soaked in the cabin.

"May I see it?"

"Sure." She ushered him inside, and he took a few minutes to walk from room to room, pausing reverently outside the kids' bedrooms. He knew what her siblings had meant to her, how deeply she'd been affected by their deaths. He didn't ask to go in, just placed a palm on each door, a sacred pause, a small offering. After a few minutes, he met her in the living room, sank into one end of the couch, and gestured around.

"I'm confused."

"Confused?"

"This place is spotless. I thought you said it was a disaster?"

"Oh. Well, I had some unexpected help." Her cheeks warmed.

"From?"

"An old friend. He owns a construction company."

"And by 'old friend' you mean 'boyfriend.'" Jack grinned and crossed his arms. "Who may or may not still be in love with you."

She reached across the couch and smacked his arm. "Hardly."

"Then why are you blushing, Archer?" Jack smirked again. He had an almost uncanny ability to suss out the truth from what someone said. It was why he'd nabbed that Pulitzer, among other awards. It was an uncanny skill, and right now, she hated it.

"It's hot in here." She fanned her face, cleared her throat, and situated herself to look at him. "In all seriousness, I'm at a loss. I feel like I might be searching for something that doesn't exist."

He cocked his head. "How so?"

She filled him in on her theory that her mother might have taken her own life.

"Well, the timing fits. Anniversaries are often catalysts." He gripped the back of his neck, bit his bottom lip, and sighed. "You already searched the house?"

"Not yet."

"Not yet?" He sat up. "Izz, come on."

"What?"

He gestured around. "If it was cleaned, then it's been completely wiped."

Had she been so exhausted that she hadn't realized that? However, if someone did harm her mother, would they have really planted anything in the cabin for her to find? Hidden poison in plain sight? She doubted it. And if it was her mother who did it, she wouldn't stash thallium in a cabinet or drawer. She would hide it. Make it hard to find. She told Jack as much.

"Theo mentioned we should look for cameras. I asked Harper if Gail had any, but she didn't think so."

"Seems like a good place to start."

They hopped up and stepped outside. Jack scoped the back, and she started with the front. She searched the edges of the property, up near the gutters. There was nothing there or near the front door. She turned to scope the walkway near the front door. Under the cover of trees, the breeze was cool, and Isabelle was immediately shuttled back to her childhood. If she closed her eyes, she could picture Harper, Celia, Ben, and Jude. Their footsteps cracking over dead branches. Their voices. Their laughter.

"Hey."

She jumped a foot and then rested a palm against her chest. "Jesus, Jack."

"Sorry. The back's all clear."

"Yeah, so's the front." She glanced at the cabin again, her eyes resting on the front door. As if tracing an invisible line, she rotated and followed that sight line to a cypress about fifteen yards out. She pointed to it. "This tree. It's got a clear shot of the front." They hurried toward it, snaking their hands over the furry bark. Jack was taller, his tan hands combing across, probing branches.

"Aha." On tiptoe, he grabbed ahold of something and brought it down to eye level. It was clearly a trail camera, about the size of a tiny lunchbox. He turned it over in his hands until he found the compartment he was looking for. "It's got an SD card."

Isabelle felt a little spark of hope. "Got your computer?"

"What kind of journalist would I be if I didn't?" He smirked, and she rolled her eyes because she hadn't brought hers.

They crunched back inside. Jack extracted his laptop from his sleek backpack and sat back down on the couch. She snuggled in beside him as he put the SD card into the reader and double-clicked on it. "Most of these have infrared light, so we should be able to see anything from night too. Do we know time of death?"

Isabelle pulled the preliminary autopsy report back up again. "They estimate between noon and four."

"That certainly shrinks our timeline."

"If she was given a lethal dose of poison, you mean," Isabelle corrected. "If whoever did this was smart, perhaps they kept increasing it until she died, making them not look guilty. Or if she did it to herself."

"So we're looking for patterns, to see who might have brought over food or drinks?"

Isabelle nodded, but she wasn't really sure. This was a flimsy theory, but they had to start somewhere.

The feed was grainy, but then she and Jack popped up on the screen.

"Rewind it to May ninth," she said.

Jack fiddled with the controls until they approached the day of her mother's death. He rewound all the way back to midnight on the day of May 9, so they wouldn't miss anything. After minutes of no activity, she asked him to fast-forward. The hours ticked by on the screen, one after the next. The occasional deer walked by, but nothing out of the ordinary. Then, they approached the window of death, but still nothing. No one came, and no one went. Isabelle sat back, disappointed.

"All this means is someone didn't come through the front door," Jack said. "Right? Maybe there's another camera out back that I missed? I didn't search the trees."

She nodded, suddenly buoyed. "How far back does this thing go?" Isabelle asked.

Jack checked the file. "About a month."

"Get comfortable, Pearce. We're going to be here awhile."

He shot her a devastating smile. "Wouldn't rather be anywhere else, Archer." He rewound the footage and pressed play.

Isabelle was both nervous and excited to see what they might find.

13

One hour bled into the next.

Though there wasn't a camera out back, they made a log of who came and who went near the front: As Harper said, her own visits were sporadic and short. She'd pop by and then leave maybe an hour later. Rita came by two weeks before Gail died. They were creeping closer to the time of her death, and Isabelle was nervous.

"Who is that?" Jack removed his readers, paused, and tried to zoom in as a man walked into the frame. He turned to look at her. "He look familiar?"

Isabelle's heart slammed against her ribs. One week before her mother died, Theo visited Gail. He'd lied to her. "That's the sheriff. Keep going." They'd moved to the dining room table, and Isabelle was now pacing behind Jack, her fists opening and closing as she shuffled through scenarios in her head. She didn't want to jump to conclusions here, but she scribbled down Theo's name and the time stamp once he entered the house. He left two hours later.

Jack ripped his readers off. "Two hours? That's the longest visit yet. What do we think?"

"I have no idea. Frank told me they used to be romantic."

He hiked an eyebrow but kept going. A day after that, another figure entered the frame, wearing a tool belt, and had a toolbox in hand. Isabelle froze.

"And this guy?"

"Yeah, I know him too." River Foust had also visited her mother a week before she died, and he hadn't mentioned it either? Instead of knocking, River walked around the side of the cabin. After a few hours, he moved back to the front and vanished from sight.

"Handyman?" Jack asked.

River did do construction, so perhaps he was helping her mother around the house or with something outside. "Maybe." She squeezed her bottom lip between her thumb and index finger, thinking. "I'll ask him."

"You think he's just going to volunteer answers?"

She shrugged. "Why not?"

"Because maybe he killed her."

"Then he should have a pretty good excuse ready, shouldn't he?"

Jack kept speeding through the footage. The hours crept by on the screen, then days. Five days before Gail died, then four days, then three. Finally, another figure in a ball cap sidled up to her door. A man. He lifted his fist, hesitated, then knocked. Isabelle could see her mother open the door, and like in the frames before, Isabelle was shocked by how much she'd aged, how slight she'd become.

When she was young, Isabelle would have described her mother as formidable. Now, she looked like any other aging woman who had lost too much. After a moment of back-and-forth conversation, the man stepped inside.

"You know this guy too?"

She couldn't be sure. "I don't think so."

They watched the time stamp. After an hour, the man slipped back out of the house, but he strategically kept his head down, as if he knew right where the camera was.

"What the hell?" Jack said. He stabbed his pen toward the screen. "This might be our guy." He scribbled something down and gnawed on the end of his pen. "Doesn't show his face, wears a hat, keeps his head down. Classic moves if you don't want to be seen."

"Knowing the placement of the camera would also suggest he's been here more than once." Isabelle looked over her shoulder toward the front door, as if the man would appear, like a mirage. "Narrows the pool down, at least."

Jack looked up at her. "Does it?"

"I mean, yes and no. There's only fifty people in this town. Can't be that hard to figure it out, right?"

"Let's keep running it." Jack stabbed the camera forward until one day before Gail's death. They already knew no one came to visit her the day she died, which, if she'd been delivered a lethal dose of thallium, meant that she had to ingest it *on* the day she died, but maybe it was through other means. But none of the visitors she'd seen had brought anything: no gifts, no food, no drinks. Was their theory completely off base?

A day before, the hours crept by, but no visitors. They were about to give up when the camera switched to night and they both watched as Gail opened the front door and barreled outside, yelling at someone just outside of the camera's frame. Gail was animated, flinging her arms, getting big, like she used to. For a second, Isabelle wondered if she was trying to scare off a bear, but she wouldn't be talking like that. Who was it?

They watched on pins and needles as Gail lunged forward, stomping toward whoever it was, and then disappeared off camera. She and Jack looked at each other, breath bated.

"This is certainly interesting," Jack whispered. "Some sort of confrontation the night before she died?"

Suddenly, Gail staggered back into view, but her body was all wrong. She was veering left and then right before collapsing to her knees.

"Jack." Isabelle gripped his shoulder and squeezed. "She's hurt."

"Or poisoned."

Even though they both knew how this story ended, they couldn't take their eyes off Gail. She gripped at leaves and sticks, dragging her hands through the earth, as if the ground could somehow save her. Isabelle felt a pang of remorse as her mother heaved herself up onto the porch steps, then reached up for the handle of the door, missed, and collapsed, breathing heavily. They waited for someone to appear, to either help her or harm her, but whoever it was also knew to stay out of the camera's lens, which made the mystery man their number one suspect.

After a moment, Gail forced herself to her knees, gripped the doorknob with both hands, and twisted. She fell into the cabin's entryway, slithered inside, and then shut the door. There was nothing after that.

They fast-forwarded all through the next day again to be sure. How long had Gail suffered before she died? Why hadn't she called anyone?

"Do you want me to stop it?" Jack's voice was kind, but she insisted he keep going. She knew Harper found her mother's body, but she hadn't thought to ask how long Gail had been dead before she made that discovery. Once Isabelle got the call from Harper, she didn't ask questions. She got in the car and drove straight here.

A full day after her mother died, Harper appeared, a bag of groceries in hand. She fumbled with balancing the bag and knocking on the door. Harper waited, adjusting the bag to her other hip, and obviously called out. When Gail didn't answer, Harper tried the door. Once it opened, she went inside. Moments later, she burst back outside, crying, grabbing her phone to call for help. Even from here, Isabelle could see how distraught she was, and she felt for Harper, she did.

Out of all the kids, Harper had the very best relationship with Gail, and Isabelle was sorry she hadn't been more sympathetic to her loss. Seeing it now, that impact, made her understand how deep Harper's empathy went, and how much more conditional Isabelle's was.

They continued to watch as paramedics arrived and her mother was removed on a gurney, a white sheet draped over her body. Isabelle sighed, deflated. So that was that.

Jack paused, wiped a hand down his face. "Wow."

"The police obviously need to see this." Even as Isabelle said it, she wasn't sure Theo was the right person to give it to, especially since he'd seen her mother before she died and kept that fact from her. But who else was there?

"I think we need more information first," Jack said.

Isabelle pointed toward his laptop screen. "More information than that?"

"Yes." His eyes were bloodshot, his hair disheveled. "Someone obviously hurt your mother. That's clear. This rules out suicide. Well, for the most part. We can't account for what happened once she went inside the cabin, and since we don't see an actual person in the footage, it might not be enough to hold up in court."

Isabelle knew how fickle the courts could be. Did she even want this to become anything official? A very dark part of her wondered if this was some sort of justice. If Gail's life was taken in the same manner as the poison she'd doled out to the kids.

"Do you think her death could be tied to what happened to the kids that night? Or unrelated?" Jack asked.

She hadn't talked about that night in so long and never in full detail with Jack. He knew what he'd read in her thallium article, and they'd discussed it from time to time, but Jack understood she wanted to forget about that part of her life. He accepted it, accepted her, and never pushed. But now those details might matter if they wanted to get to the bottom of what happened to Gail. Did she think it was related? Absolutely. But Isabelle had buried the mystery of that night with her siblings. The only time she'd tried to dig deeper had been through her article, but even then, answers didn't come.

The image of Gail's dying body still hung in Isabelle's mind like a shadow on the wall. She could feel Jack watching her, but she didn't look up. Not yet. "I think it's related."

"I do too." Jack placed a hand on her arm. "Can you take me through that night? What you remember?"

She swallowed, but nodded. "We egged Theo's house," she began. "He was outraged."

Jack pointed toward the screen. "You think his visit has any connection between then and now?"

She considered it. "I'm not sure." Isabelle told him about the wine, truth or dare, and what happened after they got back to the tree house. She paused. "I fell asleep, and that's when I must have started sleepwalking. Harper found me and guided me back home, tucked me into bed. I woke up, disoriented and disappointed we weren't going to sleep in the tree house, but she was worried that if I slept there, I'd wander off again."

"So she was with you."

"Yes, the whole night."

"And the others?"

This was the hard part. "Well, we don't know really. We were only able to piece it together by what the authorities found. They think the others found an old fallout shelter, or bunker, probably left over from the Cold War. There was a hatch. They either fell in or the ladder broke. But they were trapped."

"And how did the fire start?"

While Jack already knew the basic details, it was important that she recount everything now, lay it all out. "Jude had a lighter. He must have lit it for them to see and either dropped it or caught something on fire. It was extremely dry down there. He could have accidentally lit leaves, paper, whatever. Ultimately, after all the questioning, they ruled it as an accident." Her voice was raw but even.

"But wait," Jack said, interrupting. "If the three of them were down there, someone would have had to close the hatch, correct?"

Isabelle's hands were shaking. She clutched them in her lap. "The wooden top had been burned completely through, so they don't really know. The bunker went up in minutes. But the fire burned for a long time. There were no cabins out there. Luckily, it stayed contained to the fallout shelter."

"And you and Harper were at home. What about your mom?"

Icy chills traversed her skin. "That's the thing. My mom *wasn't* at home. Harper looked for her when we got back, to tell her we were home, and she wasn't in her room or in the cabin."

Silence descended between them.

"And Harper reported this to the police?"

Isabelle hesitated. This was one of the first rifts between her and Harper, because Harper had lied to the police. It was what made Isabelle almost certain that Gail had something to do with it. "No. Because Harper lied, she effectively got my mother off the hook, even though many townspeople had already made up their minds that she was guilty." She swallowed. "Especially because Marcus had also vanished."

"Why did Harper protect Gail?"

"Because she loved her," Isabelle said simply.

"What happened after? Who found the kids?"

"A hunter. When the kids didn't come home the next morning, Gail told a few neighbors. The bunker was a couple of miles off property, abandoned, like I said. Because they were minors, there was a full investigation, of course. The fire department, the coroner, everyone did what they were supposed to do. But no one had definitive answers."

Jack leaned forward slightly. "And there were autopsies?"

"Kind of. There was little left to test. No real soft tissue. No blood. Only calcified bone. Official cause of death was listed as 'thermal injuries and suspected smoke inhalation.' But like I said, it was presumed accidental."

Jack's jaw flexed as he tapped his pencil against the table but said nothing.

"There were no accelerants found. No signs of foul play. And the bunker was filled with flammable materials. They found Jude's lighter. It seemed to be a tragic accident. The end."

"And then your mother buried them on property."

"Yeah." Isabelle combed her fingers through her hair again, winced when a knuckle snagged on a tangle. "She filed the permits. Registered the family plot. She insisted she didn't want them in a cold town cemetery. She dug the graves herself. Harper and I helped."

"That must have been hard."

"It was. But now I'm . . ."

He sat up straighter. "Now you're what?"

"Now I'm starting to wonder if everything we accepted as truth was just . . . convenient. Too convenient. Because it was easier than asking what we were really looking at." Isabelle pointed back to the laptop screen. "You saw what happened to my mother, Jack. Someone wanted to silence her. Which means . . . if this isn't just about revenge against my mother, then someone still has something to hide."

Jack's fingers tightened around the edges of the table. "So what do you think our next play is?"

Isabelle dreaded saying what needed to be said. "In all my research, I found that thallium can be detected decades later through bone or teeth. I've always wanted to prove my theory: that the kids were purposely poisoned and killed."

"And you want to do that how?"

She looked at Jack, her lips forming the words before her brain was sure. "I want to exhume the bodies."

14

Jack looked at her.

"You mean like legally or . . . ?"

"I was hoping you maybe had a guy."

"Izz." He gave her a look and shook his head. "We can't go around the authorities on this. I could get in trouble. You could get in trouble."

"Hear me out." She kneeled in front of where he was sitting. "If the media gets wind of this, Cedarloch will become a zoo. Theo already said there's a reporter sniffing around. We need to have clear evidence first before we do anything here, especially if this was a murder. If we examine the bodies and can check for thallium, then that gives us a clear, direct link. That proves that someone poisoned Celia, Ben, and Jude. Someone set that fire. Someone poisoned my mother."

"You mean someone who wasn't Gail?"

The words nearly stopped her cold. She hadn't truly considered that someone else could have started that fire back then besides Gail. Or, like the authorities concluded, that it truly was a tragic accident. But still, someone poisoned the children. That part she was almost sure of. That was a detail that was simply overlooked back then, and it had never sat right with her. "We won't know until we know," she said. Isabelle leaned toward Jack, and he spread his knees to make room for her. She placed her palms on his thighs and squeezed. "I know this is a big ask. I know it seems insane. But can you at least ask Omar? See if he has anyone who could help us?"

"God, woman, you're killing me." He removed her hands and stood, pacing back and forth. "I'll make some calls, but if I do this, and that is a big if, we have to cover all our bases. No one can know. We have to put everything back as it was, do you hear me? And then we can go to the authorities, but they'll have to come to the thallium discovery on their own."

She considered. If they dug up the graves and the authorities were involved after the fact, they'd be able to tell the bodies had been disturbed. "What if we don't take this to the cops at all?"

Jack blinked at her, clearly confused. "What the hell does that mean?"

"I mean, why get them involved? Why go through all the red tape when you and I can follow the breadcrumbs?"

"Um, because it's illegal? Because we could go to jail?"

She sidled up next to him and cradled his elbows with her hands. "But what if we don't get in trouble? What if we can find the truth before anyone else?" She slid her hands to his chest, rooting around to feel the strong thump of his heart.

"Isabelle Archer, are you *manipulating* me?"

"Is it working?" She smirked, despite the grim possibility of exhuming her siblings' bodies. Though she'd seen plenty of dead bodies, she couldn't actually imagine doing what she was suggesting.

He leaned forward and kissed her forehead before cupping her hands beneath his. "Like a goddamn charm."

"Good." She patted his chest twice and moved back. "Call your people. I'm going to make a copy of this footage and email it to my guy back in Portland. Maybe you should do the same. I don't trust that this footage won't somehow disappear."

"Roger that."

Jack went to make his calls while she backed up all the files, pulled up her email, and shot herself a copy and then another to one of her most trusted contacts, Ethan. Isabelle checked the time. Somehow, it was already after lunch. They needed to check on Maisy. She sent a quick text to Harper, realizing she couldn't tell her about any of this. Watching how distraught she'd been after finding Gail . . . how would Harper handle knowing they were going to potentially dig up the kids' graves?

No, they had to do this alone. No one could find out.

Before Isabelle could decide their next move, a sharp knock at the front door startled them both. Jack lowered his phone. "Expecting anyone?"

Isabelle frowned. She wasn't. Maybe it was Rita again. Or even Harper and Maisy. "I'll check. You take care of that." She ushered for him to go out back for privacy as she walked to the front door.

On the other side stood a tall, blond woman smartly dressed. She smiled when she saw Isabelle.

"Hi, Isabelle Archer? I'm so sorry to show up like this, but I wondered if you had a few minutes to talk."

Isabelle eyed her warily. "And you are?"

The woman stuck out a thin, manicured hand, a simple gold band secured around her wrist. "Eliza Harrell. *The Cedarloch Sentinel.*"

Theo had already warned her about Eliza. Isabelle hesitated only a moment before shaking her hand and stepping onto the front porch, firmly shutting Eliza out of the cabin. "Since when do newspaper reporters show up on private property?" Isabelle crossed her arms. She knew the woman was just doing her job. Maybe she should have even felt a camaraderie of sorts, because they were essentially in the same profession. But this was different. This was Isabelle's life, and she knew, more than anyone, how media could interfere with uncovering the truth.

"Since the daughter of a supposed child killer returns back home after twenty years." Eliza didn't flinch, her answer at the ready. Isabelle was impressed.

"I already told the press I have no comment."

"I know that. But recent findings have come to light that I thought you might want to comment on?"

Isabelle knew she was dangling bait, but she couldn't help it. "Such as?"

"Did you know that Gail was looking into the deaths of the children again?"

Isabelle was genuinely thrown off guard. "Meaning?"

Eliza rooted around in her satchel, which was slung across her chest. "Meaning, she sent me this."

Isabelle gripped an envelope with Eliza's name scribbled on it in her mother's handwriting. She unfolded a single sheet of paper and read.

> Eliza,
>
> You don't know me, but you probably know of me. My name is Gail Archer. Years ago, three of my foster children died in a tragic fire, and I've always been convinced it wasn't an accident. Someone wanted to make it look like I did it, but I didn't. I may have been tough, but I wasn't a killer, and with the anniversary of these kids' deaths coming up, I want to do right by them. I've sat for far too long and done nothing, but I'm ready to do what it takes to find the truth. Please reach out to my biological daughter, Isabelle Archer. I have tried to get in touch with her many times, but she won't return my calls. But I know she will get to the bottom of this. I think I know who may have been involved. Tell Isabelle to follow her instincts, and ask her if she remembers what she said to me all those years ago. Her fears about the children? I have those same fears too. Then and now. I fear if I write any of this to Isabelle, she'll just throw it away without reading it. But please tell her. Please find her. It has always mattered to me that she knows I'm not a killer, that I would never harm any of those kids. It wasn't me. But

> I do believe that fire wasn't an accident. It's been too long. It's time for the truth.
>
> Gail

Isabelle read the note twice, then folded it. Her mother was right. Gail had tried to call many times, but Isabelle never returned the messages. She sorted through her memory, wondering if her mother ever wrote her a letter. If she had, Isabelle certainly hadn't opened it. "How long have you had this?"

"She sent it two weeks before she died, and I don't think it's a coincidence."

Isabelle peered at Eliza. Could she be trusted? Even if she could, Isabelle didn't have nearly enough information to share anything of value beyond the video footage.

Eliza motioned to the letter. "What did she mean when she talked of your fears about the children?"

Isabelle knew exactly what Gail meant. She'd told her mother she thought someone had intentionally poisoned them, but she certainly wasn't going to share that information with Eliza. "I have no idea." She huffed. "Look, my mother was manipulative. All this proves is that she didn't want people to think she was a killer. She didn't want *me* to think she was a killer. But I do. And I did. Her being dead doesn't change that."

Eliza nodded. "And you think your mother died from natural causes?"

"I know she did."

Eliza let that statement linger, fished in her wallet for a card, and held it out to Isabelle. "Well, that's all, then. Please, call me if you decide you want to *actually* tell me the truth." She waved, then headed back the way she came.

Isabelle exhaled, searching the trees for any more sets of eyes or surprises before going back inside. Jack was waiting for her.

"Who was that?"

"Reporter." She pocketed her card. "Any luck on your end?"

"Omar's checking, but he thinks we'd do better with someone we have ties to here. Someone who might want to do you a favor, not me."

Isabelle almost laughed before she realized. "Frank."

"Frank?"

"The local coroner. He's . . ." Well, he wasn't a friend exactly, but he might be willing if she explained everything. "Maybe worth a shot to ask?"

"Can he be trusted?"

"I think so."

"Then lead the way." Jack swiped a hand through his hair. "What about Maisy? Is she good?"

"She's fine. We'll grab her after." Isabelle relaced her shoes and led Jack into the forest. Together they forged a plan: They'd talk to Frank and see if he was willing to help. Then they would try to get to the bottom of why both River and Theo were at Gail's house and who the mystery man could possibly be. She wondered if showing the tape to Harper would help. She knew everyone in this town, but Isabelle also didn't want to upset Harper any more than she already was.

"It's got to bring up a lot," Jack said now. "Being back."

She stopped, turned to him, felt that ache expand in her chest. She rarely came apart. But with Jack, she could almost let her guard down, could almost show him how much pain she was actually in. "It does," she said softly.

He wrapped her in a hug, and she allowed herself to be held, the sounds of Cedarloch crescendoing around them. After a few moments, he kissed the top of her head, and released her. "So that River character. Anything I need to know there?"

"Besides him being my first boyfriend? No."

"Ah." He cleared his throat. "Was it serious?"

How did she answer that? Yes and no. It was serious in the ways all first loves were serious, but also faded quickly like most teenage relationships do. It mattered, and it didn't. It was deep, and yet it wasn't. "Well, he was my first love, I guess." The truth. Just like with Maisy, she always settled on the truth with Jack.

He whistled. "Serious, then. Who ended it?"

"He did." She ducked under a low-hanging branch, telling Jack to watch his head.

"Well, he's obviously an idiot."

"Obviously."

"Why, though?"

"I was young. I wanted it to be more than it was. River was what you would call a bad boy, I guess." She shrugged. "It was never going to last."

"And now?"

She stopped, and he nearly rammed into the back of her. "And now what?"

"Well, I mean, you're single. Anything left there, you think?"

"What is this? Some reverse psychology play?"

He flattened a palm against his T-shirt. "Me? Reverse psychology? I would never."

She smacked his chest and kept walking.

"Can I ask you a serious question?"

"I'll pay you a million dollars."

"Why aren't *we* together?"

He slowed after he asked it, and she was forced to stop again, turn, and really look at him. This man that she trusted. This man she'd had a child with. This man she'd almost thrown away all her rules for because she loved him so damn much.

"You know why," she said.

"No, I don't." He took a step toward her. "I know that you're scared to get too close. I know letting people in isn't easy, and I understand why. I've never pushed you to be someone you're not, Izz. But I love you. I love you so much. I love our family, and I'm telling you—not because some ex-boyfriend is here, but because it's true—I want you. I choose you. And I will wait for you."

The words were right, but the sentiment was off. "You don't need to wait, Jack." She walked again, picking up her pace. She hated having the same conversation but hearing a slightly altered version of it. As though if he could keep explaining how much she meant to him, then she would have to change her mind. It was romantic and infuriating, and she was over it.

"But I want to wait," he said, jogging to catch up.

"No." Isabelle turned, her voice sharp. "You live a big life. A transient life. You need to find someone who is all the way emotionally available, who wants all the same things you do. The marriage. The house. The white fucking picket fence."

"See? You can't stand the thought of me having a white picket fence with someone else."

"Ugh. Get over yourself, Jack."

"No, it's true." He reached for her arm and missed. "You can't admit that we were blissfully happy in our own way, and that I don't care about any of that stuff. You think I do, but I don't. I want you. I've always wanted you, and that's what scares you. Because you, as you are, with all your fears and trauma and that tough exterior . . . it's exactly what I want. I don't want to *change* you, Isabelle. I just want to love you." He reached again for her hand, but she tugged it away.

"I'm not good for you!" Her voice echoed off the trees. "I'm not good for anyone." She gestured wildly around her. "Here we are, trying to figure out if my mother was murdered by someone in this town because she may have poisoned and killed my siblings. They died in a fire that I should have been in too. Yet I was spared for some unknown reason, and while that seems like a gift, it has always felt like a curse." Unexpected tears streamed down her cheeks. Jack's eyes were pained, his fingers lifting to brush them away, but she took another step back. "The kind of guilt I carry doesn't go away because some great guy walks into my life and offers to love me, Jack. It doesn't even go away with someone like Maisy, who is the biggest, most incredible gift of my life. It doesn't change with all the success in the world, even if I win a Pulitzer, like you. It lives inside me, this *thing*. This dark, scary thing. It chews up all the good. *That's* why I can't be with you." She knifed her hand in the air. "I don't want it to chew you up too."

Before he could offer some sort of platitude, Isabelle turned yet again and made the final few yards toward the town's edge.

After a few moments, she heard Jack's footsteps race to catch hers.

Then

Jude

"Did you hear that?"

Jude stopped in his tracks and shot his arm out. "Was that Celia?" He rotated, glancing at Ben, Harper, and Isabelle, concern in his eyes. "Where's CeCe?" He panned the trees behind them. "Crap." He jerked his head and threaded his way back toward Theo's house. Maybe this had been a dumb idea. Of all the people to get caught, Celia not only didn't deserve it but was also the least likely to handle it well. Out of the five of them, he worried about her the most.

Celia often made Jude think of his real sister. They'd been taken into different foster homes when they were kids, and he hadn't seen her since.

It was one of the reasons he was most excited to leave Cedarloch. Once he was on his own, he could find her. Make sure she was okay. And yet, when he thought of branching off, he remembered who he'd be leaving behind.

Who he'd be leaving them with.

"CeCe!" he called out, looking for her among the trees. As they neared Theo's house, the deep thunder of a man's voice cracked the silence. So he'd found her. Jude, unafraid of getting caught, sprinted forward until he spotted Theo, jerking Celia around like a rag doll. She was crying, snot and tears flying from her nose.

"Hey! Let her go," Jude barked. He ripped Theo's hand away and stood up to his full height. Jude was a few inches taller than Theo, but Theo was still the sheriff. He practically ran this town and didn't let anyone forget it.

"I ought to throw your asses in jail right now!" Theo yelled. "I've got you on vandalism and trespassing, for starters."

"So do it then," Jude challenged, lifting his chin. "Arrest some kids for having a bit of harmless fun."

"Harmless?" Spit flew from Theo's mouth as he pointed toward the door. "Eggs aren't harmless, son. I'm calling your mother."

"Wait." Jude panicked at the thought of Gail getting that call. "We'll clean it up. Don't call her. Please." He didn't want to wreck this night for his siblings. If Gail knew what they'd done, she'd never let them have another sleepover again. He took a breath, swallowed his pride. "I'm sorry, sir. You're right. It was stupid. We'll clean it up."

Theo's scowl softened as he glanced down at Celia, who was still trying to stanch the flow of tears. Isabelle's arm was hooked protectively around her. Ben stood nearby, looking at his feet, and Harper shot daggers at Theo. "Christ." He dragged one hand down his face and flicked his other toward the woods. "Go on back home. Be here first thing in the morning to clean it all up. You hear?"

Jude exhaled, his entire body relaxing. "Thank you, sir. We will. First thing. Guys, come on." He jerked his head, and they all fell in line, walking back the way they came. The entire mood had been punctured. What a dumb idea. Ben was right. He should have listened. When they were about a hundred yards out, he turned to the group. "See? What did I tell you? Fun, right?"

They were quiet at first, and then Isabelle erupted into nervous laughter and the others joined in. *There.* That was what he was after. This night could still be salvaged. He was sure of it.

When they got back to the tree house, he suggested they build a fire and roast s'mores. Something to bring the mood up. They weren't little kids anymore, but who didn't love a good s'more? Isabelle grabbed the box of graham crackers and bar of chocolate. Celia and Harper stabbed marshmallows onto rusted metal skewers. Ben helped Jude with the fire, and in moments, it was raging, the flames licking dangerously close to the tree house.

"Is the fire too close?" he asked. It was windy tonight. He'd wanted the firepit near enough so they could hang out by the tree house but not so close as to be a fire hazard.

Ben shrugged. "Looks good to me, man." He sank down on a stump, and the girls did the same. They fanned out in a semicircle, watching the flames turn their marshmallows from white to brown to a bubbly black. Jude slipped his between two graham crackers with a rectangle of chocolate, then smashed it down, like he had as a kid. That first bite was delicious: sweet and sticky and crunchy all in one. He licked his fingers as the girls laughed because they couldn't get a proper bite. Ben watched Jude. There was so much pain in his little brother's eyes, so much uncertainty about what lay ahead for all of them.

The truth was they were sick. Something was definitely wrong, and though Jude wasn't one to worry, he *was* worried. He'd thought about taking them all to the urgent care a couple of towns over, but he knew Gail would find out. She didn't believe in Western medicine, had deprived them of the most basic care for the last three years. In all honesty, he was used to suffering, but this was on a whole different level.

They ate and recapped how scary it was getting caught and how none of them wanted to clean up the mess tomorrow.

"Maybe it will rain," Isabelle said, glancing at the sky. "Wash it all away."

"Here's hoping," Celia sniffed. Her face was still tearstained. Jude glanced at her bare arm, which he knew would bruise in the morning. How would she explain that to Gail? To anyone?

"So what now?" Ben asked. "Since that was a bust."

Harper jumped up. "I know!" She ran to her bag, rummaged around, and held up a Ouija board. She shook the box, and Celia groaned.

"I hate ghosts," she said.

"All the more reason to get to know them," Harper said. "Can we?"

Isabelle shrugged, as did Ben and Jude. Jude didn't believe in stuff like this, but maybe it would cheer them all up. They moved to the Parlour so they had a flat surface to play on. Harper set up the board and placed the plastic triangle in the center. "Okay, who do we want to summon?" She grinned and wiggled her eyebrows.

They were all silent, but finally Ben spoke up. "What about Marcus?"

Harper's face changed, as did Isabelle's. Their eyes locked, and something passed between them. Jude knew they'd lived with him only for a short time before he went missing. Both girls were pretty tight lipped about him. They'd only been ten when he vanished. Marcus was fifteen at the time.

Once that case went cold and Marcus was deemed a runaway, Celia, Ben, and Jude had been taken in by Gail. He'd heard the rumors about her, of course, but since she wasn't charged with anything and there was no one else who fostered nearby, Jude had convinced himself that she must be okay. Now, he wasn't so sure.

"What was he like?" Celia asked, pushing in closer to Isabelle.

"He was okay, I guess," Isabelle said, glancing at Harper. "He wasn't with us for long."

"Kind of kept to himself," Harper agreed quickly.

"Do you think he really just went missing?" Jude asked. "Or do you think Gail killed him?"

Celia inhaled sharply, as did Harper.

"Why would you even say that?" Harper asked. She had such a boner for Gail. He didn't get it.

"I mean, pretty suspicious, right? Vanishing in this town, never to be found?"

"How long did they look?" Ben asked.

"I don't remember," Isabelle said. "Awhile, I think."

"Well, let's see if we can find out some answers," Jude said, suddenly eager to play. If Marcus had died out here, maybe they could make contact with him. Stranger things had happened, he supposed.

"Okay, you all have to close your eyes and be open to the possibility of there being a presence here. If you're not, it won't work," Harper explained.

Everyone closed their eyes, but Jude squinted one eye open. Ben was looking right at him and smirked. Then Harper spoke.

"Marcus Brown, if your spirit is in these woods, make yourself known."

Jude opened his eyes again, as did the others. Ben started to laugh, then Jude. The girls looked annoyed, but did they really expect this thing to start moving on its own?

Then, as if by magic, it did. The triangle started to slide to the top left where the word **YES** was.

"Stop moving it," Harper said.

"I'm not moving it," Isabelle and Celia insisted.

"Well, *I'm* not moving it," Ben said.

Jude wasn't pushing it, but someone had to be. Finally, it rested on the word **YES**.

Harper took a breath. "Did you die in these woods?"

They waited, but the triangle didn't move.

"Does that mean yes?" Ben asked.

Harper shrugged.

"Ask him something else, something he has to spell."

They all struggled to think of what to ask, and then Isabelle jumped in.

"How did you die?" she asked.

They waited. Seconds ticked by, and then the triangle began to move. Though Jude was sure one of them was moving it, he held his breath, eager to see where it would land.

P. U. S. H. E. D.

"Pushed?" Jude asked. "He was pushed? Pushed where?"

Before they could ask more, a stick cracked behind them, and they all screamed.

"It's him. It's Marcus!" Celia said, burying her face in Isabelle's shoulder. Ben laughed, but his eyes looked uncertain.

Sometimes deer were attracted to the heat of the fire. Jude squinted, and there, beyond a tree in the distance, stood someone. "Holy shit. Do you guys see that?" He closed his eyes, counted to five, and opened them, but the figure was still there. It was easy to imagine things out here, to mistake shadows for animals. Or humans.

"See what?" They all huddled near him, but when they looked that way, the figure was gone.

"There was someone standing out there," Jude said. "I swear."

"Har har," Isabelle said. "Very funny."

"No, I'm serious." He stood, his heart thumping in his chest. "There was literally someone standing right there watching us." Before his siblings could call bullshit, he stalked toward the trees to find out who.

15

They walked silently toward the funeral home.

Jack's words kicked around in her head. The last thing she wanted to do was push him away, but deep down, she felt he could do better. When they got to the edge of the water, he stopped, gently gripped her elbow, and turned Isabelle toward the lake.

"Look at this." His voice was quiet, filled with the type of reverence and awe nature often brought out in him. She'd seen him do the same thing all over the world: in front of lakes in Italy, at the base of pyramids in Egypt, on a peak of the Swiss Alps. And then she'd seen the flip side, when he glimpsed unspeakable tragedies: bombs, war, dead children scattered along the charred earth like litter.

Before they had Maisy, they'd trekked all over the world on Jack's bigger assignments. Once she'd become a mother, things changed. Now, he was here for her. Had the tables ever been turned like this? Where it was her story they were chasing, her mystery to unfold?

"I've seen it," she said. But she loved this lake, always had.

"It really is spectacular here," he said. "I'm sorry it was ruined for you."

"Thanks." They continued walking, and Isabelle allowed herself to remember some of the good moments too. She shared them with Jack now. Madison manning the ferry. Dr. Hollis at the pharmacy. Mary, the town tutor. How the five of them would burst from the forest onto the main strip and make their rounds for supplies and conversation. It was all so easy, once. So peaceful. At least for a while.

"Jack. Nine o'clock." Isabelle stopped him, tugged Jack behind the side of a café. There, on the wharf, stood Theo and River, arguing in hushed tones. Something about their body language seemed off. Theo was gesticulating with his hands. River was pacing. After a moment, Theo said something to River. River offered a harsh laugh and turned, before the two parted ways.

Jack looked at her. "Were those the guys from the video?"

"Yep. Theo and River." Isabelle's uneasiness grew. She tried to think about the tethers they might share, especially now. It had to be about Gail.

"Are they close?"

Isabelle shrugged. "I honestly have no idea. I don't think so." But she had no way of knowing that, did she? Who was close and who wasn't? Maybe she could ask Harper.

At the funeral home, they knocked on the door. When Rita didn't answer, they tried the knob, but it was locked. Isabelle checked the time and glanced at the business hours sign hanging on the front door. It was after lunch. "Someone should be here," she said.

Jack peered in the window, tenting his fingers around his eyes. "Izz." He pulled back, moved in again. "Look."

She pushed in beside him to peer through the window. Some files were strewn along the carpet, their contents spilled haphazardly. "Looks like the files were ransacked."

They stared at each other. Isabelle thought about the papers she'd signed, the autopsy Frank had shown her. Did this have anything to do with that, or was it unrelated?

"Isabelle!" Jack's voice was sharp. He was looking back through the window. He stood up and started shouldering the door.

"What are you doing?"

"Body," he said.

"What?" She looked back through the window, searching through the detritus for what he'd seen. There, in the far back corner, she saw a lifeless arm. Rita?

A sharp crack brought her back to her body as Jack burst through the door. Inside, the place was a wreck. Isabelle covered her nose with her sleeve. "What is that smell?"

Jack rushed over and knelt down to where the body was. Expecting to see Rita, she gasped when she saw who it was.

Frank. She knelt down, rooted around for a heartbeat, and felt a slight, shallow pulse. "Call 911." She thought about calling Theo, but could she trust him? "Frank? Frank, can you hear me?" She tapped lightly on his cheek. His skin looked gray. She checked his body for wounds but saw nothing visible.

Jack was on the phone. He gave the address to the dispatcher and hung up. "They're sending an ambulance."

"I'm going to look for Rita. Stay with him."

She and Jack swapped places as Isabelle stood on shaky legs and did a quick lap. Someone had gone to a lot of trouble to find whatever they needed. The filing cabinet Frank had dipped into the other day was completely empty, turned on its side. She took in the complete disarray, wondering what happened. It seemed there'd been some sort of struggle. Once she'd swept the main floor, she paused at the top of the stairs that led down to the morgue. She'd never been in a morgue, had steered clear her whole life.

Carefully, she took the steps and paused at the bottom. The room was dark and cold. What if Rita was down here somewhere, harmed? What if someone was waiting to harm her?

Utility knife in hand, she slid her hand on the wall and flipped on the lights. The room was empty. The overhead lights buzzed, and she shivered from the sudden drop in temperature.

"Rita?" Isabelle called her name, even though it was clear no one was down here. Thank God there wasn't a corpse splayed on one of these cold metal tables. She stared at the lockers in the wall, where she knew bodies were stored once their autopsies were complete. After a quick perusal, she took the stairs back up. Frank was barely conscious. Jack had helped him sit up.

As she stepped forward, a wave of dizziness overtook her.

"We need to get outside," Jack said.

"Should we move him?"

"That smell? Might be something toxic. Smells like rotten eggs. Let's be safe. Help me get him outside."

She moved quickly, even though her balance felt off. After hoisting him to his feet, they stumbled outside and placed Frank gently on the porch swing. A little color was coming back to his face.

"Where's the ambulance?" Jack asked, searching the street.

"Next town over," she said. "First rule of Cedarloch: Don't have an emergency."

Jack paced back and forth, then pulled a bandanna from his back pocket and secured it over his nose and mouth. "I'll be right back."

"Jack, what are you doing?"

He went back inside before she could stop him. While he was inside, she checked Frank's pulse again, which was slightly stronger. A good sign, at least.

"Isabelle? What in the world?" Rita approached the steps, two large to-go paper coffee cups in hand. She glimpsed Frank and rushed up the stairs, some of the hot liquid sloshing free from one of the tops and burning the back of her wrist. She winced but gestured toward Frank. "What happened?" Genuine shock distorted her features as she looked from Isabelle to Frank.

"We found him like this. Someone ransacked inside."

"What are you talking about?" She set the coffees on the railing and rushed inside, immediately shouting about the smell. Rita gasped as she took in the state of the place.

Jack appeared back out front, a few files in his hands.

"Who the hell are you?" Rita asked.

"This is Jack Pearce. Maisy's dad."

"That smell." Rita took out her phone. "Need to get poison control down here. Good Lord. Could be formaldehyde. One of the vents might be blocked."

"Can that happen?" Jack asked.

Rita frowned. "It can, though we're usually careful about checking."

"We've already called an ambulance for Frank," Isabelle assured her.

"I don't understand how this happened." Rita lifted the phone to her ear, then lowered it when her call didn't go through. She eyed the files in Jack's hands. "You can't take anything."

"They're empty," he said, showing her the bare file folders he was holding.

She looked between them. "Why are you two even here?"

"We were coming to see Frank."

Just then, a sharp whine pierced the air as an ambulance pulled up.

"Oh, thank God. Over here." Rita gestured to two EMTs who spilled out. In moments, they had Frank on a stretcher, and Rita rode in the back with him. Jack and Isabelle watched them pull away. She hoped Frank would be okay.

"What did you find?" she asked, finally turning to Jack.

"It's what I *didn't* find," he said. He held up the folders, labeled with her mother's name and then Celia's, Ben's, and Jude's.

"What do you mean?"

"Their files are gone. I searched as best as I could, but they're not here. The initial autopsy report for your mother, the kids' death certificates. All gone."

Isabelle scoped the street, as if the culprit was lurking, watching. Who was doing this? And what were they really after?

"I don't like this, Jack," she finally said.

"Me neither. I especially don't like Maisy being here."

Maisy. If anything happened to their daughter, she'd never forgive herself. Maybe she should suggest that Jack take her back to Portland.

Before she could say anything, Theo sauntered their way. "Hey, folks." He gestured toward the road. "Was that an ambulance I heard?"

His tone was light. As if nothing were wrong. As if they hadn't witnessed him and River in an argument. As if Theo hadn't lied to her face.

Isabelle and Jack stepped off the porch and stood in front of the funeral home. Jack introduced himself before they filled him in on what happened, both she and Jack gauging his reaction.

"Poor Frank." His eyes took in the funeral home behind them. "I'm glad Rita's with him."

"We saw you with River," Jack said. "Looked like an argument."

Theo scratched his head, slowly pulled his eyes away from the funeral home. "I don't think that's any of your business, son."

Jack gave Isabelle a pointed look. Before she could confront Theo about what they'd seen and why he'd lied to her about seeing Gail before she died, a sound tore through the air like the sky splitting open, a low, concussive boom that shoved her forward and stole the breath from her lungs. Heat slammed into her back, singed the edges of her hair. The ground pitched. A roar filled her head, then nothing but ringing. Suddenly, she was weightless, propelled forward, before she hit the ground hard, the skin peeling from the palms of her hands. Dust and debris rained down around her.

The ringing was deafening. She gripped her ears and rolled to her back. She tried to sit up, but couldn't. The world in front of her was fire and ash and thick, black smoke. Two bodies lay splayed feet from her, one of them bent at all the wrong angles. She called out Jack's name but couldn't hear her own words.

Smoke and bits of paper billowed in fiery bursts above her, like clouds. People spilled out of businesses, rushing toward them. Her eyes fluttered closed, then open, then closed again. Even as she lost consciousness, the ringing faded, replaced just as violently with sound. People screaming. Shoes on pavement. Fire crackling. More sirens. Sifting through rubble.

Chaos, everywhere, all at once.

16

Isabelle cracked one eye open, then the other.

She was no longer outside but in a hospital bed. She heard the beeping of machines, smelled the antiseptic in the air. She attempted to move, and her ribs ached. Her mind went straight to Jack. Those crumpled bodies she'd seen. What if he wasn't okay? What if he didn't make it?

"Mama!" Maisy burst through the door and gave her a hug. Harper trailed behind with Ivy, a cup of coffee in hand.

"Ooh, Maisy. Be careful, sweetheart. Your mom might be in some pain." Harper placed a warm hand on Isabelle's leg. "How are you feeling?"

"What happened?" Her voice was hoarse, and her head ached. Her ears felt stuffy, as if she'd gotten water clogged in them after a long swim.

"There was an explosion at the funeral home. They think something to do with the vents or some of the chemicals. I'm not sure. Thank God you weren't inside. Why were you even there, Izz?"

Harper was talking too fast. It took a moment for Isabelle's memory to catch up. The place had been ransacked moments before they arrived. Frank was unconscious. Whether it was the vents or not, someone had gone through the files. "I was there to see Frank." She glanced at Ivy and Maisy, who were sitting on the window seat, chatting. "Do you know if Jack . . . ?" She couldn't bring herself to ask. How many moments had she watched the news as some horrible calamity unfolded live, with bombs and deaths and so many casualties, all the while knowing Jack was there one minute and might not be the next? Work like theirs sometimes led to situations like these. But she never would have thought that would be possible here. Not in Cedarloch.

"Jack's fine. Minor injuries," Harper assured her. "But Theo's in critical."

So it was Theo she'd seen, limbs bent the wrong way. "And Frank?"

"He's going to be okay, they think. God, Izz. What a damn day for this city. This is probably the most action anyone's seen in years." She sat on a chair and scraped it closer to Isabelle's bedside. "We were so worried." She glanced behind her. "Maisy was so scared," Harper whispered. Tears filled her eyes, and she cleared her throat. "I only just found you again. I couldn't bear the thought . . ." Emotion swallowed the rest of her words.

Isabelle sometimes forgot all that Harper had lost the night of the fire too. "What's my prognosis?"

"Bruised ribs. A possible concussion. Nothing that will keep you here overnight, thankfully. And I've already told Jack, but you two are staying with me. You'll be fed and taken care of, and it will be easier with Maisy."

"Harper." It was futile to protest, but Isabelle's depth of appreciation continued to grow.

"Thank me later. I'll come to Portland, and you can take care of me for the weekend."

"Deal." Isabelle winced as she moved. She'd taken some boxing classes years ago and had gotten into sparring for a few months. She'd forgotten how bad bruised ribs could feel. "Is Jack up and about, or . . ."

"I am." Jack appeared in the doorway, hair disheveled, a few superficial lacerations sprayed across his right cheek. His elbow was in a sling, but his eyes were full of life. Something about nearly dying made everything more crystal clear, he always said. It was an adrenaline high, even when you were exhausted and faced with the staggering truth that you could have died. Isabelle often asked if he believed in quantum theory, where there was another version of him out there who didn't survive. Every moment, every decision, branching them into thousands of different iterations of themselves, all living out alternate timelines. In this one, he was alive. They both were. That was enough for her. He rushed over, kissed her gently on the mouth, and swept her hair from her face.

"I can't take you anywhere," he said. His eyes filled with tears as he looked down at her and then over at Maisy, who flung herself into his arms. "Oof. Careful, kiddo. I've got a few bumps and bruises."

"What's Theo's prognosis?" Isabelle asked.

Jack glanced at the girls and shook his head. "Not good."

"River was here to see you earlier," Harper said. She gestured to the small table by the window. "Brought you tulips."

Isabelle clocked the look on Jack's face. Tulips were once her favorite, but she loved wildflowers now. River couldn't know that, couldn't know all the ways she'd changed.

"Harp, can you find a doctor and see when we can get out of here?"

"On it. Girls, let's go." They obeyed immediately and trotted after her without a backward glance.

Jack whistled. "Can we hire her?"

Isabelle groaned as she sat all the way up. "I just might. She insists we stay with her."

"Oh, I know. She's already told me." Jack laughed. "Somehow, I don't think you argue with a woman like that." He took a few steps toward her and slipped one of her hands in his. "I'm so glad you're okay."

"You too."

There was a quick knock at the door. She expected the doc, but it was a woman in jeans and a blazer. She flashed her badge and stepped into the room. "Detective Sheila Murdoch," she said. "I live in Crossings, about an hour west." Crossings was the biggest city nearby. Isabelle assumed she'd been assigned to look into the explosion. "Mind if I ask you both some questions?"

They told her exactly what happened. Arriving at the funeral home to find it raided. The missing files. Frank. Theo. That rotten-egg smell. Isabelle decided to omit any more information about her mother's possible murder, the note from Eliza, or what they were digging into. Detective Murdoch gave Jack her card and left.

"You don't think we should have mentioned your mother?" Jack asked quietly when she was gone. "Maybe she could help."

"I don't really trust anyone right now," she said. "Not even someone with a badge." And she didn't. River. Theo. Even Rita she wasn't sure about. Not to mention the mystery man in the ball cap. Could he have been behind what happened at the funeral home today?

After a few more minutes, Harper appeared with the doctor. "Ta-da." She waved her hands as Dr. Carrie Stevens walked in, checked a few vitals, and issued their paperwork for release. After another hour of waiting, they were discharged. Isabelle was given a strict concussion protocol and instructions to call if anything got worse. She refused the pain meds and changed back into her clothes, and they were outside in minutes. She winced from the sunlight, her head throbbing. The hospital was in the next town over. Insane that she had no memory of being transported here.

"I've got the van," Harper said. "Pasta for dinner? That okay, Izz?"

Isabelle hadn't eaten since breakfast. "Sounds great."

Maisy slipped one hand into Isabelle's and the other into Jack's, walking between them toward the van. Ivy chatted up ahead with Harper.

"How are you doing, Maze?"

"I'm glad you and Daddy are okay," she said, squeezing Isabelle's palm. It stung where the skin had peeled away.

She squeezed back anyway. "Me too, Bug. Me too." When they approached the van, Harper fished something from under the windshield wipers.

"Uh, Izz? This is for you."

It was an envelope with her name on it. She glanced around, then opened it. Inside was a small note card with one sentence in blocky letters.

NOW DO YOU WANT TO TALK?
CALL ME. 509.699.4235 E.

"Who is that from?" Jack asked.

"That reporter." She stuffed it into her bag. They piled into the van and rode silently back toward Harper's house. Isabelle's head was spinning. She had so many new threads to consider. If she'd been pondering whether to go back to Portland or stay, she got her answer.

She wasn't leaving Cedarloch until she got to the bottom of everything.

17

When they were back at Harper's house, Isabelle and Jack got Maisy settled, then shut themselves in the guest room to strategize while Harper made dinner.

If she was worried she didn't have anything substantial to look into before, now, with the funeral home, Frank, the ransacked files, her mother's note, Theo and River's argument, the video footage, and the autopsy report, it seemed hard to ignore. Jack kept checking in on Theo, but there was no change. They were waiting for Frank to regain consciousness before they talked to him. Considering what happened, Isabelle hoped she didn't have to plead her case so hard for him to help them exhume the bodies.

"Do you need anything?" Harper peeked her head into the guest bedroom, where Isabelle was propped up in bed with her laptop, Jack beside her.

"We're good, thanks."

Harper hesitated, as if she wanted to say something more, then nodded and closed the door. Isabelle sighed and looked at Jack. Her head was still sore, ears stuffy. "I feel bad not telling her everything," she said now.

"Do you trust her?"

"Of course I trust her. I wouldn't leave Maisy with her otherwise. I just . . . she's always had such a soft spot for my mom. We used to argue about it after the kids died. Even though Harper was sick, too, she never accused my mother of anything. We could never agree. Eventually, we stopped talking about it altogether. And then, when I moved away, she was the only one to make an effort to stay in touch."

"She doesn't seem like she held much of a grudge," he said, crossing his legs and placing one arm behind his head. He winced. "God, my body does not feel like a wonderland right now."

"Same."

"Okay, what do we know?" Jack asked now, tilting his head her way. "Let's review."

Isabelle didn't feel like focusing, but what choice did she have? They'd nearly died today. The stakes couldn't be higher. And there was no way in hell she was convinced the explosion was from a faulty vent. While whoever clogged the vents might not have wanted to harm them specifically, they had certainly wanted to destroy something. Maybe the files were a diversion. Maybe it was something else.

"Okay," Isabelle said, ticking things off on her fingers. "It's clear my mother died under mysterious circumstances. We know that now, as we have visual proof. We have River and Theo on the video footage before my mother died, and then they were arguing about something today, so we need to understand how they're connected. We have the mystery man. We have missing files. We have my mother's note. We have thallium in my mother's autopsy report." She dropped her hands. "What we *don't* have is a clear connection between what happened back then and what happened to Gail on that video."

"Yet," Jack supplied.

"Yet," she affirmed. She glanced at him. "I'm not sure Frank will be up for helping us. He could lose his license, like you said. Or worse."

"Correct. I think the smartest play here is to call Detective Murdoch, show her the video footage and the preliminary autopsy report photos from your phone, and see if it's enough to have the public health department sign off on exhumation."

She sighed. "It probably won't be."

"You never know."

"But then that makes this a possible homicide, which will turn Cedarloch into a media circus."

"Not if you call that Eliza lady and give her an exclusive. Maybe she can call off the dogs."

Isabelle considered. She wanted to do all of this privately and off the books, but there were too many repercussions for that. While she wanted to be certain of what they had before she brought this to the authorities, if they tampered with the bodies, nothing would be admissible in court. She knew doing this through proper channels was the only way. "I'll call the detective. Maybe she can even talk to Frank for us about the exhumation."

He nodded. "I think that's the best-case scenario." He looked at her. "Have you ever considered it could be more than one person?"

Isabelle adjusted back against the headboard, blinked, and considered his question. "No, I haven't." She glanced at her short list of suspects and made a figure eight around Theo's and River's names and then the mystery man. Her brain kept snagging on River. He'd been so young back then, like them. Why in the world would he want to hurt any of them? And what ties could he possibly have to her mother? "The only tether I can think of that involves two people is that the night of the fire, we saw Theo *and* River."

"That's pretty vital."

Was it? She wasn't sure yet. She chewed on a ragged cuticle until she tasted the sharp tang of blood, then slapped her notebook down and rested her head back against the pillows. Downstairs, she could hear Ivy and Maisy singing a song on a karaoke machine and laughing. "I know one little person who is completely unaffected by all this, at least," she said.

"Thank God for small miracles." Jack smiled at her.

Isabelle reached a hand up to trace the small cuts on his face. "Are you in pain?"

He shrugged. "If by 'pain' you mean it feels like I've been beaten with bats, then sure. A little. You?"

She shrugged back, though every part of her ached.

Jack opened his mouth to speak, then closed it and shook his head.

"What?"

"It's just . . ." He swallowed. "When I saw you in that hospital bed, our entire relationship flashed before my eyes. A life without you isn't one worth living. That's what kept going through my head."

"Jack."

"No, let me finish. Please." He grabbed her hand and entwined her fingers with his. "I love you, Isabelle. I want you in my life, in whatever capacity you'll have me. Almost losing you today drove that home even more. I want you to know that. It's important for you to know how much I care." He squeezed her sore palm. Before she could say anything, his phone rang. "It's the hospital." He took the call, lifted a finger, and stepped into the hall to take it. Probably news about Theo.

She exhaled and let Jack's words work their way into her system. For once, she didn't immediately dismiss them. She let them land because it was how she felt too. Hiding behind all of her stubbornness was good old-fashioned fear. Fear of loving Jack so much only to lose him. Fear that once he got too close, he would want to leave. But shouldn't she take the risk, cling to that type of love while she still could?

He came back into the bedroom, his face pale. "Theo didn't make it."

"What?" She felt like someone had dunked her in ice water. "Oh, my God." She pressed a hand to her mouth. "That's awful." If Theo was their guy, now they'd never know. She looked at Jack, understanding passing between them. That could have been her instead of Theo. It could have been Jack.

"Frank's awake too. I'm going to call the detective, see if she can meet me at the hospital, so we can both talk to him. Maybe he saw someone at the funeral home before he passed out?"

"I'll come with you."

"No, you stay and rest."

"You sure?"

"Absolutely. I'll let you know what they say."

"Thanks, Jack."

"For?"

For being here. For loving her. For sleuthing. For being a safe space to land. "For everything."

He leaned forward slowly, bracing on his good arm. When his lips were inches from hers, he moved slightly and kissed her cheek instead. His lips were warm and familiar, and everything in her body sparked to life. "You're welcome. Get some rest."

He left before she could course correct, before she could pull him into her and devour his lips with hers. That would complicate things, wouldn't it? When he was gone, she closed her eyes and attempted to nap, but she was too stunned by the news of Theo's death. That, coupled with the girls' voices from downstairs, ensured she wasn't going to be able to sleep. Plus, she couldn't just sit here. Grabbing her phone, she shot off a quick text to River, asking if he was around. He responded almost immediately.

I tried to visit at the hospital, but you weren't awake yet. How are you feeling?

I'm fine, she replied. Isabelle needed to talk to him, to get to the bottom of what he and Theo were discussing today, but she wanted to get him in his own territory, where he felt most comfortable. Though she wasn't in any state to trek through the woods, she'd do it anyway. Can I come see you?

He shot back a quick yes. She asked for his address, then mapped it. Only about a quarter mile from Harper. She told him she'd be there in half an hour. Dragging herself from bed, Isabelle took a shower and changed into fresh clothes, then tiptoed downstairs. The girls were still playing, and Harper was busy making a from-scratch tomato sauce. The smell of onions, garlic, and basil made her stomach growl.

"Hey, you okay? Do you need something?" Harper cut through a bunch of Roma tomatoes and wiped her hands on her jean shorts.

Isabelle didn't want to lie to Harper, but she didn't want her worried either. "I'm going to get a little fresh air."

"You sure? The doc said you needed rest."

"I'm sure. Just a short walk. Clear my head."

"Okay, don't be gone too long. Dinner will be ready in an hour or so."

"I won't." She crossed into the next room, kissed Maisy, and headed out, pulling up the directions to River's.

The woods were a knot of thick pines, cedars, and firs. As she walked, the sun disappeared beneath the cover of trees. The cool breeze and smell of dirt calmed her. Isabelle sought out a walking path that fanned toward a thin, winding trail. She remembered walking to River's house as a kid, first to play, then to make out.

He lived in a different house now, his own house, but she often wondered if it was strange to come back to the place you grew up, the place you once tried to leave. He'd been destined for a bigger life. Was he disappointed that he now lived a simpler one? Or was he grateful? These were the types of answers she sometimes sought out in her stories, though she reminded herself River wasn't a subject. He was a lead.

Her head pounded, and her throat burned. Even beneath the leaves, the late-afternoon sunlight made her wince. Clearly, she wasn't thinking, too blinded by the incessant need to find answers to listen to her body. It was what always drove her work. A search for secrets. The desire to uncover what was buried. The need to *know*, even if she might never uncover the truth.

Isabelle forced one foot in front of the other and then took a moment to rest. She braced a hand against a pine, the bark firm beneath her palm. The needles tickled her skin, and she closed her eyes and inhaled. It was a familiar scent, as familiar as her favorite home-cooked meal.

After a moment, she pushed off again at a slower pace and finally stepped through a clearing to River's house. It was a modern prefab home that looked Scandinavian, with floor-to-ceiling glass windows and a black metal exterior. Did he build this himself? It was gorgeous, more modern than she would have imagined, but it was clear he'd put a lot of effort into it.

River stepped onto the wraparound front porch, as if sensing her on his property, his dark eyes concerned as he swept them over her. "Jesus, Belle." He jogged down the steps toward her and gently cradled her arms in both of his hands. "You look terrible."

"Thanks." She smiled weakly and let herself be guided up the steps.

Inside, the icy slap of the air conditioner made her shiver. River walked her into the living room, which was off to the right. Everything smelled like pine. Funky art peppered the walls, surrounding mismatched furniture, a guitar collection, and various plants. It was eclectic and weird and so completely River that she stopped in her tracks. "This is beautiful, Riv." Riv. The nickname slipped out before she could take it back, but he beamed.

"Thanks. It was definitely a labor of love." He gestured to the brown leather sofa. She sank down into the cushions. "Coffee? Wine? Tea?"

"Tea would be great, thanks."

"Coming right up." The kitchen was directly off the living room. She watched him move to the kettle, flip on the burner, and pull down two teacups. His muscles flexed beneath his gray T-shirt, his jeans slung low on his hips. Something about him had always magnetized her, made everything and everyone else simply disappear. For a second, she felt a pang of guilt about the moment she'd just shared with Jack, about how vulnerable and open he'd been with her. About how she'd imagined him kissing her. And now, in River's presence, it felt like all of that was wiped clean. Perhaps it was because River was forbidden. Their story was cut short, shoved into that dangerous category of what-if. Maybe this was a terrible idea. If she couldn't stay objective, then she'd never get to the truth.

"Here you go." He placed a tray with a teapot, two cups and saucers, and a few snacks on the coffee table between them.

"River Foust, are we having a tea party? Who even are you?"

He smiled, his cheeks reddening, but said nothing.

She took her tea and sipped. It was a black tea, and he'd put a dash of cream and cardamom in it. "This is delicious, thank you."

"You're welcome." He sipped from his own mug, propping a boot over his knee, and the image made her smile. River Foust, whose hands could once make her come apart almost instantly, was sitting across from her, cradling a teacup.

Isabelle lowered her tea and sat forward. "Did you hear about Theo?"

He cocked his head. "About the explosion? Yeah. I heard he's in bad shape."

She hesitated but then decided to tell him. "He didn't make it."

River's eyes went dark. "That's awful."

"It is." She let the silence expand a moment before continuing. "I have a question for you."

"Shoot." He set his own cup back in the saucer, popped a few grapes and a piece of cheese into his mouth.

"Earlier today, before the explosion."

He winced.

"I saw you and Theo arguing. Can you tell me what that was about?"

She could have beaten around the bush, tried to warm him up to conversation, but she wanted to shoot straight with him in hopes that he'd shoot straight with her too.

She could sense he was calculating how much to say. "That's a little complicated," he said.

"How so?" she asked.

He scratched his buzzed head and sighed. "Because he was worried."

"About?" Isabelle wondered if it had anything to do with the video footage, since Theo was the one who'd suggested she check for it. Had he known about the cameras?

"That reporter had been sniffing around, bringing up the past."

"Why would that worry him?"

"Because Theo was in the woods that night," River said. "The night the kids died."

Then

Harper

"He's just trying to scare us," Harper said, stuffing the last bit of s'more in her mouth. "No one's out there."

But even as Harper said it, she wasn't so sure. Could it be Marcus's ghost, somehow watching them? Haunting them? She hadn't thought about Marcus in a while. There was nothing good to remember. Harper didn't miss him at all.

She registered the tortured look on Ben's face. Harper knew Ben wanted to be the kind of boy who could also march blindly into the woods, fearless and ready to protect his family. The truth was, he wasn't brave like Jude. Everyone could sense it. He seemed afraid to be himself. Not all men had to be big and brave. There were other, quieter ways to make an impact. That was what her real mother had taught her, anyway.

They were silent for a few moments, waiting for Jude to return. Harper glanced over at Celia, who was rubbing her arm. "Are you okay?" She hated how rough Sheriff Mullins had been with her, shaking her like that.

Celia dropped her hand but nodded. "I'm okay. He just scared me."

"Mullins is a dick," Isabelle said. "Always has been. Always will be."

"Do you think he'll tell Gail?" Ben asked.

"I hope not," Harper said. She couldn't imagine what punishment Gail might drum up for them if he did.

"Of course he will," Isabelle said. "Then we can kiss nights like this goodbye."

Ben groaned, and Harper sighed. Sometimes she wanted things to go back to how they were before Celia, Ben, and Jude arrived. Before Marcus. When it was just her, Isabelle, and Gail. Though she missed her real mother fiercely, she, Gail, and Isabelle had found their own rhythm. And then Marcus moved in. And now the others.

Some nights, she fantasized about a different life. Two parents. Dinner on the table by five. A real school in a real town. Friends. Sports. A normal life. But Harper understood that she wasn't normal, that her time on this earth wasn't about doing things like everyone else. But it didn't mean she couldn't still wish for it sometimes . . . that she couldn't wish for something else.

Ben dropped his head, scrubbed his hands back and forth over the buzz cut, and sighed.

"What's wrong, Ben?" Celia's eyes were glued to him when he lifted his head.

Harper knew he didn't feel good. They'd all been feeling so off lately. Well, everyone except Isabelle.

"Everything," he finally said.

"What do you mean by 'everything'?"

He found the second open bottle of wine and took the last swig, then started ticking things off on his fingers. "I don't know what I want to do with my life. I've never kissed a girl. I've never been on a family vacation. I've never been anywhere other than Washington, and sometimes I feel so claustrophobic I could die. It's like I'm trapped but afraid to leave or something?" The words emptied out of him in a rush, and they were all stunned into silence. Ben had never been this open with any of them before.

"Oh, Ben." Isabelle leaned over and pulled him into a hug. "I think we all feel like that sometimes."

He wiped a few tears away, clearly embarrassed. "Really?"

Harper and Celia nodded. Ben opened his mouth to respond when a figure ran up, arms raised.

The girls screamed and scrambled to stand. Ben jumped up, fists raised, as they all glimpsed a teak mask. Jude's mask.

Jude ripped it off, laughing. He gripped his belly, and Ben rolled his eyes.

"You suck," Isabelle said, crossing her arms. She jerked her chin toward the woods. "So who was it?"

"No one. I guess my eyes were playing tricks on me."

Harper didn't buy it. He'd looked genuinely scared. She pushed the Ouija board away. No more of that. "What about if we do something fun?" she suggested.

"We already tried that, remember?" Jude said, palming another marshmallow from the bag. They all drifted from the Parlour back around the fire.

"Let's play hide-and-seek," she said.

Celia balked. "At night? In the woods?"

"What? Are you scared?" Harper lifted her fingers and wiggled them.

"Duh," Celia said.

"We haven't played in forever," Isabelle said, sitting up straighter. "It'll be fun."

"Lame," Jude said, but he had a smile on his face.

"It's not lame." Harper went over and gripped his shoulders, shaking him. "This might be the last time we ever play a fun game together. You're going to be too cool for us next year. Come on. Please? The tree house will be home base."

"What does the winner get?"

"No dish duty for a month?" Isabelle suggested.

"Deal!" Ben and Jude said at the same time. They all stood up. "Who's it?"

"I'll count first," Jude said. "You young'uns scatter. I'll count to one hundred."

"Wait, we can go anywhere?" Celia said. "Shouldn't there be like boundaries or something?"

"What's the fun in that?" Jude asked. "Go. I'm counting."

Harper grabbed Isabelle's hand, and they bolted through the trees. Isabelle glanced back to find Celia, still uncertain, standing alone, but they both knew she couldn't run as fast to keep up. Suddenly, Harper felt light and happy, like when they were kids. Just like before, when it was only the two of them. They ran until they were both winded and then stopped, slumping against the trunk of a tree.

"How far should we go, do you think?" Isabelle asked.

Harper still held on to Isabelle's wrist. "I don't know. Maybe not too far so we can make it back to base?"

Isabelle yawned. "Sounds good to me." She attempted to tug her arm free, but Harper held on. "Harp, let go." She jerked her hand free, examining yet another set of nail marks on her skin.

"Sorry." It was a bad habit, left over from when they were kids. She glanced around and pointed to a grove of trees about fifteen yards out. "Let's hide there. And then we'll make a run for it once we hear him call out?"

Isabelle nodded. Harper gripped her wrist yet again and led the way.

18

Isabelle was sure she'd heard River wrong. "You mean when we egged his house?"

He shook his head. "No. After."

"Why would he tell you that?"

River shrugged. "I don't know, but he did. Wasn't sure who he could trust, I guess."

"And he can trust you?" It was a rhetorical question, really. Something was still nagging her about the other night in the woods with River . . . something she was struggling to remember. Isabelle thought back to that night when they were playing with the Ouija board. Jude *had* seen someone in the woods. Was it Theo? He was livid after they'd egged his house. Could he have followed them back to the tree house, watched them, biding his time?

"Did you ever do work up at the cabin?" Isabelle scooped up her tea and took another sip, thinking about the footage she'd seen.

He hesitated. "Gail asked me to do work on the cabin from time to time. She was a proud woman, as you know. Capable. But over the last few years, she really stopped taking care of the property. So, I would drop supplies, clear out branches, tend to the gutters, things like that. She always paid me, and then one day, she stopped. But she kept asking me to do work. Finally, I told her I couldn't do things for free anymore. She wasn't happy about it." He shrugged.

"When's the last time you were up there?"

He scratched his head as he thought. “I don’t know. A week or two before she died? She seemed a little off, like she didn’t feel well.”

Isabelle frowned. He was telling the truth. “Why didn’t you tell me any of this when we had dinner?”

“I don’t know. You didn’t ask me, I guess.”

“Well, now I am. Anything else you’re not telling me?”

Silence bloomed between them, and this time it wasn’t friendly. His eyes darkened. “Like what?”

“Like the fact that you’re on security footage at my mother’s property before she died. Or that I saw you arguing with the cop who handled the original case with the kids, and now he’s dead. And you were in the woods that night too, River. Like Theo.” As she said it, alarm bells pinged in her head.

“I know you’re not insinuating I had anything to do with that fire.”

They sat in awkward silence for another moment, as Isabelle tried to process what she knew. “Did you have anything to do with what happened at the funeral home today?”

“Are you fucking kidding me, Belle?” His eyes went steely, his shoulders stiff. His teacup clattered back into its saucer, sloshing tea onto his thumb. “I would never hurt Frank or Rita. Never.” He sliced a hand through the air for emphasis. “Or anyone, for that matter. Especially you. You should know me better than that.”

“The truth is I don’t know you at all,” she said. “Not really. I haven’t seen you for twenty years.”

“I think we’re done here.” He stood, and Isabelle was thrown by the sudden shift in his demeanor, by how quick he was to dismiss her. Was he guilty or just insulted? She wasn’t sure.

She turned at the door. “Anything else I should know? Anything I might be surprised to find out?”

He smirked. “You’re the journalist, right? Why don’t you figure it out.” With that, he slammed the door in her face, leaving her more unsettled than when she’d arrived. She searched for reception and shot Jack a quick text.

Anything on your end?

She waited for the text to go through and glanced around River's property. Before heading back into the woods, she decided to do a quick lap, hoping he wasn't watching her through the windows. Deep down, she didn't really think River was a threat, but at the same time, he hadn't said or done anything to prove his innocence either. He'd gotten defensive quickly, which was usually a sign of something. In the back, she saw a barrel sauna, an ice bath, and a garden, and then a few yards out, a shed.

Glancing over her shoulder, Isabelle scurried toward the shed and saw there was a padlock on it. The planks of wood were large enough that she could squint between the gaps. She pressed her face to the door and tried to get her eyes to focus.

"Hey!"

She jumped back and turned as River stalked toward her. "What are you doing?"

"I'm . . ." What was she doing? Searching for clues?

He stopped mere feet from her, and the hair on Isabelle's arms pricked up. They were completely alone out here, nothing but trees. She swallowed, her throat dry again.

"I'm only going to say this once, Belle," he said, his voice low. "I had nothing to do with what happened today or back then. It's time to get back to your side of the woods." He stabbed a hand toward the trees. She didn't want to give him the satisfaction of scurrying off, but everything in her told her to run.

Slowly, she turned and headed back to the trail. She could feel his eyes on her the entire way.

19

Once Isabelle was a few hundred yards away from River's house, she slumped against a tree and took a few shaky breaths.

Something was nagging her about River: the way he'd behaved just now, how eager he'd been for her to leave. She closed her eyes, reconstructed what she'd seen of his home, the items in it. Were there clues in plain sight? And what was in the shed that he was so squirrely about? Her phone dinged, and she read Jack's text.

> Just met with Detective Murdoch and Frank. She's willing to play ball. Some red tape to get through, but we might be able to exhume the bodies. Be home soon.

Home.

This place wasn't home. Not for them. And not for her, not for a very long time. Isabelle slid the rest of the way down the trunk and closed her eyes. Her head throbbed. Up until now, the exhumation had seemed like a far-fetched idea. Her idea, but crazy, nonetheless. And now she might actually learn if her theory was right. And if it was? Maybe she'd be one step closer to finding out who poisoned the kids back then. Who had access to thallium. Who wanted to make them suffer before they ultimately died.

That night they played hide-and-seek looped in her head. Harper had blamed herself for years, insisted if she hadn't suggested they play in the first place, then the kids wouldn't have wandered off so far.

But really, it was Isabelle who felt guiltiest of all. If she hadn't sleepwalked that night, Harper wouldn't have taken her back to the cabin, and maybe they could have helped the kids or ended the game earlier. There were so many factors that went into Celia, Jude, and Ben finding their way into that bunker and never making it out again.

Isabelle would do anything to know the truth about that night, of what really happened. Though testing the kids for thallium wouldn't tell her the truth, it would validate that someone *was* trying to hurt them. She could prove that, at the very least.

Isabelle thought about her mother's note that Eliza had shared. Isabelle was a stubborn woman, had always been stubborn, but what if she'd been wrong about her mother? What if she wasn't the monster Isabelle had always assumed Gail to be?

Isabelle pulled herself up as another thought entered her mind: *But what if she was?*

Back at the house, Harper practically ran out the side door. "Izz, I was worried sick. I thought you might have passed out in the woods or something." She glanced behind her into the copse of trees. "Did you get lost? Where did you go?"

"To River's," Isabelle said, as she bypassed Harper and collapsed inside on the couch.

"River's? Why?"

Isabelle waved a hand in the air. "It's complicated. Can I have some water?"

"Sure." Harper poured her some water and gave it to her, chewing on her bottom lip. "I feel like there are things you're not telling me."

Isabelle swallowed and nodded. "There are."

"Izz, you can trust me."

"I know I can. That's not it. I just . . . I need more information first. I don't want to bring anything to you until I have more facts."

Harper waited for her to say more. When she didn't, she slapped her thighs. "Got it. You'll tell me what I need to know when I need to know it." There was an edge to her voice, and Isabelle couldn't blame her. "You missed dinner. Let me fix you a plate."

"I'm not hungry." And she wasn't. Her exchange with River had killed her appetite.

"Then let's get you back into bed."

"Thanks, Mom."

Harper rolled her eyes and gripped Isabelle's arm as she helped her up the steps. When she got her settled into her room and shut the door, Isabelle glanced at her bicep. There were small indentations from Harper's nails. She'd forgotten about how she used to do that.

When they were younger, Harper would often grip her hand, wrist, or forearm, and dig her fingernails into her flesh. It used to drive Isabelle nuts, one of those quirks that had always been between them. She ran her fingers over the small marks now. Harper used to tell her she did it so that Isabelle would know she was there. Isabelle could get so lost in her head sometimes, and then, when she began sleepwalking, Harper would do it to try to gently shake her awake. It rarely worked, but the habit stuck.

What a terrible friend and sister she'd been. Isabelle had left Harper to deal with her mother, with the tragedy of this place, the heaviness of it. Deep down, she wouldn't be surprised if Harper hated her. She would.

A few minutes later, Jack entered the bedroom, looking a hell of a lot better than her. He slid into bed beside her, sighing.

"You don't have to tell me. I already know," Jack said, adjusting his arm in his sling.

"Tell you what?"

"That I'm amazing."

She rolled her eyes. "Murdoch give you any idea how long all this will take?"

"Not sure. Being such a small town, it could be a few days. Could be longer. But we're getting closer, Izz. I can feel it."

"I hope so." Her eyes drifted closed. She was suddenly wiped out.

"Hey, hey. Let me see your pupils. You're not feeling off balance or anything, right?"

The doctor had told her she could sleep, as long as she wasn't exhibiting any concerning symptoms. Isabelle sighed. "I'm fine."

"Here." Jack opened his good arm, and she snuggled into that spot on his chest she loved. "I'll tell you the details of all the horrible women I've been dating to keep you awake."

"Nice try. You hate dating." Even as she said it, her stomach flipped at the thought of Jack seeing anyone.

"You know me too well." He kissed the top of her head. "What do you want to talk about?"

Right then, Maisy burst through the door and hopped onto the bed. She climbed up and settled between them.

"Want to watch a movie, Bug?" Isabelle asked.

"Yeah! Ivy's going to her dad's tonight."

Isabelle glanced at Jack. So the dad was in the picture? Interesting. Harper hadn't mentioned that. She filed that away to ask her later.

Maisy grinned, looking between them. "Can I pick?"

Isabelle pointed out where the remote was, and she snuggled in closer to Jack as Maisy struggled to work the buttons. Finally, she pulled up Netflix. It had been so long since it had been the three of them together like this.

She wanted to hold on to the moment as long as she could.

From the bedside table, her phone dinged. Maisy stabbed the volume up, and Isabelle promised to silence it. She rolled off Jack and checked the message. It was from an unknown number.

I know it was you was all it said.

Isabelle shook her head, responded wrong number, and deleted the text.

A minute later, another text came through.

I know you killed those kids, and soon the world will too.

Isabelle froze. She sat up too fast, and her head pounded wickedly.

"What is it?" Jack asked.

Maisy was already lost in the first few minutes of a new Disney movie that had just been released.

"Nothing. Wrong number." She deleted the text, blocked the number, and settled back against Jack's chest. She was suddenly very wide awake.

The words were seared into her head.

I know you killed those kids, and soon the world will too.

20

The next few days brought more answers.

The funeral home explosion was deemed an accident, something Jack and Isabelle didn't buy. After reviewing the video surveillance footage from the cabin, Murdoch had pressured the public health officials harder, and the DA signed off on exhuming the bodies. Isabelle didn't know how she'd gotten it done so fast, but she was grateful, nervous, and dreading the moment of truth.

"You ready for today?" Jack poured her a cup of coffee from Harper's fancy Chemex. She still hadn't told him about the cryptic text message. Luckily, she hadn't received another one.

"No." She took a sip and leaned back against the island. "It's the one thing I felt I did right back then," she explained now. "Not seeing their bodies. Harper didn't either. We both decided we wanted to remember them like they were that night. Even if they were sick, they were still alive when I fell asleep in the woods." And then, when she'd woken up the next morning in her own bed, they were dead. Regardless, today, she would face the remains of her siblings and admit, after all these years, that they were really and truly gone.

"Izz . . ." Jack gave her a look. "Maybe you should tell Harper. This might be an opportunity for her to get some closure too."

She ignored him, removed a few bobby pins from her hair, and resecured her bun. "Is Murdoch meeting us there?"

He sighed as she ignored his suggestion. "Yep. So are the medical examiner, Frank, and the DA. Meeting us there at eight."

She nodded. She was looking forward to seeing Frank and was relieved he was okay. If they hadn't arrived when they did, he would have died in that explosion. They gave a goodbye kiss to Maisy, who was happy as a clam now that Ivy was back home, hugged Harper, and told her they had some things to do at the cabin.

They set out together on the short walk. Isabelle's ribs still hurt, but her head was better. No real concussion symptoms, thankfully. Jack's arm was already out of his sling, though he was still babying his shoulder a bit.

They walked in silence until they butted up against the edge of the property. Red tape had cordoned off the area around the graves. There were already workers with shovels standing nearby. Detective Murdoch and two men stood chatting beside them.

"Here we go," she said.

"Detective Murdoch." Jack announced himself, and she introduced them both to the medical examiner, Ishmael Mathews, a well-put-together man in his forties, and the DA, Harris Boyd. Frank was standing off to the side. The detective glanced toward Isabelle, her face softening.

"I know this is hard. Just let us know what you need today, okay?"

Isabelle had shared everything she knew with the detective by now, and Murdoch seemed to think this case had legs. The autopsy report, coupled with the video footage, had sealed the deal. They'd rewatched it together, and Murdoch had asked her over and over again if she recognized the man in the ball cap, but she didn't. It made Isabelle feel good that she and Jack weren't completely on their own.

They would get to the bottom of it, one way or another. After everything was in place, the men were signaled to start, and the workers began shoveling, with strict orders to dig slowly and shallowly since her mother had decided on natural burials.

Jack appeared beside her. "You helped dig the graves, right?"

Isabelle shivered. *Bones. Dirt. Shovels.* "I did. Harper too." She remembered standing there, shovel in hand, digging and crying, in utter disbelief about what was happening. At the time, it had felt like some sort of punishment.

"That must have been torturous."

"It was." They only dug for a short time before Gail took over. Now part of her wondered if she should have let Harper come today, if she should have told her the truth. Harper was smart and could easily sense *something* was happening, but she hadn't pushed too hard to ask what. Isabelle's stomach clenched, and she pressed a palm gently to it. Jack noticed.

"You okay?"

"Fine."

The first grave was Celia's. They were going one at a time.

After several silent minutes, save for the sound of dirt thudding rhythmically against the ground, one of the workers barked out, "Body!" Ishmael, Harris, Frank, and Detective Murdoch descended around them like vultures. In moments, just as she'd imagined, a tarp-wrapped bundle was hoisted from its resting spot and placed gently on the earth.

Isabelle's world tilted. How horrible, to disturb someone from their grave. She knew Celia wasn't in there; that it was only her body and nothing more. If souls really existed, then she was somewhere else. But it felt sacrilegious to unwrap that cloth, to extract teeth or bone tissue from her sister's corpse in order to run labs on them. To prove a theory. *Her* theory.

Isabelle held her breath and took a few shaky steps closer. The medical examiner carefully peeled back the tarp with his black rubber gloves until pieces of Celia were revealed. Isabelle shut her eyes but then forced them open. Frank stooped across from the medical examiner, sighing as Celia came into full view.

Her sister wasn't intact. The head lolled on its own, detached from the rest of her. From this vantage point, Isabelle could only see her clavicle, half of an arm, one hand, two femur bones. It was like she'd been dismantled. Was this all that had been recovered from that night? Good Lord. Isabelle's stomach bucked, and she squeezed her eyes shut again and counted to ten.

Jack placed a hand on her back and rubbed small, soothing circles until she came back to her body. Once again, she forced her eyes open and took measured breaths. The medical examiner was using tweezers to pluck something from the skull. She turned away, marched a few steps toward the trees, and began to shake.

Jack followed. "Just breathe," he said. "Breathe."

No one knew what this was like. No one except Harper. To see the result of either a murder or an accident and to wonder for the millionth time why she and Harper had survived when they didn't.

The men started on Ben's grave next. This one took longer, his body deeper. His tarp was larger, and again, there were simply fragments of him: skull, rib cage, parts of arms and legs. Either he wasn't fully recovered, either, or the fire, along with time, had disintegrated his limbs. Maybe the worms had gotten to him. A chill worked its way through her body as she stared down at her sweet brother. Ben had been so nervous about his life, about where he would go and who he would become in the real world. She remembered the night he died, when he'd made that big confession. He'd died without ever kissing a girl or going on vacation.

Tears stung her eyes. She swiped them away angrily, then folded her arms against her chest. Last was Jude. You weren't supposed to have favorites, but Jude had always been her favorite person, period. He was loving, kind, and smart, and she'd imagined their adult lives a million times. They'd be close. She would always be able to rely on him. She watched again as the men began to dig shallow and slow, the clop of dirt smacking the earth. Thud, thud, thud.

After about twenty minutes, they still hadn't pulled him out. Perhaps her mother buried him deeper because he was the largest. The oldest. She couldn't watch. Pacing back and forth between the trees, she tried to remember the actual day of the burials. She'd kept herself busy in her room. Isabelle and Harper hadn't wanted anything to do with the bodies. They'd dug the graves. That felt like enough. Isabelle didn't want to see the bodies placed inside. She'd only come out once they were already lowered into the earth.

"Isabelle." Jack's voice brought her back to the present. So they'd found him. She would face Jude, get some closure, and move on with her life. Taking one more deep breath, she stalked over but didn't see the tarp anywhere.

"Where is he?" she asked.

Detective Murdoch was crouching by the grave. She stood and turned to her. "Well." She tented her gloved hands on her hips and took a step toward them.

"What?" Isabelle asked, her heart hammering so hard against her ribs, she could hear it whooshing in her ears.

"There's no body," the detective said now. Her eyes were bright, and Jack let out a sharp cry of disbelief.

"What do you mean there's no body? Of course there's a body." Isabelle walked forward and stared down into the empty pit of the grave. They'd dug about six full feet. Could they have missed him? Was he just fragments, maybe? Bone shards? She spun in a circle, then hopped down into the grave and began to sift through the dirt herself. She knew she needed gloves and could be contaminating the soil, but she didn't care. Her brother was *in* there. He died. She was 100 percent positive.

A collective hush fell over the group as she maniacally sorted through the dirt, gripping handfuls like sand and letting them sift through her fingers. But there was nothing there other than bugs and rocks. "I don't understand," she said, standing back up slowly, dirt staining her clothes. Was this a joke? Where was Jude? A small glimmer of hope, as quick as a flash of lightning, streaked through her heart.

Could Jude be alive?

Murdoch stabbed a number into her cell phone and began talking in hushed tones. Jack lowered in a hand to help her climb out of the grave. She swiped her muddy palms against her jeans. "I don't understand what's happening," she said. "Where is my brother? Where's Jude?"

"I don't know," Jack said. "Wherever he is, he's not in that grave."

Part II: The Bones

Then

Jude

Once Jude reached one hundred, he cupped his hands around his mouth and shouted, "Ready or not, here I come!"

When was the last time he'd played this game? Definitely before he moved to Cedarloch. A memory, quick and brutal, materialized. Him and his biological sister running around their yard, playing hide-and-seek. Him catching her as she squealed. Later, them being yelled at and spanked when their dad got drunk.

With his hands on his hips, he listened for any giggles or rustling of leaves. Now that he thought about it, it was a pretty stupid idea, having zero parameters around how far they could go, but he was certain they couldn't have gotten too far. He also knew catching Celia first was probably his best bet. She was the slowest, and if he caught her, she could come back to the tree house and rest.

Jude had been trying to figure out what was happening with all of them. Symptoms seemed to flare with food. He'd been keeping a journal and trying to eat out of the house when he could. When he did, he felt better. He thought maybe the cabin had mold, but Isabelle and Gail seemed fine.

He set off north, unsure of how he was going to find anyone. He knew Harper and Isabelle would be together, and he hoped Ben hadn't ditched Celia. She didn't like to be out in the woods after dark. In fact, this whole night seemed like a nightmare for her—truth or dare, getting caught by Theo, the Ouija board—and now this.

Jude fished out his Zippo lighter and lit it, studying the ground. He was a good hunter, prided himself on it, in fact. He could see sets of shoe prints heading slightly east. Jude followed the tracks until they stopped. Sighing, he realized this could take a while.

He stalked every which way for close to half an hour, ready to give up. Maybe they were already back at base. Up ahead, there was a rustling of leaves and then a sharp cry. Jude heard voices. He tiptoed and rushed behind a tree, waiting. Then he sprang forward, hoping to find someone to tag. As he stepped into a clearing, he could definitely make out voices. But it was pitch black back here, no light pollution of any kind.

"Hello?" He waited, realizing he shouldn't give himself away, but he was a fast runner and could easily tag someone before they made it back to base.

"Jude!" Celia's voice sounded relieved. "Jude! Down here!"

Down here? She sounded frantic. Jude followed her voice but came to an open clearing. He didn't see anyone.

"Where are you?"

"We're in here!"

Jude approached what looked like some sort of underground bunker or fallout shelter. He noticed a wooden cover, scattered with leaves, had been slid from the top. He peered down into the round hole, into complete darkness. Was Ben down there too?

"Jude! We're stuck down here, man!" Ben's voice echoed its way up to the top.

Jude covered his nose with his arm. "Ugh, what reeks? Are you guys okay?"

"There was a ladder, but it broke," Celia said. Her voice was thick with tears. "We're stuck, Jude. I feel like I can't breathe. I . . ." Her voice drifted as Ben tried to calm her.

"Can you throw down your lighter? We can't see anything. Maybe there's another way up."

"Why did you guys go down there in the first place?"

"Dude, when there's a secret underground lair on your property, you check it out," Ben said. He sounded more confident than he probably felt.

Jude sighed. The last thing he wanted to do was to go down into some creepy dungeon, but he had to get them out. Maybe once they saw how deep it was, Ben could lift Celia onto his shoulders, and he could pull her up. Then they could figure out how to get Ben out. "You ready? I'm going to toss down the Zippo." He extracted it from his pocket. It had belonged to his real father, a man who'd been a mean drunk, but it was the only thing he had to remember him by. He tossed it down and heard it chink against the ground.

"Sorry, man. It's dark in here." Ben tried to light it a few times, and finally a flame grew, a small plume of light around them.

Jude frowned. He couldn't see much, but they were pretty far down. He'd need to rig something to lower in so he could drag them back up. Maybe a sheet, or a rope. He hadn't tracked how far he was from the cabin. "Put out the flame, Ben. You don't want it to run out. Look." He contemplated what to say so he wouldn't scare Celia. "I'm going to try to find the girls to see if they can help get you guys out. We need something to bring you up."

"There's some old rope where we used to have the tire swing," Ben said. "It's all coiled up. I think it's under some leaves or something." Three years ago, when they'd moved into Gail's, they'd piled on the tire swing and broken it. None of them had fixed it since.

"All right. Can you guys hang tight?"

"Yep," Ben called up. Celia was still crying.

"Hey, CeCe, listen to me, okay? I'm going to get you out of there, and then we can have more s'mores and all pile up in a big pallet to go to sleep. How does that sound?"

She sniffled, but finally he heard a small "Okay."

"Okay. I'll be back as fast as I can. Meanwhile, see if there's another ladder or something you missed."

"Copy," Ben said, as if they were on a mission.

Jude was suddenly wide awake. Not only did he need to find his way back to the cabin, but he also needed to find the girls, grab the rope, and remember exactly where this bunker was. Why hadn't they ever found it before? And why did Ben have to stumble upon it tonight of all nights?

He stalked through the woods, determined. A thrill raced through him at being able to save his siblings. He could already see himself throwing the rope down and pulling them up, one by one. Clapping Ben on the back and hugging Celia. It would be a crazy story they'd get to tell.

The night he got to be the hero.

21

Isabelle couldn't breathe.

"How could this happen?" she asked again to the group. "Jude was declared dead. There was a body. There were three bodies."

"Did you see them?" Detective Murdoch asked now.

Isabelle hesitated. Technically, she hadn't seen them. And Frank hadn't worked on her siblings back then. Had Theo seen the bodies? She assumed he had. That did nothing to help them now. "No, I didn't."

"We'll get to the bottom of it," the detective said.

But how? Isabelle felt like she was going to be sick. Bile climbed her throat, but she choked it back down. The only people who could answer any questions about the three bodies were the original medical examiner, her mother, and Theo. Had they hidden something back then?

Once again, Isabelle recounted in her head what happened that night. It was all so clear until she fell asleep waiting for Jude to find them during hide-and-seek.

"Got something!"

Everyone's head turned on a swivel, and they rushed toward Jude's open, empty grave. The medical examiner brought up a strip of fabric. A small fragment of a red T-shirt. She could see the letters *D* and *E*, faded. She gasped. "That's part of Jude's Deftones T-shirt. He was wearing it that night." Could fabric survive a fire? She swallowed. Might there be other pieces of him in there, just more decomposed than Ben and Celia?

"Keep digging," the DA barked. He swiped a hand over his face, possibly realizing that there was more to uncover here than he originally thought.

Isabelle tried to think rationally. Maybe Jude really was there but much deeper than the others. She paced back and forth, Jack beside her. Isabelle couldn't figure out how she felt. Did she want them to find his bones, or didn't she? Because if he wasn't in there, that meant he was somewhere else. Celia's, Ben's, and Jude's deaths had plagued her for so long, she wasn't sure she could deal with a possible disappearance on top of everything else.

"How are you doing?" Jack gripped her shoulder and gave a gentle squeeze.

"I'm in shock. I just . . ." She ripped a hand through her hair, snagging her bun. "I don't know how Jude could have been declared dead if he's not in there."

Jack nodded. "We don't know that yet. Let's not jump to conclusions."

"Right." Isabelle shuffled toward the grave again, where the medical examiner had pulled up more torn fabric. "Still no bones?"

Ishmael shook his head and then stopped as his fingers rammed into something hard. He was standing inside the grave. Crouching forward, he barked to the others, and Isabelle's stomach lurched once again. He brushed away the dirt and lifted a hunk of something into the air. Which body part would it belong to?

"What in the world?" His voice faded as Isabelle saw what he was holding.

It was one of Jude's carved masks. He had it the night of the fire. The mouth was twisted in agony, caught in a perpetual scream. It was how she felt now, trapped in a nightmare with no way out.

Why were all these belongings in here but no skeleton? No traces of her brother? Did her mother do this? Her phone buzzed. Unknown number. Again, her heart pounded in her chest.

You're looking in all the wrong places.

As if in slow motion, everything around Isabelle faded. The workers. The noise. The birds. She rotated, her eyes tracking the trees. They were being watched, she was sure of it. She remembered Maisy seeing someone through the trees. Who was it? Who was watching her?

"Izz?"

Isabelle pushed past Jack and slowly searched left and right. Who had eyes on her? She remembered the cameras. Could someone have video out here too? She began walking from tree to tree, hunting. When she couldn't find any cameras, she finally typed out a response.

Where should I be looking then?

She held her breath as she waited for a response.

The bunker was all it said.

What could be left in the bunker after all these years?

"Ma'am, this is private property," Detective Murdoch barked.

Isabelle shook herself from the cryptic text message as she saw the reporter approach. Annoyed, Isabelle stalked her way over, looped a firm hand around Eliza's elbow, and steered her back toward the cabin.

"Doing some gardening?" Eliza asked lightly.

Once they were out of sight of the diggers, Isabelle let her go and thrust her phone in her face. "Is this you?"

Eliza squinted at the phone. "As you've seen, handwritten notes are really more my thing. I don't even have your number because you haven't texted me."

"You really want me to believe you can't get my cell phone number?"

"I didn't say I *couldn't*. I said I didn't have it." She jerked her head toward the diggers. "What's that all about?"

"A private matter."

"I see that." Eliza gauged what to say. "Look, Isabelle, I know that to you, I'm following a story. But to me, it's more than that. I want to help."

"Help with what?" Isabelle gestured around her. "Bringing even more confusion and awareness to my family's darkest secrets?"

"It's not just your family," Eliza said.

Isabelle looked at her, perplexed. "What's that supposed to mean?"

"Jude was my biological brother," she said now. "I'm doing this for him."

22

Isabelle was stunned into silence.

She took a few steps back and shook her head. "How?"

"Not sure how much Jude ever told you, but we grew up in Portland. Drug addict mom, deadbeat dad. Abusive. Alcoholic, the whole nine yards, blah, blah, blah. When it was clear they couldn't care for us, DCFS was called. No relatives wanted to take us, so we were split up. I don't have to tell you what a nightmare some of those homes were." She was quiet for a moment, and Isabelle experienced that same sad pang from when the kids used to share their foster home stories.

"I had no way to find Jude, no way to contact him," she continued. "We were bounced from home to home, and then the next thing I heard was that he died in some horrible fire." She shook her head. "I was devastated, naturally. But I was a kid. I couldn't do much about it."

"And now you can?"

"I'm trying to," she said. "I want the truth to come out, but in order to do that, I need you to work with me."

"By doing what?"

"By trusting me," she said. "I know you have no reason to."

"No, I don't." Isabelle stared at Eliza, clearly confused. She was doing all this to get answers for her dead brother, but did she know that her brother might not even be in his grave? "What does trusting you look like?"

Eliza glanced behind her and then pointed to the woods. "It means you follow me." She took off before Isabelle could stop her.

Isabelle wavered only for a moment, but the journalist in her won out.

She almost called for Jack but instead shot him a quick text to share what was happening. Isabelle's instincts were sharp, always had been. She didn't think Eliza was a physical danger, but she would keep her distance just in case.

Isabelle pushed branches out of the way as they veered off the path. There was no trail back here, but it seemed Eliza knew where she was going.

"Must be hard, watching them dig up the graves like that."

So Eliza did know what they were up to.

"If Jude's your brother, then it must be hard for you too."

Eliza said nothing. Of course, Isabelle had no proof that what Eliza said was true. She could say she was anyone's sibling. Was Isabelle just supposed to believe her? The two walked silently for what felt like an hour, but in reality was only about twenty minutes.

Finally, they came to a clearing, and Eliza spread her arms. "The bunker."

Isabelle thought about the text message she'd received. What were the chances of receiving a clue to go to the bunker and then being led there by someone else? "How do you know where this is?"

"Because I'm good at my job," Eliza said. She crouched down and pushed the new reconstructed top off, groaning with the effort. "You ever been down here?"

"Of course not." Once the kids had been found, Isabelle and Harper had steered clear of this part of the woods. She hadn't been back since.

"Here's the thing about small-town investigations," Eliza said, standing again. "They miss things. They bury things. They don't want to draw too much attention. Small-town cops want everything wrapped up in a neat little bow so they can look like the hero."

"Are you talking about Theo?"

She nodded, removed a flashlight, and flipped it on, even though it was daytime. She crouched again, and her knees popped. She shined the light down into the bunker. "The thing to remember is, when you get things wrapped up so fast, it's usually because you don't want people to look too hard at what you're wrapping up." Eliza motioned Isabelle closer.

Isabelle wavered. She'd never once looked into the bunker. She hadn't wanted to see the aftermath. She didn't want to imagine what her siblings had gone through. But there were no dead bodies down here now. That, she knew for sure. Taking a breath, Isabelle squatted beside her and followed the cone of light toward the bottom. It was small and circular, nothing but soot and ashes, broken tree branches, and a few dead birds. Eliza snaked the light around the perimeter and stopped on the ladder. It had been repaired in order for the investigative team to go up and down so many times like they did.

"Up for an adventure?"

Isabelle blinked at her. "An adventure?" She gestured to the bunker. "It's a tiny space. There's nowhere to go but up."

"Isabelle, please." Eliza pocketed her flashlight and moved over to the first rung of the ladder. "Don't you know by now that things aren't always as they seem?"

Before she could argue, Eliza descended the ladder.

It was up to Isabelle whether or not to join.

Then

Ben

Ben was putting on a brave face, but he was scared.

He'd been running and had tripped over a buried handle. He should have left it, kept directing Celia to a hiding spot, but curiosity had gotten the best of him, and now, here they were.

It smelled like rot down here. When he'd struck the lighter, he'd only seen a few feet around them. The bottom was cramped, full of dried leaves and dead bugs. The floor was nothing but pine needles and dirt. Had someone ever stayed down here? Or maybe it had been an old well. Or shelter from the war? Ben liked thinking of the history of places, of what came before him. And what would come after. He'd research it once he got out. Maybe it was famous.

His fingers itched to light the Zippo again, but Jude had told him to save it, in case the lighter fluid ran out. Celia's cries had finally quieted. He felt so bad for her. This night was not turning out like they'd hoped. With her sore arm from Theo, and now falling the last few feet from the broken ladder, she was pretty banged up.

"Let's talk about what we want to do tomorrow," Ben said. Celia loved making lists and plans. She was always writing, writing, writing in her journal, though he didn't know what she was really writing about. He got so bored sometimes, he'd stare off into space and hours would pass by. But not Celia. She was always in her head, always chronicling things.

Celia sniffed. "Well, I'd love to go into town for the farmers market. Maybe get something to make a nice family dinner." Her voice strengthened as she talked, some of the fear slipping away. He tried to listen, but he was coming up with contingency plans in his head, large, looming what-ifs that made him tremble with fear.

What if Jude couldn't find his way back to the bunker? What if he couldn't find the rope? What if he couldn't get them up? What if they died down here? Even as he thought it, he knew that wouldn't happen. If Jude couldn't get them up by himself, he would go get Gail, and she would get them out. People could call Gail many things, but *incapable* wasn't one of them. He thought about her now, about what Jude had been whispering lately to him in the night.

He thought Gail was poisoning their food, making them all sick. But every time Ben tried to grab onto that theory, it didn't stick. There would be no reason for her to want to make them sick. She didn't even take them to the doctor, so if anything, being sick was a nuisance. Maybe the three of them had weaker immune systems. He reminded himself they were young. Whatever it was, this would pass. He was almost sure of it.

Ben flipped the cap of the Zippo open and closed, the sound satisfying in his ears. Celia stopped talking, and the sound of the metal cap filled the space.

They heard rustling above, and Ben felt relief crack against his ribs like a bat. "Jude! You back, man?"

There was commotion, and then someone's head lowered over the empty opening. He couldn't see, but he knew from the shape of him it wasn't Jude.

"Who is that?" Ben asked.

"Who's down there?"

Celia sighed. "It's River. River, we're stuck down here! Jude went to get help, but maybe you can help us? If there's any way—"

"What do you mean you're stuck?" River asked. He had an almost amused sound to his voice. Ben knew the girls were crazy about River, but there was something about him that he didn't like.

"Why are you even out here at this time of night?" Ben asked, suddenly suspicious. It was late, and this was their property. He shouldn't be anywhere near here. Celia elbowed him in the ribs, which made him wince.

"And who is that down there with our Celia? Ben Archer? You're not doing anything inappropriate with your pseudo-sister, are you?" He snickered.

Ben's entire body flushed. What a disgusting thought. River was a bully, and he wasn't in the mood tonight.

Celia ignored his crass joke. "River, this is serious. There was a ladder, but it broke. Do you have anything at your house that might help bring us up?"

"Well, let me think." They could see him tapping his chin in thought under the moonlight. "What are you going to give me for it?"

Celia seemed shocked. No boys in town flirted with her, least of all River Foust. "Whatever you want, okay? Just stop dicking around and help us!"

Ben was proud of her for speaking up, for putting River in his place.

After a moment, River laughed. "Nah, I think I'll let you two sweat a bit, see if that sweet brother of yours comes to the rescue. And if not? I get to be the hero." Before they knew what was happening, River was sliding the top back on the bunker, causing debris to flutter down. They shielded their faces as acorns and rocks pelted their shoulders.

"What the hell, man?" Ben cried.

Celia began to whimper again, and he draped an arm around her shoulder. When he got out of here, he was going to put River Foust in his place. Now it was completely pitch black. The Zippo was cold in his palm.

"Look, I'm going to light this real quick so we can see if there's anything down here that can help us get back up, okay?"

"But Jude told us not to," Celia whined.

Ben contemplated. He knew how quickly lighters could run out of fluid, but Jude could top it off when they got back home. "Just real quick." He hit the striker a few times, and the Zippo sputtered but didn't light. Was it out already? Finally, an inch of flame flared above his thumb, and Ben held his hand out, snaking it slowly around the room. The walls were dirt. It smelled so awful down here, he wouldn't be surprised if there were dead animals under some of the leaves. Celia clung to him as they slowly rotated together in a circle. They'd nearly made it all the way around when they stopped. Ben's hand began to shake, and the lighter went out.

They were both breathing heavily. He could feel Celia trembling beside him.

"Was that what I think it was?" Ben finally asked.

In response, Celia began to scream.

23

Right as Isabelle was set to descend the ladder, her phone buzzed.

It was Detective Murdoch. We found something.

Then one from Jack. Get back here now.

She searched for another cryptic message from the unknown number, but there wasn't one. Was that because the messages were from Eliza? Isabelle paused on the rungs and called down. "Eliza, they found something. I need to get back."

Eliza groaned. "But we were just getting to the good stuff." She climbed back up, and they began to walk back toward the grave site.

"How do you know this property so well?"

"I've studied it for years."

"Studied or trespassed?" Isabelle asked, an eyebrow cocked.

"Studied. I'm not an idiot. I don't think your mother would have taken kindly to trespassers on her property."

Damn right, she wouldn't. But still, there was a lot Eliza wasn't telling her, and she wanted to know why. What was in that bunker? What did she want Isabelle to see?

Once they were back at the site, sweat clung to her hairline and pooled in the crevices of her clothing. It was only ten in the morning, but the sun was fierce, even though the temperature was mild. Eliza hung at a safe distance, away from the commotion.

Isabelle fanned her face. What could they have possibly found? She tried to remember what other items Jude had with him that night, but her memory was faulty, scrubbed by time and grief.

Jack shot her a look and motioned her over. There was a separate tarp laid out. On it was a third human skeleton. Her breath slipped from her open mouth, and she staggered forward. *Jude.* His body was mostly intact, pieced back together by the medical examiner. Isabelle pressed a hand to her chest. So they'd found him. At last. Her eyes found Murdoch's.

"He was buried about a foot to the right of where we dug," she explained.

Jude was dead. He was actually dead. Isabelle suddenly felt foolish for that tiny flicker of hope. Her gaze rested on the skeleton. The ME was brushing away dirt, examining the bones with precision. She walked over to Frank, who stood on shaky legs from being crouched for so long.

"We had to work for this one." He wiped his forehead with the back of a gloved hand. "Sorry to put you through all that, Isabelle."

She could barely speak. How could Isabelle have really thought there was a world where Jude had survived? Behind her, Eliza was watching, one hand at her throat. If this was hard for Isabelle, she knew it must also be hard for Eliza, especially since she had seemingly devoted her professional life to uncovering the truth. But there was a stark difference between knowing someone was dead and seeing it with your own two eyes. Frank removed his gloves, grabbed a bottle of water from the crew, and greedily drank.

"So what happens now?"

"Now, we'll see if we can get some viable samples to test for thallium." He whistled. "I gotta tell you, though, looking at the state of the bodies, I wouldn't get your hopes up."

Had they done all this for nothing? Even if the tests confirmed the children did have thallium in their systems, what did that really prove?

What did that change? Anything? Jack came over and placed a hand on the back of her neck and squeezed gently.

"Let's let them work, Izz."

They moved out of the way, and Jack gestured to Eliza, who was standing out of earshot. "What does she want?"

"She took me to the bunker. She wanted to show me something. She says she's Jude's biological sister."

Jack's eyes swung back to Eliza, reassessing. "You believe her?"

"I'm not sure yet."

"Want to go see what she was going to show you?"

She stared at the three bodies. It certainly beat sitting around here to watch them test, poke, and prod her siblings. "Do you need anything from us right now?" she asked Detective Murdoch.

Murdoch turned from the DA. "Not immediately, but don't go too far, please." She eyed Eliza but said nothing.

Isabelle nodded, gestured to Jack to follow, and approached Eliza. "Take us back to the bunker."

Eliza eyed Jack. "All three of us?"

"All three of us," Isabelle confirmed. She motioned toward the woods. "Lead the way." Right before they hiked through the forest, something caught her eye on Jude's left wrist. She stopped and gripped Jack's arm.

"What?" he asked.

Isabelle lurched forward. She was sure it was a trick of her eye, but she stopped at the edge of the corpse anyway, where Frank was busy gathering samples. He looked up and squinted at her from the break in the clouds.

"What's that?" She pointed again to Jude's left wristbone, where it appeared there was some melted metal wrapped around it.

Carefully, he lifted and peered at it. "Seems to be a watch. A . . ." He squinted again. "A Timex, maybe. Looks like the metal fused into his skin and bone. Miraculous really. These things really hold up. They should put that on the advertising." Frank was flippant because death was his subject, but it certainly wasn't hers. She spun in a circle and then took a few shaky steps back.

Detective Murdoch sidled up beside her. "What is it, Isabelle? What's wrong?"

She stabbed a finger toward the skeleton, toward the Timex that had somehow lasted through a fire and twenty-five years beneath the earth. "That watch," she said.

"What about it?"

"Jude didn't wear a watch."

Then

Harper

Harper wasn't sure how much time had passed, but she was falling asleep.

Isabelle was already out cold, her mouth open, snoring slightly. Harper laughed. She considered waking her, but it had been a long night, and she didn't know when they might make a run for it back to base.

They weren't far from the cabin, and Harper wanted to grab a different set of pajamas. The ones she brought were going to be too hot. Maybe she could run to the house real fast and then wake Isabelle up, so they could sprint toward base.

Deciding, she jogged toward the cabin and thought about tonight. It had been pretty crazy so far but was still one of the most interesting nights they'd had in a long time. Except for the Ouija board. She hadn't liked thinking about Marcus.

At her bedroom window, she paused, then lifted the glass and pulled herself up and inside. She listened for her mother but didn't hear anything. She quickly grabbed her pajamas and was headed back out when she remembered the new bar of chocolate she'd bought at the farmers market. They could use it for more s'mores. Wincing, she cracked open the bedroom door and began tiptoeing toward the kitchen. It wasn't that her mother would mind if they were back, but she didn't want Gail to start asking questions or encourage them to come on home.

At the entrance to the kitchen, she stopped. She heard voices, then Gail's unmistakable laugh. Everyone said it was more like a cackle, but she loved it. Mainly because she didn't hear it very often. Was she watching a program in the sunroom? But then she heard a male's voice, and the hairs on her arms pricked up. Who in the world could that be?

Staying pressed against the wall, she rounded the corner and crouched on all fours to peer into the sunroom. All had gone quiet, and when Harper peeked, she saw why. Sheriff Mullins was groping her mother, kissing her and pushing her back on the sofa.

Harper scrambled to stand, and her stomach bucked. What was he *doing* to her? But then, right when she was about to interrupt, Gail moaned and wrapped her legs around Theo's back. Harper stood there, shocked, and scuttled backward, her heel jamming into the oven. It made an awful clanging sound, and she heard her mother gasp.

"Hello?"

Harper didn't know why, but she didn't want Sheriff Mullins to know that she had seen them together. Especially not after he'd caught them on his property tonight. Carefully, she scurried back to the bedroom and out the window, and she had begun to sprint back toward Isabelle when she stopped. In the distance, she spotted Jude up ahead, but it looked like he was carrying something.

She knew they were playing a game, but she had to tell someone what she'd seen. Sheriff Mullins must have come over here to tell Gail what they'd done tonight . . . and then had he thrown himself at her? Gross.

"Jude!" She hissed in the distance, not wanting her mother to see them if she came outside.

Jude didn't turn, so she ran to catch up to him, nearly out of breath. "Jude! Wait!" When she got closer, she could see that he had a giant coil of rope looped over his right shoulder. "What's that for?"

Jude turned, his eyes determined. He blinked when he saw her. "Hey, Harper. Want to help me with this?"

"Help you with what?" Even as she asked, she hoisted the back end of the rope, and Jude automatically quickened his pace. "Where are we going? Are we not playing anymore?"

"Ben and Celia are in trouble. We need to get them out."

Out? Out of where? She followed along wordlessly, feeling bad for leaving Isabelle sleeping under that tree. "Can I tell you something crazy?"

"If you walk faster while you tell me."

She rolled her eyes but picked up the pace. "I went back to the cabin to grab some different pajamas, and you will never believe what I saw."

"What?" He looked over his shoulder, genuine interest in his eyes.

"Gail and Sherriff Mullins, like full-on making out. It was disgusting."

Jude stopped, and she rammed into the back of him. "What?" He glanced back toward the house, as if they might be standing there on display. "Are you sure?"

"Of course I'm sure. I know what I saw. Did you know about them?"

"Ew, definitely not."

They walked in silence for a while as Harper tried to work out why her mother would be involved with a married man. She asked Jude as much.

He shrugged under the weight of the rope. "It's a small town. Not too many fish in the sea, if you know what I mean."

"But isn't he worried about getting caught?"

"Some men think they're invincible."

She didn't know how he knew that, but from the way he said it, she believed him. "So where are we taking this? Where are Ben and Celia?"

He didn't respond for a few more minutes, and before Harper could ask again, he dumped the rope and stretched his back. She let her end pool on the ground and looked around.

"Jude? Where are they?"

He shuffled over a few steps and then groaned as he pulled back a wooden cover and shouted down. "How did this top get put back on?"

"Jude! River was here. He slid it back on. He wouldn't help us. And you won't believe what we found!" Celia sounded hysterical.

Harper stayed rooted to the spot. Celia and Ben were somehow underground. River had been here. She glanced to the left. Was he still out here somewhere, watching them? Was that who was in the woods earlier? Harper glanced down at the rope. Her mouth went dry. She felt sick.

"I need to get Isabelle," she said. "She can help." Before Jude could stop her, Harper started sprinting back the way she came, memorizing directions in her brain.

Celia and Ben were in trouble. River had left them there. Sheriff Mullins and her mother were having an affair. With every step, she ran faster and faster until she was out of breath. Isabelle could help make this right. Isabelle would know what to do.

When she got back to the tree, Harper was gasping and had a stitch in her side. She rested a palm against the trunk and walked around to the other side. But the moment she got there, she could see that Isabelle wasn't.

"Izz?" she called out. If Isabelle had woken up and seen that Harper wasn't there, she probably would have headed back toward base. Taking off again, Harper jogged that way, keeping her eyes peeled. But at the tree house, Isabelle wasn't anywhere to be found. A fist of worry began to press against her chest. What if she was sleepwalking? Though it wasn't Harper's responsibility to prevent Isabelle from sleepwalking, sometimes it felt like it was.

"No, no, no." She didn't know what she should do or where Isabelle could be. There were too many things going on. Her brother and sister needed her help, but so did Izz. Who did she choose?

Making up her mind, she grabbed a flashlight from the tree house and set out to find Isabelle.

24

Isabelle stared at the watch.

She felt like she couldn't breathe.

Detective Murdoch frowned. "Well, maybe you don't remember him wearing one that night?"

"No, Jude didn't wear a watch. Ever." But she knew who did. She lurched backward a few steps. Her words failed her. After a moment, she approached Frank.

"Frank, is anything different about this body from the other two?"

The DA and Detective Murdoch stopped talking and turned, clearly interested in whatever she had to say.

Frank looked at her, concern in his eyes. He huddled with the medical examiner, pointing things out and talking in a hushed whisper before addressing the now small crowd. "In short? Yes." He pointed to the skeleton. "You see these chalk-white fragments? It's what we like to call microcracking." He then pointed to Ben and Celia. "In contrast, Ben and Celia have some soft tissue shielding and patchy charring."

"Which means?" the detective asked impatiently.

"Which means those patterns are typical of fresh bodies in a fire." He turned back to Jude's skeleton. "But after the extra weathering and brittleness post-burial, it would be my estimation that this person has been dead longer."

There was a collective intake of breath. "How much longer?" Murdoch asked.

"I can't officially say . . ."

"If you had to," Isabelle asked. "Ballpark."

He rubbed his cheek with the back of a glove. "Two, three years maybe?"

Isabelle closed her eyes. It confirmed what she already knew. That this skeleton wasn't Jude. It was her missing foster brother, Marcus, likely buried here *before* Jude. She told the detective as much. That was Marcus's watch. He never took it off.

"So you're telling me your foster brother, who was reported missing, has been buried here this whole time?" Murdoch asked.

"I'm not sure." What did this mean? Had her mother known? Had she killed him herself? Was Gail a serial killer? Maybe this was why her mother wanted to bury the kids right here: because it would look like there were three bodies instead of two. She had no idea what that meant for Jude.

"We need to confirm," Murdoch said. "If he's in the system, we'll look at the dental records."

"What would this mean, then?" Isabelle asked. "About Jude?"

Detective Murdoch gripped her hips, looking from one skeleton to the next. "That's the million-dollar question, isn't it? Excuse me." The DA beckoned Murdoch over, and Isabelle's head began to pound.

Marcus was dead. All this time, he'd been buried in her brother's grave.

"I don't understand," she said to Jack now. "None of this makes sense."

"It will," Eliza said. "Come with me."

Before she could say no, that she needed to stay, that she needed to figure all this out, Eliza once again slipped through the trees.

25

Another twenty minutes, and they were at the bunker again.

Isabelle's brain worked overtime. The dead body in the grave might be Marcus. So where was Jude?

Jack peered down into the bunker, then scratched his head. "I don't understand. Why do we need to go down there?"

"Just trust me," Eliza said.

"Maybe take me to dinner first," Jack joked. He motioned to Eliza. "After you." Once Eliza was down the ladder again, Jack cocked an eyebrow at Isabelle. "You really think this is a good idea?"

"No." She followed suit anyway, taking her time on the rungs. The char had long since faded, but as she eased down into the cramped space, a full-body shudder tore through her. After the fire, they discovered this bunker had most likely been on the property since the Cold War, abandoned ever since. Isabelle flipped on her phone light and glanced around as she waited for Jack.

Once he was at the bottom, Isabelle felt her impatience flare. "Okay, now what?"

"After the fire," Eliza said, dragging a palm against the wall and walking in a complete circle. "It was chaos. When authorities were called, it was a recovery mission, as you know. It was too late." She paused a moment and settled her hand against the dirt wall opposite the ladder. "When they got down here, all they saw were the remains of three children. A tragic accident gone wrong."

For some reason, Isabelle's heart began to race. So there *had* been three bodies down here. Was the third body Marcus?

"Once they retrieved the bodies and found Jude's lighter, it seemed like a pretty open-and-shut case. One of the kids accidentally caught something on fire. Jude came back to rescue them with the rope. But somehow, the rope came undone from the tree, and they had no way out." They all looked up, freedom impossible without the ladder.

Isabelle took a shaky breath. She'd never stood in this exact spot, and now that she had, she could almost feel the panic of her siblings, wanting so desperately to get out and realizing that no matter what, they were going to die down here. She shivered, and Jack touched her arm.

"They removed the bodies, a few samples were taken down here, and that was that. The bunker sat undisturbed."

"We know all this," Isabelle said.

Suddenly, Eliza crouched down and ran her fingers along the seam where the dirt floor blended into the wall. She flipped her palm up and tugged hard until a tiny door creaked open into the bunker. "What none of them knew was that there was another way out."

Isabelle was speechless. She rushed forward. Moments before, this door had been completely invisible to the naked eye. Now, it was here. *Obvious.* She ran her fingers over it.

"How do you know about this?"

"More importantly, where does it lead?" Jack asked.

Isabelle could hear the excitement in his voice. But Isabelle wasn't excited. She was devastated. All this time, there'd been another way out. The realization hit her hard, caused her to shuffle back a few steps.

"It's a tunnel," Eliza said. "Follow me." She ducked down to fit inside the tiny door, Jack close behind. Isabelle's stomach cramped. How had the authorities missed this? How had any of them not known this was here? Like Eliza said, maybe they were in such a hurry to wrap up the case, they hadn't looked any further than they had to.

She extracted her phone again and turned on the flashlight. A long, cavernous tunnel stretched in front of her, all made of dirt.

Eliza and Jack chatted up ahead, guessing what the tunnel could have been used for, but Isabelle lagged behind, feeling like Jennifer Connelly in the movie *Labyrinth*, heading toward either freedom or sudden death. Roots dangled above her, tickling her hair. The smell of damp soil and decay filled her nostrils.

They walked for what felt like a mile before the tunnel ended at another bunker with a metal ladder that seemed to butt up against a hatch. Isabelle glanced behind her, the tunnel fading into total darkness, her stomach in knots. If her siblings had only known about this tunnel, they would all be alive. Her entire life would be different.

"Izz, you coming?" Jack ascended the ladder, and she reluctantly followed. Eliza had already pushed back the hatch, which opened onto a patch of scruffy, unkempt land. A small, dilapidated cabin sat in front of her, maybe a third of the size of theirs. It had a wonky chimney and a rotten wood porch. It looked abandoned.

Isabelle glanced around. There was no car here, no signs of life. She flipped off her flashlight and rotated in a circle, gesturing to the cabin. "Why are we here?"

Eliza crossed her arms and looked down at her boots. "Because you need to see this place. It's important."

"Why?"

"You'll see."

Isabelle was tired of the runaround. The three of them walked around the property, searching for signs of life. The windows were too caked with dirt to peer in. Back at the front door, Eliza tried the knob. It was open, and she went inside. Was this where Eliza had been staying? Was this how she knew about the tunnel and the bunker in the first place? Because she'd discovered them?

Isabelle and Jack looked at each other, and he motioned for her to follow. So many things that didn't make sense were clashing for space in her brain, but she couldn't get a firm grasp on anything.

Inside, it was clear someone had been here. There were two twin beds, a two-burner stove, and a mini fridge. A pair of shoes and a duffel bag were tossed on the bed. She sniffed. There was something familiar that clung to the air.

Isabelle moved toward the duffel bag and glanced inside. Pants, T-shirts, underwear, socks. No ID. Nothing to let her know who was squatting here if it wasn't Eliza. There was a small nightstand by the bed. She opened the drawer, which was offset and nearly toppled to the floor. In it was Viktor Frankl's *Man's Search for Meaning*.

Isabelle was almost positive that whoever was staying in this crappy cabin wasn't going to find the answers here. Jack opened the tiny fridge, which was nearly bare. The remnants of coffee sat in a mug in the sink, a few boxes of mac and cheese by the stove. In the bathroom, which was so cramped, she could barely stand inside, she spotted a bar of Dial soap and a razor. There was that smell again.

Isabelle caught her reflection in the mirror. She looked tired. *Haunted.* She gripped the sides of the sink. Why did Eliza bring her here? What did she expect to find?

Back in the main room, she lifted her arms and dropped them. "What are we looking for, Eliza?"

But Eliza didn't direct her or Jack. She simply waited, arms crossed, perched on the edge of one of the beds. As Isabelle neared the front door, there was a flash of movement outside. She knew how territorial people were about their land. Growing up, they'd learned early and fast that they should be careful about whose property they disturbed, lest they get shot.

"Eliza. Someone's outside."

The knob jiggled, turned. She held her breath.

A man shuffled inside, shut the door, and bent to unlace his boots. Sensing something was off, he stiffened and stood to his full height.

Time stilled, transformed, broke apart. He looked different than Isabelle remembered, older, weathered, with a full beard and a baseball cap, thick brown hair spilling from under the bill and out the sides. Both arms were severely burned, the patchwork of scars disappearing under his T-shirt. But she'd know her brother anywhere.

"Jude." Just saying his voice out loud felt like a prayer. He was a ghost, a figment. But then he opened his mouth, and she realized everything she'd thought was true for the last twenty-five years had all been a lie. Here was the proof. She'd found it. Jack and Eliza faded into the background, not daring to say a word.

Finally, the ghost of her brother spoke.

"Hello, Isabelle."

Then

Celia

Celia couldn't stop thinking about what they'd seen.

A body. A *dead* body. A boy, pale and decomposed, shoved in the corner like an afterthought. Had he fallen down here? Had he gotten stuck just like them?

But they were getting out of here. Jude was back with the rope.

Worry number one thousand: Dying next to a dead body before her thirteenth birthday.

When she got out of here, she might never be able to step foot in the woods again.

The rope descended over the side.

"Give it a tug!" Jude called.

She did as she was told. She assumed he'd tied it around a tree for support. What if she got halfway up and it came loose, and she fell and broke her back?

Worry number 1,001: Dying next to a dead body with a broken back before her thirteenth birthday.

"All right, Celia. You're going to prop your foot against the wall and use it for leverage as you climb. Almost like you're walking up the wall. But you're going to have to pull real hard with your arms, okay?"

Celia was panicked. She didn't have upper body strength, could barely do a push-up, and the boys constantly made fun of her for it.

Now she wished she'd joined in on all the physical activities, because it might save her life. She told herself to focus. She'd be like those mothers who got a huge surge of adrenaline when they needed to lift cars off their babies. She could do it. She had to.

She braced one foot against the wall and gripped the rope. Ben stood behind her to help her stay steady.

"You've got this," he said.

She hoisted herself up, and immediately, her arms began to shake. The rope cut into her hands, ripping the flesh. She bit the inside of her cheek and forced herself to keep climbing. But she couldn't see anything. She felt like she was dangling in space. When her arms couldn't hold anymore, she fell back to the start, tears burning her eyes.

"Hey, that's okay. That was a good effort. Let's try again."

Her palms stung, the flesh flapping below her fingers, torn, like paper. She blew on them, but that made it worse. "I don't think I can do this," she said.

"Yes, you can." There was an edge to Ben's voice, but she knew he wouldn't climb up until she'd made it safely to the top.

"I can't do it, Jude," she said, craning to look up. "I'm not strong enough."

He cursed from above, and then before she knew what was happening, he lowered himself down. It took only moments, but then he was there with them, her big brother, come to save the day.

"Dude, why did you do that?" Ben asked.

"We have to figure out a way to get her up," Jude said. "Maybe she can get on my back, and I'll pull us both to the top. Once we're up, then you go, okay?"

"Okay."

"Celia, hop on my back." Jude lowered himself so she could jump up. It had been years since she'd done a piggyback. She did as she was told and wrapped her arms around his neck, squeezing her shaking thighs around his middle. Jude grabbed the rope between his hands. "You good?"

She took a shaky breath. "I'm good."

Before he could start to climb, they heard commotion up top.

"I think Harper was going to get Isabelle."

All of a sudden, the top of the rope came raining down and landed with a thud at the bottom.

"Hey!" Jude called. "Hey!"

Celia's heart began to pound. She gripped Jude harder. And then, like something out of a horror movie, the top slid back into place, sealing them into utter darkness.

They all stood there, completely stunned. Celia hopped down, violently shaking from head to toe.

"Was that River again?" Ben asked, his voice full of rage. "I swear, I'm going to kill him."

"He probably thinks it's a joke," Jude said.

Even though he tried to keep his voice light, Celia could hear it: There was real fear there. "Didn't you say Harper was coming back?"

"Yes, she was going to get Isabelle to help. I hope she remembers where it is." His voice faded, and the three of them stood there, shocked into silence.

"Let me see the lighter," Jude said.

They hadn't told him about the dead body yet. They didn't want to panic him any more than he already was, but if he lit it, then he'd see. Should they warn him first?

He hit the striker a few times, and then the flame illuminated Jude's face as he glanced around and got his bearings.

When he saw the lump in the corner, he stepped closer, then jumped back in surprise and dropped the lighter. The flame still flickered, and as if in slow motion, the dry leaves caught. He cursed, lunged forward to stamp out the flames, but he was too slow, and the fire began to spread.

Celia hurled herself back against the wall.

Worry number 1,002: Dying next to a dead body because she burned to death before her thirteenth birthday.

Celia honestly couldn't imagine a worse way to die.

Jude ripped off his shirt and began trying to beat the flames, but they were too strong. Ben shuffled back, too, but his eyes were wild and fearful. "Help me!" Jude yelled.

The heat was already licking toward her face. Thick black smoke curled around them. It was getting so hot, she'd broken out into a sweat. The three of them looked at each other, panic consuming as much space as the flames and smoke. They all began to scream for help as the fire crackled and grew. Jude jumped up, fingers splayed, searching for purchase, searching for something to grab onto, to climb up with. The dirt crumbled beneath his fingers as the fire spread toward them, reaching.

There was no way out.

Celia slid down the wall. She made herself small, just like she'd done her entire life.

The smoke was gagging her. Her eyes watered. The fire threatened to consume her.

She closed her eyes and prayed for a miracle.

26

Isabelle was too shocked to move, to hug him, or even to demand answers.

Instead they stared at each other, a world of hurt and disbelief between them. Finally, she found her voice. "How are you alive?"

He ripped off his ball cap, smoothed back his unruly hair, and fitted it back on. **NYU**. Had he gone there? It seemed impossible, like every true thing she knew about existing in the world—graduating high school, moving, going to college, landing a job—all hinged upon having an actual identity. How could you do any of that if you were presumed dead? Jude gestured to the tiny, soiled couch in the corner of the makeshift living room. Begrudgingly, she sat.

"I don't know where to begin." His voice pierced her heart. It was the same but also different. Weary but strong. All she wanted to do was pummel him, hold him, ask him why he'd left her all alone, when he could have come back for her anytime.

The anguish built inside her until she thought she'd burst. "At the beginning." Her voice trembled, and she knotted her hands in her lap, willing herself to stay calm enough to listen.

Jack and Eliza hung in the background. Finally, Jack spoke up. "Maybe we should give you both some privacy."

Isabelle nodded, and Jack and Eliza let themselves outside. Once they were gone, Jude sighed and swallowed. He swiped a scarred hand across his beard.

"I'm sorry I never let you know I was okay."

"Why didn't you?" Since he was presumed dead, he'd had a thousand opportunities to reach out. Isabelle was close to tears, and she hated herself for it, but she hated him too.

"I couldn't. For so many reasons." His fingernails were rimmed with dirt.

"I thought you died, Jude. I thought . . ."

"I know."

"Well?" Isabelle snapped. "What happened?"

He filled her in on the basics: He went to get a rope to try to help Ben and Celia. Harper was supposed to come help. That was news to her. Harper had never told her that she'd seen Jude that night or that she'd gone to the bunker. Something in her gut began to ache. He told her about River and that someone untied the rope and pushed the top back in place. She'd never heard about any of this.

"Who did it?"

He scratched his beard, and again, her eyes clamped on his patchwork of scars. "Always assumed it was River, but . . ." He shook his head and didn't continue.

River Foust. A killer. If he hadn't untied that rope, then maybe they'd all be alive.

"Then what?"

"There was a body down there with us."

"Marcus."

He nodded. "I had no idea who it was at the time."

"We exhumed the graves today. They found his bones where yours were supposed to be. They have to confirm it first, but the corpse had on Marcus's watch."

Jude let that land, exhaled, flung his arms back against the sofa. "What a mess this is going to be."

She had too many questions: Who killed Marcus? Who untied the rope? Where had Jude been this whole time? Why hadn't Harper told her about what she'd done that night?

"It was my fault the fire started. When I saw the body, I dropped the lighter, and the whole place went up in seconds." He snapped his fingers. "I tried what I could, but . . ." His voice faded, and Isabelle couldn't imagine the atrocity of watching Ben and Celia burn to death. The screams, the smells. "I was desperate. I moved back against one of the walls and slid down to the ground to see if I could dig or do something, *anything*, and I found a door."

"Why couldn't you take them with you?"

"They were already engulfed, Izz. It was . . . it was too late." He took a steadying breath. "But I knew they were going to find three bodies down there. They were going to assume that Marcus was me." He looked at her. "I thought Gail was poisoning us. I knew that everything was going to change after that night anyway, and I just . . . I took my opportunity. I ran. I shut that door, and I crawled through that tunnel until I found this place." He gestured around. "There was a nice older couple, Ruth and Jim, who took me in. They took care of my wounds. Then they caught wind of what was going on and agreed to keep me away from Gail. They packed everything up, and we left. I took on their last name. They gave me a new life." His eyes filled, and he cleared his throat, swiping the tears away angrily. "I owe everything to them."

"I get wanting to start over, wanting to get out of this place, Jude, but . . . why are you here now? Why didn't you let me know you were alive sooner?"

"It's complicated." He was quiet. "Eliza found me first. She's been digging into what happened for years." He sighed. "I guess when Gail saw the bodies after the fire, maybe she knew it was Marcus because she killed him? I don't know. But a few months ago, Gail reached out. Said she wanted to tell me everything."

"What do you mean she reached out? How would she even know you were alive?"

He motioned outside. "Eliza. She convinced me to talk to her. So I came back. Gail had a bunch of crazy theories."

"Such as?"

He readjusted his hat. "Like I said, they were crazy."

Isabelle studied him, suddenly putting two and two together. The ball cap. The mystery man from the video footage. Chills crept up her skin like spiders. "Did you kill her?"

He balked. "Kill her? Jesus, Isabelle. Of course not."

"But you think someone did?"

"I don't know."

"Well, I do. I have the video footage to prove it." She considered something. "But you knew there were cameras, right? It's why you kept yourself hidden."

"I did, but I didn't know anyone hurt her. I thought maybe she did it herself. Or maybe she died from natural causes."

"Well, she didn't." She filled him in on the thallium and her theory back when they were younger. "What's more pressing to me is who untied the rope. Who shut you all in?"

Jude looked at her with a tortured expression. "Well, that's the thing Gail wanted to talk to me about," he said.

"Did she see who it was? Could it have been Harper?" Even as she said it, that didn't quite compute.

"Mom was with Theo that night. They were having an affair. Harper saw them kissing and ran out to tell me."

Again, something Harper had omitted after the fact. Why? Was that why Theo had turned on Gail after the investigation? Because maybe Gail had threatened to tell his wife about the two of them? So many theories, and no way to know the truth.

"Harper was looking for you first before she came back to the bunker," Jude said now, softly. "But when she couldn't find you, she made her way there. She saw who did it." He swallowed. "She saw who put the top back in place. At first, she kept that information to herself. But she finally had to tell someone. So she told Gail."

"And Gail wanted to tell you? Why?"

He sighed. "It's complicated."

Isabelle sat up straighter, desperate to know. "Was it River?" Or maybe Theo?

His eyes slid from his scarred hands up to her eyes. "It wasn't River, no," he said at last. "It was you."

27

She almost laughed. "Me? What are you talking about?"

He hesitated. "You were sleepwalking, as you know. Harper looked everywhere for you, and when she couldn't find you, she ran back to the bunker. Somehow, you found it too. She literally watched you untie the rope and slide the top back on."

They could have heard a pin drop. Isabelle's face was on fire, her heart thudding against her ribs. "That's not possible," she said. But wasn't it? Hadn't she watched Maisy sleepwalk in the same way? Hadn't Isabelle woken up in strange places, over and over again, not remembering anything? "I didn't even know where the bunker was."

He gripped the back of his neck, closed his eyes, then opened them. "But you did."

Isabelle's world began to tilt. "*No*, I didn't."

"The night Marcus died. You sleepwalked. Marcus followed you. Harper didn't trust him to be alone with you, so she went after him. You somehow found that bunker. Marcus must have startled you. You pushed him. He broke his neck. Harper was horrified. She replaced the top, guided you back to the cabin, and never told anyone. She . . . she was trying to protect you, Izz. And I guess when she saw the bunker that night and knew Ben and Celia were trapped in there, she knew Marcus was down there too."

How in the world could Jude know any of this? And why would Harper never tell her? As if reading her mind, he spoke up.

"I went to see Harper after I talked to Gail. Part of me assumed Gail was lying, that she'd lost all touch with reality. But when I confronted Harper, she finally came clean. She . . . she's been protecting you all this time, Isabelle. I'm sorry."

Isabelle felt like she was floating. She jumped off the couch, clawing at her chest and throat. Stumbling outside, she startled Eliza and Jack, who were mid-conversation. When he saw the look on Isabelle's face, he followed her as she hurried down the porch stairs and gripped the nearby trunk of a tree.

"What's going on, Izz? What did he say?"

She shook her head and pointed to the woods. "I need to see Harper."

"Harper? Why?"

Without saying a word, she started stalking through the woods. She roughly knew her way to Harper's farm if she could circle back toward her own cabin. All this time, Harper had known and hadn't said anything? All this time, *Isabelle* was the villain? She nearly stopped as another thought crossed her mind. What about the thallium? Had that been her too?

No. She had no access to thallium, no way to poison anyone. Her legs trembled as she stalked through the forest, Jack close behind.

"Izz, stop. Tell me what's going on. Please." He gripped her shoulder, forced her to stop.

She was breathing too heavily and crooked forward, bracing her hands on her knees. "Harper saw me that night," she said. She straightened, looked off into the distance. "I was sleepwalking. I untied the rope. I . . . I sealed them in."

"What?" He looked as shocked as she felt. "That's ridiculous. How would you know where the bunker was?"

She explained what Jude had told her about Marcus. Jack took a few steps back, both hands gripping his hair. "Okay, look. Let's be rational here." He dropped his hands. "Do you really believe that? Maybe Harper is lying?"

She laughed. "Why would Harper lie about that? She let the whole world think it was Gail, a woman she loved, a woman she protected at all costs. The only person she loved more than Gail was . . ."

"You." He finished her sentence.

"I need to talk to her."

"Okay, we'll talk to her. Let's take it one bombshell at a time."

She resumed her pace, her thoughts all over the place. Because of her, her siblings were dead. Because of her, Marcus was dead. What did she *do* with that information? Turn herself in? And beyond that, Harper knew Jude was alive. How long had she known? And how could she keep something so important from her?

By the time Harper's fence came into view, she felt like she might explode. Wordlessly, she let herself through, walked around to the front of the house, and knocked on the front door. After a moment, Harper opened the door, her entire face lighting up. "Hey, you." Once she clocked the look on Isabelle's face, she frowned. "What's wrong?"

Isabelle felt sick. "Where's Maisy?"

"The girls are upstairs taking a post-lunch nap. They're exhausted." She glanced at Jack behind her. "What's happening?" She reached for Isabelle, and Isabelle jerked back.

"Whoa, Izz. What is it?"

"Maybe we should go inside," Jack said, stepping onto the front porch.

Harper opened the door wider, and the three of them moved inside. Isabelle and Jack sat on the couch, and Harper perched in the chair beside them.

"You're scaring me." Harper's eyes searched Isabelle's face.

How did Isabelle start this conversation? *Where* did she start this conversation? "Do you know Eliza Harrell?"

Harper's face paled, but she nodded.

"Then you know Jude is alive, has been alive all this time."

Harper's eyes filled with tears. "No, I haven't known long. I swear. I wanted to tell you, but Eliza told me not to. I . . . I'm sorry. I should have told you the truth."

Isabelle barked out a laugh. "The *truth*? Just like you told me the truth about the night of the fire? Just like you told me the truth about Marcus?"

Harper's eyes went wide, and then she dropped her head into her hands and moaned. After a moment, she composed herself. "Look, I'm sorry. I thought I was doing the right thing. If I'd told the police what really happened back then, you would have been *arrested*, Isabelle. Your whole life would have been ruined." Harper moved to sit beside her, but Isabelle jumped up and began to pace.

"Do you understand that I thought my own mother was a killer my entire life? Do you know what that does to a person?"

"Of course I do," Harper said. "But isn't that better than realizing it's you?"

Silence engulfed the room. Though she was getting answers to some questions, she didn't have answers to all of them. Who'd been the one to poison their mother? Who'd been the one to steal the files and possibly cause that explosion? Who'd poisoned the kids? She thought about the note her mother wrote Eliza to give to Isabelle. Was that before Harper told Gail the truth? Things still didn't add up. "So now what? Do I turn myself in?"

"No," Jack and Harper snapped at once.

"You were sleepwalking," Jack said. "Just let it be."

"Let it *be*? Jude's, Celia's, Ben's, and Marcus's bodies were exhumed today. There's a secret door that leads to an even more secret cabin in the woods where my dead brother has been living these last few weeks. We were in an explosion! Someone is sending me cryptic messages . . ."

Ivy appeared in the living room then, fists jammed in her eyes.

"Hey, baby." Harper opened her arms, clearing the emotion from her voice, and Ivy folded into them. "Did you have a good nap?"

She yawned and blinked at Isabelle and Jack. "Where's Maisy?"

Isabelle stiffened, but Harper laughed.

"What do you mean, sweetie? She's in her room."

"No, she isn't."

Isabelle took the stairs two at a time, her head thumping from the sudden exertion. She opened the door. The covers were disturbed, but no Maisy. She searched the bathroom, the rest of upstairs, and circled back downstairs. The kitchen door was flung open. "Oh, no." Isabelle took off outside, searching the farm. Harper and Jack came outside. "She's sleepwalking," Isabelle explained.

"What?" Harper was confused. "Since when?"

"Help me find her." At least it was daytime. Jack, Harper, and Isabelle split up to search the property. When they couldn't find her, Isabelle stared into the dark, yawning mouth of the woods.

Though a bomb had landed in her lap, she couldn't think of that now.

She had to find her daughter. Everything else could wait.

28

The thicket of trees consumed her.

Jack and Harper ran up behind her. "Let's split up," he said.

"If you find her, don't wake her up," Isabelle warned. "Just call out."

They divided, and Isabelle found herself winding toward River's house. All this time, Jude had been alive. Did River know too? She couldn't imagine he didn't. No secret like this could hold in a town this small. No stranger could slip in and out without being detected, could they? Especially one with scars like that.

Though Isabelle knew it wouldn't matter, she called Maisy's name. Desperation clawed at her skin. All of this had grown bigger than her journalist brain could handle. She didn't know why she couldn't accept what Jude and Harper told her.

There were massive chunks of this story still missing, but what else could she do? What would Murdoch do? With Marcus's body exhumed instead of Jude's, this changed things. They'd be looking into an active murder investigation, one that *she* was responsible for. Their attention would swing from detecting thallium in the children to a real case worth solving. Because even if they uncovered thallium, Celia and Ben were still dead. Gail was dead too. The only living person left to pay was her.

Her heart was shattered. All these years, it had never crossed her mind that *she* could have had something to do with what happened that night. It still didn't explain the poisoning, though. It still didn't explain what had happened to her mother. Or her mother's note.

"Maisy!"

Harper's and Jack's voices clashed in the distance and bounced off the trees. Overhead, storm clouds gathered, swallowing the blue sky into various shades of gray. Isabelle stopped as she felt a dizzy spell pass over her. She'd been pushing her body too hard, hadn't given herself proper time to rest. "Maisy!" she called again and saw something ahead dart behind a tree.

She picked up her pace, but there was nothing there. How far should she walk? This forest went on for miles. As if to drive home the sense of urgency, a grumble of thunder shook through the forest. They had to find Maisy before a storm blew in. Panic pushed her forward faster, made her ignore her body's complaints. She tried to tell herself that sooner or later, Maisy would wake up. They would find her. They would.

Isabelle tried to remember what it was like to wake up after sleepwalking and find herself in unexpected places. The bathtub. The front porch. The woods. Once, she walked all the way to a neighbor's swimming pool and crawled inside, though it had luckily been drained for the season. Celia and Harper started locking the bedroom door, but even then, sometimes Isabelle's subconscious mind remembered how to unlock it. And now that she knew how serious sleepwalking could be, what it could lead to, she and Jack would get Maisy whatever help she needed as soon as they got back to Portland.

Without trying to, she'd arrived at River's house. His truck was gone. The lights were out in the cabin. She hesitated and was about to circle back when her eyes swung toward the shed. River had behaved so oddly the other day when she approached it. Though Isabelle realized this was essentially trespassing, she crept toward the shed but stayed hidden in the tree line. She searched for Maisy along the way.

Another ripple of thunder pushed her to walk faster. When she approached the shed, she examined the padlock. It was a basic lock, thankfully. Isabelle fished a bobby pin from her hair and bent it into an L. She slid it into the keyway, twisting enough to feel the pins press back. With the other end, she probed gently, lifting each tiny stack of metal until she felt the faintest click. One by one, the pins gave way before the core turned, smooth and cold under her fingers. The lock sprang open, and she gave a satisfied little yelp. Glancing over her shoulder to make sure River was still gone, she pulled back the wooden door and stepped inside, closing it behind her. A sudden crack of lightning briefly illuminated a basic shed with lawn supplies: a riding mower, a gasoline can, gardening equipment, fertilizer. Rows of metal shelves were neatly arranged along the left side. But then she saw other things: a little girl's bicycle, toys, a kid's life jacket. She hesitated. So River had a kid? Was this what he didn't want her to see?

Isabelle quickly sorted through the random objects, looking under and behind them, searching for what, she wasn't sure. She was about to leave when she saw a stack of files shoved behind some pesticides. Probably instructions or warranties, but something pricked her senses. Isabelle grabbed the file folder and opened it. There, staring back at her, were the missing files from the funeral home. Celia's, Ben's, and Jude's autopsy reports and death certificates, plus her mother's.

Her heart began to hammer. Why would River have these here? Hidden? Why would he take them in the first place? This proved he was connected in some way, that he had something to hide. Or someone to protect.

Tucking the files under her arm, she exited the shed, relocked the padlock, and froze as she heard River's truck pull into the gravel lot. The sky was nearly black, the clouds pregnant and ready to unload. The wind whipped her loose hair across her face, and she scraped a few strands behind her ears. Before she could disappear back into the trees, River barked her name.

In a few short strides, he had crossed over to her, a look of concern on his face. "What are you doing here, Belle?"

Now the nickname made her cringe. She lifted the files. "Why do you have these?"

He stared at them, his face genuinely confused. "I have no idea what those are."

She snorted. "Please, stop lying, River. It's Celia's, Ben's, Jude's, and my mother's autopsy reports and death certificates, stolen on the day of the explosion."

He appeared genuinely shocked. "Why would I have those?"

"Exactly my question."

He motioned toward the shed. "I could have you arrested for trespassing, you know."

"So do it," she challenged. As she said it, she was reminded of the night the kids showed up at Theo's house. How he'd threatened to arrest them. How Jude had told him to do it. But she wasn't a kid anymore, and whether River was bluffing or not was none of her concern. She had what she needed and could focus on finding Maisy. "If you turn me in, I'll be happy to share these."

"Like I said, I have no idea what those are, Belle. I swear."

"Whatever you say, *Riv*," she said, stalking toward the trees.

Before she was back on the path, he moved behind her and gripped her arm, hard. She twisted, but he didn't let go. She turned, and his eyes seared into hers.

The sky opened up, and fat raindrops pocked their shoulders and the dirt beneath their shoes.

"You have no idea what you're doing," he growled now, shaking her arm. "Go back to your life and leave us alone." He shook her again before he released her. She wobbled back, shoved the file beneath the safety of her shirt, and turned to run. Her heart thudded in her ears. Once she was out of his sight, she slowed, his words echoing in her ears.

"Found her!" Jack's sharp voice rang through the trees, and Isabelle started sprinting toward his voice. Her thighs burned.

"Call out!"

He whistled once every few minutes until she spotted him up ahead on the path. The rain was coming harder now, and she wicked some of the moisture from her eyes. Jack had Maisy's hand clutched in his and was guiding her back toward the house. Isabelle knew she shouldn't wake her, but she had to. She gripped her small shoulders, shook her roughly, and called to her to wake up.

"I thought you said . . ."

"I know what I said." But it was too much. River. The files. The storm. She needed to make sure Maisy was okay. She needed to get her back inside, to safety. "Maisy. Bug. It's Mama. Wake up."

Finally, Maisy jolted awake. The confusion washed over her face as she looked from Isabelle to Jack. She shivered in her clothes as they were pelted with the rain.

"You were sleepwalking again, Bug," Isabelle said, rubbing soothing circles on her back. "It's okay." She hoisted Maisy in the air and wrapped her spindly legs around her waist. She hadn't carried Maisy in a while, often wondered when it would be the very last time before she outgrew wanting to be held. She gripped her tightly, tears stinging her eyes.

Harper was waiting for them back at the house with a yellow umbrella in hand. "Oh, thank God you found her!" She smiled at Maisy and ran up to shield them from the rain. "Go for a nice walk in the rain, sweetie?" Harper's eyes locked with Isabelle's and then slid back to Maisy's. "You hungry? Want a snack? Here, let's get you inside." Harper reached for her, and reluctantly, Isabelle passed her over. Maisy wrapped her legs and arms around Harper, and they walked back inside.

"That was really scary," Jack said. He was soaked.

Once inside, they dried off with fluffy towels Harper left for them in the mudroom. They removed their shoes, and Isabelle extracted the file folder from beneath her shirt.

He motioned to it. "What's that?"

"Found this hidden in River's shed." She left out the part about him grabbing her. Jack flipped through the mostly dry pages and wiped a hand over his mouth.

"So this means what, exactly?"

"I'm not sure yet." Her phone buzzed. It was Detective Murdoch. We need you back at the site. She showed it to Jack. "Can you tell Maisy I've got to get over to the site but I'll be right back?"

"I'm coming with you. I'll let Harper know." Jack disappeared down the hall.

Suddenly, she wanted to heed River's advice. She wanted to get the hell out of here. She wanted to go back to her life in Portland and pretend none of this had happened. But she couldn't do that now. Knowing what she knew about that night.

Knowing what she'd done.

Knowing what she had to confess.

Part III: The Shadows

29

Once the rain passed, Isabelle and Jack walked back through the woods.

They were headed to the secret cabin first, not back to the site.

"Izz, you don't have to tell Murdoch anything." There was a desperation in his voice she hadn't heard before, and she understood it. If she admitted her involvement, she could go to prison for the rest of her life. Maybe not for untying the rope but definitely for Marcus. She'd killed her foster brother, and deep down, she knew why.

She'd never shared it with anyone, but Marcus had been sexually inappropriate with both her and Harper many times. He was older, and at first, his advances came off as joking, then turned more sinister. Maybe subconsciously, she'd had enough. Was that why she'd been uncomfortable with River in the woods? Not because of anything River had done, but because of what Marcus had done to her and what *she'd* ultimately done to Marcus? A subconscious memory, tucked away? Regardless, it didn't matter. Marcus was dead, and it was still her fault.

At the cabin, Isabelle knocked and stepped inside. Eliza and Jude were still there, just as she'd left them.

"Where'd you go?" Eliza asked.

Isabelle tossed the file at her. "Found this in River Foust's shed, hidden on a shelf. Murdoch needs me back at the site."

Eliza flipped through the file.

"I'm going to tell her," Isabelle said now. "It's the right thing to do."

Jude's eyes were pained. "You didn't purposely hurt anyone, Izz. You were asleep."

She scoffed. "As if that matters? I still did it. I killed someone. I'm responsible for Celia and Ben not getting out alive. And you have the permanent scars to prove it." She took a deep, steadying breath. "I've wanted someone to pay for this my entire life. Even if it's me, it's the right thing to do."

"Izz, think about Maisy." Jack's fingers found her wrist. "Please." His eyes were full of love and need and fear. She felt it too.

"They're right," Eliza said, crossing her arms over her chest. "If you confess now, things are going to get a lot more complicated. You need to think about how this affects Maisy. About how it affects you. And Jack."

"And me," Jude said softly. "I know I've stayed away all these years, and I'm sorry for that. But I'm here now. We have a chance to start over." His voice faded into the background. They all looked at her, basically asking her to lie, to pretend that she didn't know what had happened to that skeleton on the tarp.

"What about you?" she asked Jude. "Are you going to let the world know you're alive?"

He and Eliza shared a look, and Jude gave a small nod for Eliza to explain.

"That's what I've been working on. This whole thing . . . it's a big story, and the timing has to be right."

"Which means what, exactly?" she asked. "That I need to keep my mouth shut?"

"Basically, yes," Eliza said. "For a little while longer. I've been working on this for years."

Isabelle nodded. She understood, because this was the nature of her work too. She, Jack, and Eliza shared a similar universe. One wrong step, one leak, and the story could be ruined, years of work gone, just like that. She didn't want to do that to Eliza, didn't want to out Jude if he wasn't ready to be outed. "So what do I tell Murdoch, then?"

"You don't tell her anything," Eliza said, handing her the file back. "Except you found this in River's shed. Maybe send them on a little goose chase."

Was that the right thing to do? While she didn't know the level of River's involvement, she didn't think he killed Gail. "So, who do we think killed Gail?"

Once again, Eliza and Jude looked at each other. "Theo," they said at once.

She frowned. "Theo? Why?"

"I think Gail was threatening to come clean about their affair, about how thoroughly he botched the investigation with the kids. I'm not sure why now, but she wanted to set the record straight. She wasn't feeling well, so maybe she thought she was on borrowed time? I don't know."

"Well, I guess we'll never know now, will we?" Isabelle massaged her temples. "This is like one giant riddle I can't solve. And I need to. I want to get Maisy away from this place."

"Understood," Jude said. "But we're in agreement? You won't say anything yet?"

They all looked at each other, but Isabelle couldn't say yes. Finally, Jack motioned to Isabelle. "Let's go see what Murdoch needs. Where will you two be?"

"Here," Jude said.

Isabelle glanced at Eliza. "You coming with?"

"No, I'm going to stay with Jude."

They said their goodbyes, and then Jack and Isabelle were heading back through the damp forest. She couldn't remember the last time she'd walked this much.

"Tell me what happened with River," Jack said.

Isabelle recounted as best she could, again leaving out when he'd grabbed her. "Something he said, though. It's nagging at me."

"What was it?" Jack asked.

"He said, 'Go back to your life and leave *us* alone.' Who's 'us' in that equation?"

"Good question."

Even though Isabelle didn't like Theo for Gail's murder, she had to admit it fit. Their affair. He was in the woods the night of the fire. He'd threatened them. Plus, his involvement with the kids' burial and signing off on a body that wasn't Jude's made it all the more complicated. Maybe Eliza's sudden interest in dredging all this up had made Theo desperate to silence Gail. He'd only recently lost his wife. Perhaps he felt he had nothing to lose. She thought about River again, how hard he'd gripped her arm. As she already knew, people were capable of anything.

Back at the site, the skeletons were still on the tarps but covered from the rain. Murdoch waved them over.

"What's up?" Isabelle asked, forcing her voice to sound normal.

"We can't be sure, but it seems Marcus might have broken his neck. Could have been an accident. Or not." She scratched her cheek. "I'll need to ask you and Harper some questions. What he was like. When he went missing."

She nodded. "Of course."

"The boys were able to collect what they could before the storm blew in. Not sure if we'll find anything, but we'll keep you posted."

Isabelle handed over the file. "I found this in River Foust's shed. These are from the funeral home."

Detective Murdoch flipped through them. "Seems like we might have more than a faulty vent to look into after all."

Isabelle turned her attention to the covered bodies, somehow sobered by the fact that she was partly responsible for Celia's and Ben's deaths too. But not Jude's. Jude was alive. The one silver lining in all this.

"Do we need to come down to the station, or . . .?"

"No, no. I'll come to you. You're staying at Harper's, right? Why don't you give me her address, and I'll meet you both there in an hour or so?"

Isabelle nodded. "Anything else?"

Murdoch examined her, cocking her head. She was a full head shorter than Isabelle. "Maybe I should ask you the same thing?"

Isabelle's blood ran cold, but she held her gaze. "I'm trying to get to the bottom of everything," she said, swinging her gaze back to the tarps.

"Aren't we all." Murdoch lifted the file. "Thanks for this. I'll pay Mr. Foust a visit too. See you all soon." Just like that, they were dismissed. Isabelle huffed, annoyed they'd walked all this way only to trek back to Harper's again.

What happened next depended on what Harper told Detective Murdoch. Would she tell the truth or cover for Isabelle as she'd been doing all these years? Could Isabelle really sit across from the detective and lie to save herself?

Maisy flashed through her mind. How could Isabelle possibly risk having her daughter grow up without a mother? Mothers were supposed to protect their children. Mothers were supposed to be there, no matter what.

Jack followed close behind. The wet ground squished beneath their shoes. His voice was swallowed by the trees. She couldn't concentrate on what he was saying.

Only one question bounced around her head: What kind of mother did she want to be—one who lied or one who told the truth?

30

At Harper's, Maisy and Ivy were upstairs playing.

Harper pulled Isabelle into a hug and then held her at arm's length. "Okay, please tell me what's going on. For real."

So she did. Jack made them coffee while Isabelle told her everything she'd learned so far and that Murdoch was on the way to question them both about Marcus.

Harper looked worried. "What are you going to say?"

"I don't know yet."

"Well, I'm certainly not going to say anything. So don't go get a conscience and think you're doing the right thing." Harper's voice shook. "I know we never talked about it, but Marcus wasn't a good kid, and we both know it. I'm not sorry for what happened to him."

Isabelle had buried that part of her life. The games Marcus would play. How he would touch them. She and Harper were only ten. It was such a long time ago, and as with so much of her life, she chose not to remember.

Only now did she know how dangerous not remembering was.

Isabelle asked about Gail's note, which Harper confirmed.

"That's why I told her the truth," she explained now. "She had all these crazy theories and wanted to go to the police. I knew if I told her what really happened, she'd drop it." She reached for Isabelle. "She would do anything to protect you, Izz. Just like I would."

But did she *want* to be protected? Not if it meant that the truth stayed buried.

Isabelle also shared Eliza's theory about Theo having killed Gail. She told Harper about the video footage, which Harper asked to see, but Jack said it would be best if she didn't. Harper dropped her head into her hands. "How did we get here?" She finally said, "It's all such a mess."

Isabelle couldn't argue. It was a mess, and they were at the center of it. Harper excused herself to go to the bathroom, and Isabelle looked at Jack. She wanted to ask him what he believed because he'd been awfully quiet since they got back. She knew him well enough to know he was probably gathering facts and didn't want to make any snap judgments yet. But his opinion mattered to her the most. She trusted him, and when he was ready to bring her his theories, she'd listen.

The doorbell rang, and Isabelle sighed. Harper exited the bathroom, poured them both a cup of coffee, and walked toward the door. Jack excused himself to go watch the girls.

"Liquid courage," she said, chinking her mug against Isabelle's. Isabelle smiled, took a sip of the caffeine, felt the buzz of it mix with her nerves. She reminded herself she was answering questions honestly about Marcus. She didn't have to lie.

Once Murdoch was inside, they situated themselves at the dining room table. Murdoch took her time before launching into questions about Marcus. Isabelle felt Harper stiffen beside her.

"So you were adopted by Ms. Archer when you were ten, and then how long after did Marcus enter the home?"

They looked at each other. "About six months, I believe," Harper said. "It was fast."

"And unexpected," Isabelle explained now. "My mom was trying to help."

"Uh-huh. And what was Marcus like? Quiet? Troubled?"

Harper swallowed. "He was older than us, kind of did his own thing."

So Harper was already lying. Isabelle gritted her teeth in frustration.

"And Harper, your mother. Sandy. How did she die?"

They were both thrown by the change of topic, but Harper answered. "She had multiorgan failure."

"Cancer?"

She shrugged. "They never determined. She'd been having odd symptoms, and then one day, she just . . . died." Harper's eyes filled with tears, and she cleared her throat, embarrassed. "Sorry."

"Autopsy report never determined cause of death?"

"They think she maybe had an undiagnosed metabolic disorder. Sorry if I don't remember all the jargon. I was ten," she snapped.

"Right. Of course." Murdoch switched back to questions about Marcus. How long he'd been in their home, where his room was, if he wandered in the woods often. The truth was, he'd only been with them a few months before he died.

"So how does a woman who had a missing child on her hands get custody of three more kids?" Murdoch asked now. "That one doesn't make sense to me."

"She needed the money," Harper said. "Money was always tight for Gail, but I think, deep down, she really did like helping kids in need."

Isabelle almost scoffed. "Sheriff Mullins also pulled some strings," she said, realizing it was another knock against Theo. "Gail was the only foster in town, and they needed homes immediately."

"Right here, in Cedarloch?" Murdoch whistled. "Seems kind of unlikely."

Isabelle opened her mouth to speak, then shut it. She guessed it was kind of unlikely. Ben, Celia, and Jude had all been in foster homes outside of Cedarloch, but she hadn't thought much of it at the time.

Murdoch wrote something down and then looked at Harper. "Tell me about River Foust."

Harper made a face. "Why?"

Murdoch leaned forward, crossing her arms on the table. "I want to know more about the father of your child." She glanced at her notes. "Ivy, is it? You two must be on good terms, living so close and all."

Isabelle laughed, sure she'd misunderstood. River wasn't Ivy's father. She opened her mouth to correct her, but Harper's face said it all. Then it clicked. The kids' toys, the bike. They were Ivy's. That was why he hadn't wanted her in his shed. That was what he'd meant by "leave *us* alone." He was talking about Harper and Ivy.

Harper looked at Isabelle, her eyes pleading. "Isabelle, I can explain. I . . ."

Isabelle shot up so fast, she sloshed coffee on herself. "River Foust is Ivy's father? And you didn't think to tell me that?" Her brain was working overtime as she considered what this could possibly mean. "What else haven't you told me?"

Murdoch looked between them, not saying a word but clearly interested in the sisterly back-and-forth.

"It was a stupid, nothing thing," Harper explained. "He'd just moved back. We were catching up, one thing led to another, and boom. I got pregnant." She sniffed and shook her head. "We kept it quiet. Ivy sees him, but it's not a public thing. *We're* not a thing. I was embarrassed. I was . . ." She shook her head. "I'm sorry. I thought you would be mad."

Isabelle frowned and sat back down. "Why in the world would I be mad?"

"Because you were in love with him," she said. "He was your first boyfriend."

Murdoch looked at Isabelle with renewed interest.

"So? That was a lifetime ago. I haven't been pining for him all this time, Harper, if that's what you mean." She lifted the sleeve of her T-shirt, revealing the handprint left there. "In fact, he gave me this when he caught me at his shed today."

Harper gasped, and Murdoch eyed her arm, concerned. "He did that today?"

Isabelle lowered her sleeve. "To be fair, I was trespassing."

Murdoch's phone buzzed, and she took it. She barked out a few clipped words and then hung up. "Ladies, it's been illuminating. I'll be in touch."

She left without another word, and Isabelle studied Harper. She understood why she hadn't told her about River, but she was still shocked by the depth of the secrets Harper had kept.

"You must hate me." Harper dropped her face into her hands and shook her head, then lifted it. Her eyes were red and watery. "I'm sorry."

"Harper, stop apologizing. I literally couldn't care less. I want the best for you, for Ivy. Does he treat her okay? Is he good to you?"

She waved a hand. "He's fine. A bit rough around the edges, but he's a good dad."

Isabelle nodded.

Harper bit her bottom lip. "Do you think she bought our story about Marcus?"

Isabelle shrugged as she took her mug to the dishwasher. "I mean, why wouldn't she, right?"

"Right." But Harper didn't look convinced. She glanced toward Isabelle's arm. "Did River really do that?"

"It's fine."

"It's not fine."

Isabelle suddenly felt a heavy weight pressing on every part of her. The excitement and shock from the day had left her drained. She could barely keep her eyes open. "I think I'm going to lie down for a while if you don't mind. I'm absolutely beat."

"Of course."

Isabelle went to tell Jack and Maisy that she was going to rest for a while. When she got upstairs, she noticed her bed had been freshly made, and there were a vase of wildflowers and a bottle of water on her nightstand.

Isabelle smiled, took a sip of water, and climbed into bed.

She was out before her head hit the pillow, wondering what in the world would come next.

31

Isabelle woke to her phone buzzing over and over again.

"Hello?" Her voice was clogged with sleep.

"Isabelle," Detective Murdoch said. "I need you and Harper to take me to the bunker."

Isabelle glanced at the time. It was seven at night. She'd been asleep for hours. "Now?"

"Yep. I'll meet you out front of Harper's in fifteen."

Isabelle groaned, threw back the covers, and changed into a clean outfit. Downstairs, she could smell roasted chicken. Ivy, Harper, Jack, and Maisy sat around the dining room table, eating chicken, potatoes, and a big salad.

"There she is," Jack said, wiping his mouth.

"Why didn't you wake me?"

"You clearly needed the rest," Harper said, motioning to the empty plate beside Jack. "Come, eat. Did you have a good nap?"

Isabelle stared longingly at the food. Her stomach growled. She couldn't remember the last thing she'd eaten. "As lovely as that sounds, Murdoch called. She's coming here. Wants us to take her to the bunker."

Jack turned around in his chair, his eyebrows knitted together. "The bunker? Why?"

"No idea." She stepped forward, grabbed a hunk of potato from Jack's plate, and ate it. "Hey, Bug. Food good?"

"So good." Maisy kicked her legs against her chair, and Ivy did the same.

"Do you mean 'us' as in me and you?" Harper asked.

"Yep."

Harper rolled her eyes, wiped her mouth with her napkin, and kissed Ivy on the head. "Mama will be right back. Jack, do you mind?"

"Of course not." The three of them launched right back into eating and conversation as Harper pulled on her boots and met Isabelle by the door.

"What's this all about, do you think?"

"No clue." Isabelle yawned. "Hopefully it will be quick."

Right on time, Murdoch knocked on the door, and the three of them set out to the bunker. They walked in silence for a while. Harper lagged behind, and Isabelle led the way, having memorized the directions by now.

"Did you talk to River?" Isabelle asked as they weaved on the path and stepped into the clearing where the bunker lay hidden in the earth. It was cool outside, and she zipped up her hoodie.

"No," Murdoch said.

"Why not?" Harper asked.

They stopped at the wooden covering of the hatch. Murdoch stood, hands on her hips, staring between them. "River's dead."

Isabelle felt like she'd been slapped. Harper audibly gasped.

"What are you talking about?"

"How?"

She and Harper spoke at the same time. Murdoch shook her head. "Inconclusive. He was in his kitchen, unconscious." She tucked a loose strand of hair behind her ear.

Isabelle didn't know what to say. She'd just seen him, and now he was dead? Harper's eyes filled with tears, and she shook her head, visibly shaken.

"Ivy . . ." Her voice trailed off, and she covered her mouth with her hand.

"Harper, may I ask where you were this afternoon?"

"Excuse me?" She dropped her hand. "I was at home, with my daughter and Isabelle's daughter."

Murdoch turned to Isabelle. "And you were there too?"

"Yes. I was asleep. Jack was there. He can verify."

Murdoch gave a nod and pointed to the bunker. "Would one of you mind removing the top?"

Harper and Isabelle looked at each other. This felt like a trap. Harper huffed and moved forward to tug the lid free. She gestured to it. "Ta-da. The bunker. Why are we here, Detective?"

"Tell me. The day Marcus died. How'd he know where to go?"

"How are we supposed to know?" Harper asked. "He was always in the woods."

"But you hadn't been here before? You didn't know this place existed?"

"I already told you that," Harper said.

Isabelle shook her head.

"Let's go down."

"Why do we need to go down there?" Isabelle asked.

"I find that sometimes clues crop up when you least expect them. I want you both to walk me through the night of the fire."

There was no reason on earth to walk Murdoch through that night because if she believed their story, then she'd know they hadn't been at the bunker. Neither of them moved, unsure of what to do.

Isabelle suddenly realized: Murdoch knew about the secret door. The tunnel. Did she know about the rope too? What Isabelle had done? Did she know about Marcus? About Jude? As if reading her mind, Murdoch spoke.

"Funny thing about Marcus. We did some digging into his previous homes. He'd been kicked out of every single one for sexual misconduct. And then Gail brings him into a house with two little girls? Now why would she do that?"

Isabelle felt sick. Her mother had known about Marcus? She couldn't have. "Were those records public?"

"I would imagine so, though maybe your mother didn't ask, but I can't imagine she'd be so careless." Murdoch continued. "Unless it really was all about the money." She pointed toward the bunker. "Now, we thought Marcus might have wandered out here and fallen, but then another idea popped into my head." Murdoch brought her fingers together at her temple and then opened them, making an explosion sound. "What if Marcus was hurting one of you? What if you lured him out here because you'd found this bunker, and then pushed him in? And what if, on the night of the fire, your siblings saw Marcus down there, and one of you panicked and set the fire to cover your tracks?"

Isabelle was speechless. "That's not what happened."

"I could understand it, though," Murdoch said, nodding her head as she took a few steps toward the bunker. "If I was being molested by my brother and saw a way out . . ." She mimed pushing someone into the bunker. "It would be almost too easy, wouldn't it?"

The words bubbled up on her tongue. Harper shot her a look, but Isabelle spoke anyway. "I was sleepwalking."

Both Murdoch and Harper looked horrified as she said it. "What?" Murdoch asked.

"I was sleepwalking. Apparently, he tried to touch me, and I . . . I pushed him in."

Murdoch looked between them. "But you have no recollection of this?"

"Well, no, not exactly."

"And let me guess." Murdoch pivoted toward Harper. "You told her this?"

Harper's face was beet red, her fists balled by her sides. "Why did you have to say that, Izz?"

"Because it's the truth," she said now. Isabelle was so tired of keeping secrets. Even if it complicated her life, she wanted to be honest. She'd made her choice.

Harper looked up toward the sky and exhaled. An owl hooted overhead and then swooped beneath the trees. "It's not the truth." She lowered her head and looked at Detective Murdoch. "I pushed Marcus."

Once again, Isabelle was speechless. She thought back to the night of the fire, the Ouija board that had spelled out the fact that Marcus had been pushed. Had Harper done that on purpose? "What are you talking about? You said—"

"I know what I said!" she screamed. "You were sleepwalking. That part is true. You wandered out in the woods, and I woke up and tried to follow you. But I saw Marcus in the woods first, not you, and I got this terrible feeling." She swallowed. "He was faster than me. By the time I caught up to him, he was . . . he was touching you. His hands were all over you. I didn't know there was a bunker here, I swear. I didn't know anything about it. I ran up behind him and shoved him, and he . . . he fell in. He didn't move. I panicked."

Harper looked at Isabelle. "You were still asleep. I found the top, pulled it back over, covered it with leaves, and guided you back home. For days, I was petrified that he'd be found or that someone saw. But no one did. And then the case went cold when they couldn't find him." She swung her gaze to Murdoch. "But I swear, I did not mean to hurt him. I was trying to protect Isabelle."

Murdoch and Isabelle were quiet. Isabelle's mind was working overtime. If Harper had lied about that, then what else had she lied about? "And the night of the fire . . . is what you said true?"

Harper was silent. She balled her fists and glanced at the ground. Finally, she looked up. "No."

"No?"

"Explain," Murdoch said, crossing her arms. "I have no idea what you two are talking about."

The pit in Isabelle's stomach expanded as Harper began to talk. "The night of the fire, I came to the bunker with Jude. Celia and Ben had gotten trapped. Jude had the rope to help them. I went back to find you, but you were sleepwalking. I checked the tree house, and then I started running back to the bunker. When I got there, Jude was lowering himself down. And I knew if they were down there, then they had all seen Marcus. And I knew that was bad news for me."

"Harper, what did you do?" Isabelle whispered.

She swallowed and looked into Isabelle's eyes. "I was *never* going to leave them there, I swear. I just needed a little time to think."

Murdoch stood perfectly still, but Isabelle took a step toward Harper. "What the hell does that mean?"

To her surprise, Harper let out a laugh. It was maniacal and made all the hairs on Isabelle's arms stand up. "You have no idea all the things I've done for you."

Isabelle recoiled as if she'd been slapped. "I never asked you to do anything for me."

"Oh, please!" Harper stepped forward and gripped Isabelle's wrist, twisting it. Her nails dug into her arm, just as they had when they were kids. "We were *best friends*, Isabelle. Best friends!" She shook her arm, and Isabelle attempted to twist her wrist to get out of her grip.

"Harper, let me go."

But Harper wasn't listening. "All I ever wanted was for you to look at me as something *more* than your best friend. More than a sister. When my mom died, I saw my chance. It could be just you, me, and Gail." She sneered, and her pretty face turned ugly. "But then there was Marcus. And then Celia, Ben, and Jude."

"Did you poison the kids too?"

Harper didn't respond.

"Did you kill Gail?"

Again, Harper didn't respond. She dug her nails deeper until Isabelle saw blood bubble up on her skin. She peeled Harper's fingers off and moved back, nearly toppling into the bunker herself.

Murdoch motioned to the ladder. "Why don't you go down and show me the rest."

This didn't seem like a smart move. Harper was unhinged. She wasn't thinking clearly. It could be dangerous for Murdoch, or for her. But then she saw Murdoch's hand braced near her gun.

"Why do we have to go down there?" Harper's voice shook.

"Because I want you to show me how Jude escaped."

So she did know. To Isabelle's surprise, Harper turned, stepped onto the ladder, and lowered herself down. Murdoch went next. Isabelle wavered up top. She had a horrible, sinking feeling about this.

Whatever was about to happen, she hoped she was one step closer to learning the truth.

Then

Harper

Harper couldn't find Isabelle anywhere.

She was overly worried now. What if something bad happened to her like it did that night with Marcus?

Harper thought of everything she'd learned tonight. The kids had found Marcus's body. Though there was no way to prove that she'd pushed him, what if they somehow figured it out? What if they also figured out she was the one making them sick? She'd been poisoning the kids for a while now, but that wasn't really doing what she'd thought it would. She didn't want to hurt them. She only wanted them to fade into the background so Isabelle would pay attention to Harper again.

Instead, Isabelle was even more worried about them. So Harper had pretended to be sick, too, in hopes that Isabelle would dote on her like the others. All she craved was Isabelle's attention, and she would get it however she could.

Harper marched farther into the woods, finding herself heading back toward the bunker. She still remembered that night with Marcus. What he was doing to Isabelle. What he'd done to her. Even now, she didn't feel bad about pushing him. It was an accident, but he still deserved it.

Tonight, when she'd moved the Ouija board, it had been a way to confess what she'd done. She hated living with so many secrets. There was what she'd done to her mother, which she sometimes regretted, but it had gotten her closer to Isabelle, hadn't it? Ever since she was little, she'd always had these compulsions to do bad things, but she wasn't a bad person. She just wanted what she wanted.

And what she wanted was Isabelle.

Up ahead, Harper shone the flashlight, hoping she'd see her. Maybe subconsciously, Isabelle had made her way back to the bunker, but no. Instead, she saw Jude lower himself down with the rope tied around a tree. Her heart pounded as she clicked off the flashlight.

Of course, she didn't want anything horrible to happen to her siblings, but maybe if she let them stay down there tonight, then she could "discover" them tomorrow, and become the hero! Isabelle would love that. So would Gail.

Again, she pictured what Gail and Sheriff Mullins had been doing tonight and shuddered. She didn't ever want to do that with a boy. Only with one person. Only with Isabelle. She sighed. Maybe Harper would tell the sheriff's wife what he'd been up to. It would serve him right after the way he'd treated all of them tonight.

On tiptoe, Harper crept toward the tree, untied the rope, and threw it in over the side. Then she slid the wooden top into place, just like she'd done with Marcus. But this would be different. This would give her time to think about what she'd say if questioned about Marcus. No one would ever suspect what had happened back then. It would look like an accident.

Steeling herself against their protests, she turned on her flashlight again and searched for Isabelle. Below, Celia started crying. Man, Celia was such a wimp! She needed to toughen up. Maybe surviving tonight would be exactly what she needed. Maybe Harper was doing her a favor.

Finally, yards from the house, she spotted Izz. Yes! She ran up to her and gripped her forearm. She dug in her fingernails, hoping maybe Isabelle would wake on her own, but she never did.

Back at the house, Harper listened for their mother, but it was late, and Gail was hopefully asleep by now. She helped Isabelle into bed and pulled the covers up to her chin. She stared down at her and then leaned in.

"All mine." Harper lowered her mouth to Isabelle's in a soft kiss, then crawled in beside her. She draped an arm over Isabelle's waist and smiled.

Harper was right where she belonged.

32

At the bottom of the bunker, Murdoch shined her flashlight around.

"I never meant to hurt them," Harper said. "I untied the rope and slid the top back on because I wanted to have some time with Isabelle. I was going to get them in the morning. I swear. I couldn't have possibly known there would be a fire."

Murdoch nodded. "That part I believe. Now show me the door."

"I don't know where the door is," Harper responded.

Isabelle didn't understand how Murdoch knew about the door, but Harper searched for it anyway. When she couldn't find it, Isabelle walked over to where she'd seen Eliza press her hand against the seam of the hidden door. After some effort, Isabelle tugged it open.

Murdoch shined a flashlight down the tunnel and then back to them. "You're going to show me what's on the other side. Move."

Harper stood still, locking eyes with Isabelle, but didn't duck through the opening.

Murdoch knew about Jude. That much was clear. But Isabelle still had so many questions. Who killed River? Who killed Gail? Harper was many things, but she wasn't a stone-cold killer. Was she?

"Move," Murdoch barked again.

Harper crouched through the door first, then Isabelle. Murdoch trailed behind, talking, as she shined her flashlight ahead. It illuminated Harper next to Isabelle, made her golden hair glow.

"Craziest thing happened today. Before I went to River's, I popped by your shed, Harper. The door was open, so I thought I'd peek inside. Run-of-the-mill stuff, really. Pesticides. Herbicides. But then, on the very back shelf, there was something else. Care to tell me what that was?"

Harper froze and turned, her eyes flashing as Murdoch shined the light directly in them before addressing Isabelle.

"You see, Isabelle, your thallium theory really interested me," Murdoch said. "I read your piece, looked at Gail's autopsy report. Then I got a little hunch to look up Harper's mother's autopsy report, and what do you know? Many of the symptoms were consistent with thallium poisoning."

"You can't prove that," Harper snapped.

"Oh, but I will," Murdoch said. "Which got me thinking about the kids and why someone would want to poison them but not kill them. That part I'm still not too clear on, Harper. Care to elaborate?"

Harper's chest heaved, and finally she exploded. "I thought if they were sick, then Isabelle would only want to play with me."

The words were so childish that Isabelle almost laughed.

"And you got the thallium from your mom's farm, correct? It was mostly outlawed by then, but it wasn't uncommon to have some on hand in more rural places like this. You saw it work with your mom after you poisoned her, so you experimented on the kids. But not Isabelle. And not Gail.

"And then, all these years later, when Gail started asking questions again, you began to poison her too," Murdoch continued. "So that she needed you. So that you could take care of her. Maybe she was onto you. Maybe she figured it out. So you killed her."

Harper stood still. There was nowhere to go, no way to get out of this.

Suddenly, the video surveillance flashed through Isabelle's head. Did Harper know where the cameras were? Had she been visiting her mother but coming in through the back? Isabelle thought about

Harper's reaction at finding Gail. Her shock had seemed so genuine. "You knew about the cameras," Isabelle said. Was it Harper her mother had argued with off camera? "Did you kill her, Harper?"

"It got you back here, didn't it?" Harper's eyes locked onto Isabelle's with such intensity Isabelle took a step back.

"I don't understand." Isabelle's world tilted, rearranged. "Why? Why would you do all of this? You loved Gail."

"But I loved you *more*." Harper took a step forward and gripped Isabelle's shoulders. Her lips trembled as she spoke. "I'm sorry. I never meant to hurt anyone. I didn't. Things just happened. All I ever wanted was for us to be together again."

Be together again? Isabelle shook herself free and ran back through the last few days in her head. Leaving Maisy with Harper. Trusting her, no questions asked. "Did you hurt Maisy?"

"No! I would never hurt Maisy. *Never*," she said.

Isabelle thought of how tired she'd been, how late she'd been sleeping, how groggy. "Did you drug me too, Harper?"

She opened her mouth, then looked at the ground before letting out a sigh. "It was just crushed sleeping pills."

Isabelle moved another step away as Harper closed the gap and reached for her again. "I didn't want you to leave again, and you needed the rest, Izz! That's all. I wasn't trying to hurt you. I was taking *care* of you. You have to believe me!"

Her voice was shrill, rising in the small, cramped tunnel. Isabelle butted up against the dirt wall, while Harper moved in closer, smothering her with her confessions. She needed to get out of this small space, needed to get away from this person she thought she knew.

Harper was crying now, her desperation a hot, sticky thing. "Please, Isabelle. I *need* you. I love you. You have to believe me."

Isabelle pushed off the wall and shuffled back until she was even with Murdoch. She didn't believe Harper. She would never believe anything she said again.

"Keep walking," Murdoch instructed.

Harper debated, her eyes pained as she silently pleaded with Isabelle. And then she turned and began to run.

Murdoch cursed, then took off after her, and then Isabelle began to sprint, too, her legs flooded with adrenaline. Harper's admissions swirled in her head. Harper had killed Gail to get Isabelle to come home? She'd killed Sandy to get *closer* to Isabelle? She'd only been a child. What type of child would ever do such a thing?

At the other end, Isabelle climbed the ladder to find two cops waiting. So that was why Murdoch wanted them to travel the tunnel. To get to the cops on the other side. To get Harper to confess. The moment Murdoch emerged, they had Harper in handcuffs. She protested, completely unhinged, kicking and screaming. Isabelle had never seen this side of her, couldn't reconcile the woman she'd left her child with day after day—the friend, the sister she'd known her whole life—with an actual murderer. There was a part of her that still couldn't believe it, didn't want to accept the ugly, sordid truth.

Jude and Eliza watched from the cabin porch. Murdoch nodded toward Jude.

"And this is your dead brother, I presume."

"Recently undead," he joked, raising a scarred hand.

Murdoch snorted. "Sense of humor intact, I see." She crossed her arms and watched the men yank Harper toward the trees. "Hell of a twist," she said.

Isabelle couldn't speak. Her entire body was trembling as she struggled to work through everything she'd learned. "I don't understand. She wasn't a bad person. She was . . ." Her voice faded. She was what? She was Harper, her best friend. Harper, her sister. Harper, the serial killer?

"She was in love with you, Isabelle. And people do crazy things for love," Murdoch said. Isabelle stared down at the five half moons on her forearm, now crusted with dried blood. "I'm going to need you to come down to the station this time. We can sort all this out in Crossings."

Isabelle nodded as Murdoch followed the officers through the forest. Her legs gave out. She sank to the ground and dipped her head between her knees. After all this time, she had answers. Not the answers she wanted, but at least she had them. Jude approached and placed a hand on her back before he pulled her to standing. She had to get to the station, but first she needed to see Jack and Maisy.

"Hard to believe," Jude said now. "The monster we were living with wasn't Gail after all." He tipped his chin toward the trees. The knot of officers and Harper grew smaller in the distance before they were finally swallowed by the trees.

Isabelle shook her head. She still couldn't say it out loud, couldn't really believe it. Even now, she was torn. She'd loved Harper. She'd trusted Harper.

And yet, River was dead. Theo was dead. Sandy was dead. Marcus was dead. Ben and Celia were dead. Gail was dead. Harper had done everything to try to get closer to Isabelle, not caring who she hurt in the process. And now she would spend the rest of her life paying for those choices, leaving her daughter without a mother.

Poor Ivy.

"I just can't believe it," she finally said.

"Neither can I." Jude looked down at her and then reached for Isabelle's hand. The gesture brought tears to her eyes as his fingers entwined with hers. The knotted, scarred flesh felt waxy between her fingers. "We'll get through it." His voice was hoarse, barely a whisper.

We'll get through it. The words ripped right through her. Isabelle had spent her entire life blaming her mother. And now it was too late to ever make it right. But Harper *was* a mother. And, as Isabelle was learning, sometimes mothers did bad things. Her eyes drifted to the trees, then to the sky, which was moody with clouds again.

She'd just lost her former best friend and sister, but she'd regained a brother—once her favorite person, now alive, *real.* That was a gift. They still had a lot to discuss, of course, and so much to work through, but Jude was here. And so was she.

For now, that was enough.

Epilogue

Jack and Isabelle watched the girls play outside on the swing set.

For now, they were staying at Harper's farm until they sorted out custody. Harper stipulated that if anything should ever happen to her, Isabelle retained custody of Ivy. With River dead, there was no one else to step in. The last thing Isabelle wanted to do was to stay in this place, with all its secrets and reminders. But she didn't want to uproot Ivy immediately. Her father had died at the hands of her mother, who would now spend the rest of her life in jail.

After Harper had been arrested, all the facts were laid out. How she'd poisoned her own mother using thallium from the farm, so she could live with Isabelle and Gail. How she'd killed Marcus because she wanted to protect Isabelle, even though it had been accidental. How she'd slipped thallium into the sourdough starter or the kids' drinks to make them sick enough so that Isabelle would pay more attention to Harper. How Harper had started slowly poisoning Gail and then delivered a lethal dose when Gail crept closer to the truth. How she'd been drugging Isabelle. How she'd sent Isabelle all those cryptic text messages. How she'd clogged the vent at the funeral home. How she'd stolen the files and planted them in River's shed so no one would think it was her. How, after Harper had seen what River did to her arm, she'd marched over to his house while Jack was watching the girls, and killed him too.

It felt like piecing together an insane puzzle, and sometimes Isabelle still didn't believe any of it could be true. But it *was* true. Every last bit.

It was still shocking to know that all this time, Harper had been obsessed with her. Not as a best friend. Not as a sister. But as something more. From the moment they'd met as children, Harper had been plotting ways to get closer to Isabelle. It all seemed so sensational. Isabelle's mind was still reeling from the magnitude of it.

The least they could do was spend a few months at the farm while they figured out what was best for Ivy. Jack had canceled his trip, the only time in his career he'd walked away from a major story. He looped an arm around Isabelle's shoulders as they swayed back and forth on the porch swing. She snuggled into his chest, so thankful that through it all, she'd at least come to her senses. Jack was her person. He wasn't going anywhere. He'd seen all the skeletons in her closet, literally and figuratively, and had chosen to stay.

So she chose him right back.

"One hell of a way to spend a summer vacation," Jack said, pressing back and forth with his toes.

Isabelle belly laughed. "You can say that again."

It made her sick to think she'd let Maisy stay with a psychopath when Harper could have turned on her daughter at any moment. It was hard to reconcile the best friend and sister she'd known with an actual murderer.

She watched the girls playing on the swing set. Through it all, Maisy and Ivy had grown closer. That was a silver lining, at least. Maisy was still sleepwalking, but they had found a hypnotherapist they were hoping to work with when they got back to Portland.

Jack looked around. "Not a bad way to live, really. Maybe a nice getaway from the city from time to time?"

"You're joking, right?"

"Maybe?" He laughed and kissed her head.

Just then, Maisy came up to them, crying and gripping her arm.

Isabelle sat up. "Oh, Bug, what happened? Did you get stung?"

She was gulping air and stuck out her arm.

"What is that?" Jack asked, cocking his head.

All the hairs on Isabelle's arms stood up. There, all along Maisy's forearm, were tiny half-moon indentations from Ivy's fingernails.

A chill rippled through her body as she called Ivy over. "Did you do this?"

Ivy looked remorseful. "I'm *so* sorry. I didn't mean to." Ivy blinked up at her, the spitting image of her mother. That was what Harper used to say. *I didn't mean to. I didn't mean to. I didn't mean to.* Ivy turned to Maisy, nearly on the verge of tears. "I didn't mean to, Maisy. I'm sorry. You're my best friend."

"You're my best friend too." Maisy folded her into a hug, and then the two of them ran off the porch, hand in hand.

Jack shot Isabelle a concerned look. "Isn't that what Harper used to do to you?"

Isabelle nodded, her system buzzing on high alert. When the girls got to the swing set, and Maisy climbed onto the swing, Ivy got behind her to push. Ivy's gaze swung to hers. Her eyes were cold, but she smiled. It was Harper's smile exactly.

Like mother, like daughter, she thought.

She exhaled. What could she do? She was *responsible* for raising Ivy, unless she put her into foster care, which she would never do. She'd have to keep a closer eye on her . . . because what were the odds that Ivy had the same compulsions as her mother?

Ivy continued to smile at Isabelle and finally lifted her hand in a wave.

"Izz, talk to me." Jack wasn't looking at the girls. He was looking at her.

Isabelle watched Ivy. Finally, she lifted her hand to wave back and then turned to Jack. "Is that the first time this has happened?"

"As far as I know."

The wheels were turning in Isabelle's head. After a few minutes, Maisy ran over. "Can we see if the sun tea is ready yet?"

"Sure thing, Bug." Jack stood up and took Maisy inside. The tea had been steeping all day.

Ivy walked back over to where Isabelle was sitting and stared at her.

"You need something, Ivy?"

"No." But she continued to stare, her little fists balled by her side. She was rigid, the smile on her face wiped clean. Moments later, Maisy burst out the front door with a pitcher of the sun tea, and Ivy cleared the scowl from her face and plastered on a smile.

"Teatime!" She grabbed Maisy's wrist again, her little fingernails pressing hard into her flesh. Maisy winced but let herself be tugged back toward the playground.

Isabelle stood, wanting to go to Maisy but not knowing exactly what she could do.

"Everything okay?" Jack asked, handing her a fresh cup.

"Everything's fine," she said. She took a few steps toward the swing set, the glass sweating in her hand. Ivy was busy pouring Maisy a cup. Maybe Isabelle was overreacting. But what if she wasn't? If Isabelle had known any of the signs to watch for back then, her whole life would be different. Everyone she loved might still be alive. As she was contemplating how to handle this, she froze and looked down at her cup. "Jack?" She turned back to him on the swing. He was gripping his stomach. "Jack?"

He winced and set his half-empty glass down on the ground. "Izz . . ."

"Did Ivy make this tea all by herself?" Isabelle asked.

"What?"

She was nearly hysterical. "Did Ivy make this tea all by herself?"

"Yeah, why? She . . ."

Before he could finish, Isabelle sprinted toward the girls and slapped the full glass from Maisy's hand, spilling it all over her clothes. She dumped the pitcher out, much to the shock of the girls.

"Mama, why'd you *do* that?" Maisy shrieked.

"Maisy, go inside and change your clothes."

"But you ruined it!"

Isabelle clapped. "Maisy, now!"

Maisy stomped and let out a frustrated scream, but did as she was told. Ivy followed her inside, trying to console her. When the girls were out of sight, Isabelle rushed back to Jack, who was still studying his tea.

"Are you okay?"

"I got nauseous after I took a few sips." He held it up to the sun. "You don't think . . ." His voice faded.

"I don't know." How would Ivy even be able to get her hands on anything to poison the tea? Was Isabelle being paranoid, or was there really something here to be concerned about? "Don't drink it," Isabelle warned. "To be safe."

Jack nodded and dumped the tea, right as Jude sauntered over from the horses. He removed his work gloves and wiped a hand over his brow. "Hot today."

Though Isabelle was still rattled, she offered him a smile. "Sure is. How are the mares?"

"Good." He stepped onto the porch and glanced at their empty glasses.

"Can I have some of that?"

Jack and Isabelle looked at each other and back at him.

"No," they both said.

"Wow, okay." Jude looked perplexed. "Can I have some water, then?"

"Let me," Jack said. "I'll check on the girls."

Jude took his place on the porch swing, his weight making the chains groan. He patted the empty space next to him, and Isabelle sat as they pushed back and forth. It was still so foreign to her, being with Jude, talking to Jude, learning all about his life.

While she still couldn't completely understand why he hadn't reached out to her all those years, what mattered was now. They had the rest of their lives to get to know each other, and for that, she was beyond grateful. He rested an arm over the back of the swing and smiled at her.

"How are you doing with all this?"

Jude wasn't a big talker, but he'd been checking on Isabelle every day. Helping with the farm. Doing chores and not complaining in the process. Eliza still hadn't run her story yet. She wanted to warn Jude that when she did, his life would never be the same.

She contemplated telling him about what just happened but refrained. For a moment, she wanted to revel in sitting on a porch swing with her big brother, a simple moment she'd never thought was possible. "I'm okay," she finally said. And she was. Nothing had been wrapped up in a big red bow, but she had Jack. And Maisy. And Jude. She was thankful.

The screen door squeaked open, and Maisy and Ivy sprinted back toward the swings. Maisy didn't even look her way. Isabelle would have to somehow explain why she'd dumped the tea, but luckily, her daughter didn't hold a grudge. Jack handed Jude a glass of water, and he offered his seat back, but Jack waved for him to stay.

"Look at us," Jack said, shoving his hands into his pockets. "One big happy, dysfunctional family."

Isabelle laughed. "That's the understatement of the century."

Her eyes tracked back to Ivy, who was now in the swing next to Maisy. They tried to go higher and higher until they both jumped out of their swings and landed hard on the grass. Ivy gripped Maisy's hand and swung them back and forth.

"Sweet girls," Jude said, smiling.

Isabelle wanted to believe that. She wanted to believe Ivy was nothing like her mother, but the past and present mingled together as she watched them. Isabelle might not be able to change the past, but she could certainly change the future for her daughter if necessary.

Ivy and Maisy bounded up the steps, still hand in hand. "Want to play hide-and-seek?" Ivy asked.

Jude stiffened beside her, and chills erupted on Isabelle's skin. They shot each other a look. It was only a game. The girls couldn't possibly know what it meant to them.

Jack faltered, then knelt down in front of the girls. "How about I play?"

"No, it has to be all of us," Ivy said.

"Yeah, all of us," Maisy parroted.

Isabelle looked at Ivy, who blinked at her again, wide eyed and innocent. She smiled sweetly, revealing a gap where one of her permanent teeth hadn't yet come in. But her eyes were cold and fixed on Isabelle's face. She reached out her hand and gripped Isabelle's arm hard, digging her fingernails into her skin.

"Come on, Izzy," she said, biting into her flesh and tugging her to stand. "Let's play."

Isabelle stood, casting Jack a concerned look as she let Ivy yank her toward the woods. Harper flashed through her mind again. She replayed all the moments they'd shared just like this that had seemed so innocent. Taking a friend's hand. Playing a game.

But it had never been innocent.

Isabelle wrenched her arm from Ivy's firm grip, her little nails imprinted in her skin. Jack began to count extra slow, exaggerating each number so the girls had time to hide. Ivy squealed and ran toward Maisy, and they both ducked behind a tree.

Isabelle stood there, staring at her arm, then at the girls, as Jack continued to count.

"Two, three, four."

Isabelle jogged the opposite way, her eyes still trained on Ivy, her mind still tangled on Harper.

"Five, six, seven."

Isabelle watched as Ivy pressed a hand over Maisy's mouth to keep her quiet. Maisy gripped Ivy's fingers and tried to peel them off, but Ivy wouldn't budge. Just when Isabelle wanted to intervene, Ivy dropped her hand, and Maisy sucked in a big gulp of air.

"Eight, nine, ten!"

Isabelle's stomach clenched. Everything in her demanded she get Maisy away from Ivy. What if history really was repeating itself? What if Ivy was just like her mother?

Jack removed his hands from his eyes.

Thunder rumbled overhead. A warning. Her eyes searched for Ivy and Maisy, but they were no longer behind the tree. Where had they gone?

Jack walked toward the open mouth of the forest. While she desperately searched for the girls, Isabelle couldn't help but wonder. . .

"Ready or not . . ." Jack's voice echoed among the trees.

If some monsters were made.

"Here I come."

Or born.

ACKNOWLEDGMENTS

Since 2018, I have been obsessed with writing stories about mothers. Mothers who do unspeakable things. Mothers who have secrets. Mothers who will do whatever it takes to protect their children. For this book, I even managed to get the word *mother* in the title.

While the subject matter was easy, this book was not.

The first kernel of *Dear Mother* came to me right after I wrote my debut novel, *Not Her Daughter*, in 2017. I always envisioned a follow-up to that book: *What happened to Emma Grace Townsend after she grew up?*

It became clear that the publisher didn't want a sequel, but the book floated somewhere in the back of my mind, seventy pages loosely built, stuffed in a drawer for *someday*. When I sat down with my Thomas & Mercer editor, the incomparable Jessica Tribble Wells, we were discussing what my third book for this imprint could possibly be. She liked the premise for *Dear Mother*, and I was so excited to resurrect this long-abandoned idea (while also turning it into something new).

I churned out the draft and turned it in early. My agent read it and liked it. *I nailed this one*, I thought. In fact, wouldn't it be great if my editors had NO NOTES? Surely, nine books in, I knew what I was doing?

Wrong.

Not only did they have *all the notes*, but ultimately, I had to scrap the entire draft and start over. I'll spare you the details, but the book you are holding in your hands was essentially rewritten (three times!) in less than a month. Is it better than what I initially turned in? Yes. Was I panicked about writing something brand new under such a time crunch after I'd just finished another book? Doubly yes.

But once I stopped resisting, I found that I enjoyed the painstaking process of reconstruction. My editors, Jessica and Angela James, were on board the entire way. It was the most collaborative edit I've had to date, and I am utterly indebted to their commitment to seeing me through this.

So, all that being said: I hope you enjoy the book in your hands, but if you don't? Well, I wrote it in a few weeks, so . . . too bad, so sad.

Thank you, as always, to my longstanding literary agent, Rachel Beck. We've been together for nine books, and I honestly can't think of anyone else I'd rather travel this publishing journey with. I trust you, I appreciate you, and I cannot wait until we hit it B-I-G.

To my fellow Nashville Authors crew—Jennifer Moorman, Lauren Nossett, and Melissa Collings. You three women have graced my life in so many ways, and I have loved every moment we've spent together. Sometimes, when you turn your passion into a career, you forget: This is supposed to be fun. I am rediscovering fun with the three of you, and I can't wait to see what magic we dream up together!

A special shoutout to Jennifer Moorman: I could not travel this publishing path without you. Every chat, every uplifting word, every voice note, every ounce of gratitude shared between us reminds me of the point of all of this: to create. I'm so grateful for you, friend. You are magic.

Thank you to Vanessa Lillie for our Monday Manifestations and Friday Wins weekly touchpoints. You inspire me and help me anchor in my dreams. Thank you to Nikki, my bestie of thirty-plus years, for every walk and talk. We have literally grown *together* all this time, not apart. You are my longest-standing relationship.

Thank you to all the women in my life who uplift me, create space for me, and show me what it means to live an *aligned*, embodied life. (You know who you are.) I am so fortunate to have such an incredible support system and consider myself very lucky to have such a phenomenal community. Thank you to Janina Lawrence for our adventure bucket list dates, for exhibiting what it means to be a phenomenal mother, sister, and friend. And to Chris and Gemma, the best neighbors anyone could ever have.

Thank you to all the bookstores, bookstore owners, librarians, bookstagrammers, readers, and humans who support books, share books, and spread the word. Thank you to all the authors who inspire me (of which there are too many to name). Every time I read one of your books, I want to become a better writer.

Thank you to the entire Thomas & Mercer team: my editors, the sales and marketing team, Liz Gluck, Cortni M., Darci Swanson, Annie S., my proofreader (unclear antecedents and misplaced modifiers be damned!), the cover designer and audiobook folks, and the audiobook narrator (as of writing this, I don't know who you are just yet, but I'm sure you're awesome). You all make this job so easy. Thank you to BookSparks for helping promote this baby! Thank you to my film/TV agents at IPG for constantly pushing my books to grace the screen.

And, as always, thank you to the readers. I will never tire of hearing from you. I marvel that out of all the books you could read, you choose to spend a little time with mine. I appreciate each and every one of you more than you know. (And if any of you ever want to blow up one of my books on BookTok, I won't be mad at you.)

Thank you to my family. We are a small bunch, but we are mighty. Your unwavering support to follow my creative dreams means the world. Thank you to my dog, Luna, for making me a dog mom. (I don't know how I lived my whole life without you. Now, you have to live forever. The end.) Thank you to my partner, Alex, for every warm meal, long conversation, relaxing hike, road trip, or lazy pool day we get to share. You are the best husband, lover, and friend I could ever ask for. Fifteen years in, and you are still my favorite person. This is the real win.

And last but certainly not least, to my daughter, Sophie. You made me a mother and *also* a published author. It wasn't until becoming a mother that I learned to write stories about mothers. You have been along for my entire author journey. I remember when you were only five years old, upstaging me at my first book launch. Now that you're thirteen, our conversations have evolved because you are writing your own stories, finding your own voice. You, too, are my favorite person. I love you and am so proud of you for being exactly who you are. You inspire me to be myself in every situation, and for that, I am forever grateful.

Here's to the next one, y'all.

ABOUT THE AUTHOR

Photo © 2023 Kate Gallaher

Rea Frey is the #1 bestselling author of a dozen books. As a book doula, she has helped over five hundred first-time authors land agents and publishing deals. A Silver Falchion finalist, Book Pipeline's film adaptation winner, and voted one of *Marie Claire*'s best fiction writers, Rea has had her work optioned for film and has been featured by *Good Morning America*, *CBS Saturday Morning*, and *The New York Times*. To learn more, visit reafrey.com.